M000207464

LOUISE BURFITT-DONS

Our Man In Kuwait

A Historical Spy Thriller

nc

NEW CENTURY

First published in Great Britain by New Century 2022

Copyright © 2022 by Louise Burfitt-Dons

All rights reserved. No part of this publication may be
reproduced, stored or transmitted in any form or by any
means, electronic, mechanical, photocopying, recording,
scanning, or otherwise without written permission from
the publisher. It is illegal to copy this book,
post it to a website, or distribute it by any other
means without permission.

Louise Burfitt-Dons asserts the moral right
to be identified as the author of this work.
This novel is entirely a work of fiction. Except in the
case of historical fact, the names, characters and
incidents portrayed in it are the work of the
author's imagination. Any resemblance to actual
persons, living or dead, events or localities
is entirely coincidental.

A CIP catalogue record for this book is
available from the British Library.

First edition
ISBN: 9781916449183

To my father, Ian Byres

Chapter 1

BEIRUT. JUNE 1960

Vladimir Petrov collects the letter from the communal box in the foyer of a block of apartments in The Christian Quarter. Back in his flat on the third floor, he spreads out the two pages on the Formica-topped kitchen table.

Using a combination of ultraviolet light and the heat of his small stove, he deciphers a message written in invisible ink between the ten lines.

Vladimir works for the SVR, or the Soviet foreign intelligence agency which is focused on the State's stability. His network recruit, "Alex", is a Kuwait-based deep cover tasked with providing useful information on potential targets to support Operation Oasis Palm Tree.

One of the aims of the mission is the destabilisation of British influence in the Middle East by supporting the drive towards Arab nationalism across the region. The ultimate objective is to restore the predominant position of the Soviet Union on the Arabian Peninsula. The SVR push the mantra

'Marxism as the true path to freedom for all!'

As the principle sea port, if Kuwait can be seized, the prize will be control of the busy shipping lanes of the Persian Gulf.

The sounds of the busy street waft up through the open window as he pores over the information which he will send on to his Soviet spymasters.

It is the fourth letter Vladimir has received. Alex is in full swing, harvesting the social opportunities within the close-knit Anglo-American community of Ahmadi, a town 40 kms south of Kuwait City and home to the Kuwait Oil Company.

Vladimir clips the report to the others. He lights a cigarette and paces back and forth in the small flat.

No. Alex has not disappointed. The details sent through to date list no less than eighteen names of people privy to inside knowledge either of the internal affairs of the oil industry or the political machinations going on in Kuwait.

The reports are padded with the customary fill from agents such as, 'So-and-so is the Swedish wife of high-ranking petrochemical engineer and having an affair with one of the Kuwaiti princes.'

In addition are details of several targets of significance for the SVR to assess and pass on to the KGB if appropriate.

'Went to a function at the Ahmadi Desert Motor Club and am working on a Russian-born member disaffected with colonials.'

Of real interest to the SVR are the targets vulnerable to blackmail.

'Senior pathologist driving research on cholera projects in desperate need of money due gambling debts.'

'Teacher at Anglo-American School. Former socialist activist at Cambridge University.'

'Everyone excited about the arrival of Ian Fleming in November. Opportunities to be exploited over visit.'

Those given codenames are of even greater importance. Such as MERRYWEATHER (access to the KOC l-Ahmadi Refinery Marine Department Sea Berth Loading Terminal Plans) and MADRELL (Face-to-face contact with access to plant servicing oil wells north of Ahmadi).

One in particular catches Vladimir's attention.

'DERRICK is in charge of a programme to identify anthrax spores similar to those used in chemical production by the Iraqi Secret Service. Location of laboratory unknown.'

Oasis Palm Tree is time critical. Next year, Kuwait reverts from a Protectorate under an agreement signed in 1899 in India between Sheikh Mustafa Al-Sabah and the British government because of threats to Kuwait's independence from its neighbours.

Without the assurance of British protection, its independence is at stake. Across the northern border, Iraq is voicing territorial claims based on the view they both belonged to the Ottoman Empire. In addition, support for the idea of a United Arab Republic is gaining momentum. Out of self-interest, the royal family of Kuwait is rumoured to be considering joining. Solidarity with the brotherhood also will increase the potential to restore Palestine.

Night falls and there's a ring on the doorbell.

Another Russian enters, and the two men drink coffee together. They discuss the report and decide on a plan of action. The unknown factor is can agent Alex be trusted?

Chapter 2

AHMADI, KUWAIT. AUGUST 1960

At 2.30 on Tuesday afternoon Gordon Carlisle polished and replaced his spectacles as he sat in his white-painted new office at Southwell Hospital.

Outside, the Kuwaiti heat scorched the paint off the walls, but inside the air conditioning made it necessary for Gordon to wear a long-sleeved shirt with his customary silk paisley cravat. It also made it vital to check the temperature of the cages of various live desert creatures which shared the room with him. The more poisonous, the more valuable for study into antidotes.

Gordon's wife described the office scene as something out of a horror story. It was a standing joke between the two of them. 'If I'd known it'd mean sharing you with half the desert animals in the world, the marriage would definitely have been off,' she'd jested on her first visit.

Gordon reflected on this and smiled. Newly married, after a long run as a bachelor, his friends had often referred to him in the past as wedded to his snakes. When Anita asserted on their first date she hated creepie crawlies, he'd kept quiet

4

about his reptile menagerie. Just in case it put her off.

The phone rang. It was the Head of Public Relations, John Dickson.

'Heard of Philip Foster? Also known as Pip Foster?'

The words set off Gordon's light stammer. 'P-p-p-'

'Writes for the Telegraph.'

'Can't say I have.'

'Well, he's out here. I wondered if I could send him over your way. He's doing a piece on Kuwait ahead of next year. Came in from Saudi. Travelling around the Middle East.'

Gordon Carlisle worked in the preventative medicine division. He'd been a permanent fixture in the department since arriving in the country three years after the Second World War ended.

'What perspective is he taking? Wouldn't Guthrie be of more use?' His lazy boss, who never lifted a finger but signed Gordon's reports with his own name to make out he did, would have been more appropriate.

'Fully tied up, I'm afraid. But anyway, he's bloody useless. And Pip asked for you specifically. I assume he got it from someplace.'

Puzzled, Carlisle rubbed his forehead. Why him? Had they met in the past somewhere?

'OK. Well, if I can help at all. Would be good to learn a bit more of what he's after.'

'I'm devilled if I know, old boy. Cholera injections. Household water integrity. Whatever your department does. I'll send over one of his pieces so you can check out his writing.'

'No doubt I can conjure up something of interest.'

John rang off, leaving Gordon to ponder the out-of-the-blue request.

An hour later his trusted aide Mansour, who had taken Gordon's car to the garage to check the tyres, was despatched to collect a copy of the article from Dickson's office at company headquarters.

Gordon recognised it straight away as an editorial he'd flicked through some months back.

Kuwait enjoyed prosperity long before the oil industry arrived. Although hot and humid in August, for much of the rest of the year, it enjoys a cool, dry climate. As a result, the country has always been one of the healthiest seaports in the Gulf.

In the past, its dhows plied the expanse between Basra and the Persian ports and on into the Red Sea, to India and East Africa. Kuwaiti merchants financed over 400 vessels in the lucrative pearl fishery industry and sold the catch in Bombay and the Levant.

On the landward side, Kuwait was always a busy trading hub for the Bedouin tribes, who ranged over the scrubby pastures stretching into the Najd.

Caravans travelled from there into the desert and onwards to Damascus and Aleppo. Bazaars filled large tracts of land on the edge of the town, where there was a brisk trade in guns, cotton goods, cooking oil and other staple products.

OK. General historical stuff, Gordon thought. Nothing he couldn't handle, given a broad brief.

Reading the newspapers from London was one of Gordon's favourite pastimes. Or would have been if he'd got his hands on them more often. Or if a small-minded censor had not

6

beaten him to it. The Telegraph and the Times turned up a week late normally, with large holes cut out of them and looking like a children's paper game.

He told all this to the journalist, who arrived the following afternoon in a pickup lent to him for his twenty-mile journey from Kuwait City.

They met in the car park and hit it off straightaway.

'It's all censored. Any mention of Israel or Judaism gets the scissors. Or blacked out with a pen. They don't care what's on the other side. V-v-very frustrating to read.'

He bent slightly to open the door and show his guest to a solid steel chair;

'Not very comfortable I'm afraid. As you can tell, we have just taken up occupation in this brand new building.'

At six foot four, Carlisle towered over Pip Foster by at least five inches, as he did most people he met.

'Bloody hell. You're right. Hard as a rock.'

Foster is at least ten years older than me, Gordon thought, taking in the handsome though somewhat lined face. His sandy-coloured hair had the odd silver fleck. He asked first off a general question. What attracted families from rainy old England to live in an unbearable, blistering climate like this?

'The money and a pleasant way of life,' Gordon replied, looking across his desk into a pair of bright blue eyes. 'A high standard of living. And in the winter the temperature is rather pleasanter than it is today.'

'I'm jolly certain it is.'

'Perhaps you'd like me to show you around. Ask me whatever you want. If I-I-I can help, I will.'

They spoke at some length about risks to expats, and what vaccinations they required on arrival. Also whether

7

the oil company had helped raise the living standards of normal citizens, such as the local Kuwaitis. Or just made the Westerners more affluent so they could double up on booze and cigarettes.

'Absolutely, they've b-b-benefitted. Oil money's given everyone free health care. They even treat animals on a no fee basis.'

'That's excellent.'

'Most of the medical equipment is state-of-the art.'

'So I've picked up.'

'But no point in good treatment if you don't practice prevention.'

'Which is why your department is so busy, of course.'

'Vaccination programmes and education are essential.'

Foster shifted his gaze, and Gordon watched him closely. The journalist rubbed his chin, as if preparing an awkward question.

'Something I heard on the grapevine on you which caught my interest.'

Gordon Carlisle shifted forward, all attention. 'Which was?'

'Connected to a recent outbreak of anthrax.'

'There was one, it's true. Yes.'

'Found in carpets, wasn't it?'

'Ah.'

'Understand you were the one to pick it? Rather clever of you, I thought.' The journalist took out a shiny holder from his pocket, opened it and offered a cigarette. 'Smoke?'

'W-w-word gets around,' said Gordon, taking the Stuyvesant. He searched his desk for a lighter.

'Rather fancy doing a profile on you. If you're up for it, old boy. A little more interesting than a kid getting an injection in the arm, eh?'

'I don't know that I'd be much of a s-s-subject.' He blinked in the bright morning light and searched for an acceptable refusal. 'Surprised you got to hear of that?'

Foster inhaled a thick lungful of smoke. He fished a notepad from his hip pocket with his left hand. 'You're quite the detective, aren't you?'

'It's all part of the job in a way.'

Chapter 3

A few months earlier Gordon might indeed have found the idea of an article written about him amusing. His sleuthing into an unexplained outbreak of anthrax had saved lives, for sure. As it was, five Kuwaitis had died. The common factor between the deaths had been a small carpet emporium in the city souk. And he had traced the source of the outbreak further back to a Bedouin tribe travelling south from Iraq, who had unwittingly woven the deadly spores into the rugs.

'James Bond of the Desert.'

'Hardly.' Gordon wondered how he could deflect interest from the topic. Scurrying noises from behind Foster caused the journalist to spin around in his chair. A tiny creature hopped up on its hind legs inches from where he was sitting.

'What is that?'

'A jerboa. Type of desert rat. No two moves alike.' Gordon got up to admire the small mammal he'd been nurturing, which someone had brought into his office weeks earlier. 'Helps them evade the jaws of h-h-hungry predators.'

'How many cages do you have here?'

'Eleven. I get given what people find in their gardens or yards. T-t-take a look at the yellow fat tailed scorpion.'

Gordon crossed the office to peer through the glass. 'He has his own little heater. We have to keep the cage warm to replicate the exact desert conditions.'

'An evil-looking thing.'

'Scorpions will try to kill anything that moves. Fortunately, only if it's smaller than them. So you needn't worry.'

Gordon hoisted the lid of the enclosure, put a hand in and picked up the eight-legged creature, plopping it down into the centre of his palm. It sat there waving its narrow tail from side to side. 'That's the bit you have to avoid,' he said, pointing at the stinger on the tip.

'I might not hold it all the same.'

Gordon Carlisle smiled then tenderly replaced the creature and checked the thermostat before turning back to his guest. 'Sometimes they find their way into homes. We encourage people to bring them here rather than kill them.'

'And that?' Foster appeared relieved to be safely away from the deadly scorpion and move on to the next container which housed an ash coloured snake.

'That's a horned viper. It's one of the most venomous snakes in the world. I f-f-found it myself out near the oil wells.'

'Do you have many of them?'

'No. They are becoming endangered. But I keep her cage at the bottom under another one. These snakes have a habit of escaping. She'll end up out at the Scientific Centre one of these days.'

Pip Foster flopped down again in his hellishly uncomfortable steel seat.

'Going back to the previous subject. Can I ask what became of the carpets?'

'With the anthrax? The ones we could trace had to be

11

destroyed.'

'Did they get compensation?'

'They weren't too h-h-happy, no. Not having spent their hard-earned rupees on them.'

Gordon suggested they do a walkabout of the new hospital. 'Would that interest you at all?'

By the reaction, a Cook's tour of the sterile and featureless offices was of no great interest. Nor what Foster was after, Carlisle sensed.

'That would be wonderful, old boy. But gosh, is that the time already?'

The journalist raised a wrist and checked his watch. 'I'm sure there's a lot to see. But I'm due back in Kuwait City for an evening appointment. Got to get the jeep returned.'

'Another day, perhaps. How long are you out for?'

'Just a week or two. I'd rather base out here in Ahmadi for a bit. By all accounts, it's quite a lively scene.'

'I'm sure John Dickson could arrange that. There's a comfortable Guest House here.'

'So I've heard. Would save driving back and forth, pissed as a newt.'

'Why don't I give you my telephone number at home. That way we can fix another meeting when we both have more time.'

Pip scribbled his details on a memo pad, tore off the sheet and handed it over.

It seemed to Gordon that Foster had cut the interview short because he wasn't getting the story he wanted. But that suited Gordon fine. He didn't want to elaborate on the carpet saga. Nor should he. Who was Foster, after all?

He reached across the desk to shake hands signalling the

meeting was over.

After escorting his visitor out to the front of the hospital, he returned to his paperwork. But the biro stuck motionless between his fingers and he couldn't concentrate on anything but the interview. For ten minutes he gazed out of the window at the distant saplings being planted; speed growers reaching at least forty centimetres a year and hardy enough to survive in the barren sand.

Gordon reflected moodily on Foster's blunt questions.

Unlocking a gunmetal filing cabinet he took out a carbon copy of the original anthrax report. He had relayed it on through his head of department to a case officer working for the British political agent in Kuwait City. It was a standard protocol undertaken with any virus outbreak.

He lit a cigarette, sat back at his desk and thought about it all. How he and Mansour had gone back to check on the efficiency of the antibiotics and found the seven decomposing bodies.

The disease had not caused the deaths. An autopsy revealed evidence of poisoning. Gordon suspected foul play. A sample of their primitive water supply confirmed traces of pesticide, possibly a case of inter-tribal rivalry. The mystery was still under investigation by the police.

When he delivered a follow-up report on the affair, he received the following memorandum from Whitehall.

```
The subject: Possibility of a Soviet-backed chemical
weapons experimental facility in Southern Iraq.
Documentation: Statement attached from Gordon
Carlisle on the leak of anthrax spores from the
establishment.
```

```
Action to be Taken: All information and findings on
the above are considered classified.
```

He read through it again. Classified? The British authorities had speculated the Bedouin had chanced upon a chemical weapons outpost. Maybe Iraqi. Or even some Soviet-backed laboratory preparing bioweapons to use on the civilian population of Kuwait. Far fetched? Perhaps not.

Selective scenes from that last trip into the desert ran through Gordon's head, none of them pleasant. The scorching Kuwaiti sun had been beating down on the bloated, fly-blown corpses for three days. The decaying bodies had turned black, and the stench was unbearable.

Gordon closed the file and returned it to the cabinet. Since receiving the memo from London he'd not spoken of the incident to anyone outside the department.

Once a week he stopped off at the swimming pool at the Hubara Club. Oil company employees' children spent their after-school hours dive bombing into the deep end while the parents sat gossiping on the raised terraces. His responsibility served principally to check that the attendants maintained the required level of chlorination. Occasionally, the inspection yielded a surprise result. Such as the fake bomb found under bushes close to the filtration plant.

Gordon decided to move his scheduled visit forward a day as a distraction to throw off his gloomy thoughts. He zipped up his portfolio and tucked it under his arm, pleased with the plan. In all likelihood, he would also see Anita there. By his reckoning, she would be on one of those very terraces sunning herself and reading a book.

Chapter 4

In the twelve years he'd been in Kuwait, it had been Gordon's little adventures which had kept him sane. The routine desk job had forced him to find distractions from the tedium of memoranda and long hand-written reports. Minor diversions which got him out of the office helped enormously and the range of interests soothed his restless soul.

But if he'd earned his reputation as James Bond of the Desert, it was because of the camping excursions. He didn't see it himself and certainly didn't want the ridiculous image aired around. Particularly since the news that Ian Fleming himself, creator of the fictional secret agent, was on his way out to Kuwait.

Gordon looked at his watch as he pulled up at the Hubara Club. It was three thirty. After parking the car he ran into Carl Sandberg as they walked up to the swing doors from opposite directions.

A blast of over refrigerated air met them in reception, almost sufficient to set off hypothermia. So much so, they appreciated reaching the open corridor which led to a drinking saloon called the Blue Bar.

Carl suggested they grab a beer first off. Gordon enjoyed

his company. Sandberg worked in Operations and usually had something original to say for himself.

As they'd once lived in the same block of bachelor flats, Carl was an old friend from way back. The stocky Geordie could have been described as a rough diamond. But five years of marriage and two children had taken off the edges.

'I've left them there for the time being,' he said of his family. 'Just back from six weeks leave in England, but the family wanted to stay on for a bit.'

'B-b-back to single life, then?'

'Those were good times, weren't they?' Sandberg bounced on his toes as he recalled a couple of escapades from the time they chased around in racy cars doing treasure hunts organised by the Ahmadi Desert Motor Club.

'You'll be back to living out of a tin for a while.' Gordon hoped single living didn't include a return to Carl's alcohol-induced outbursts, which had once got him into so many scrapes.

'Aye.'

'They're probably enjoying the difference. It's so pleasant in England during the summer.'

'No. They miss the pool. The diving boards. But they start school there next month. And my lad's fixated on television. Robin Hood and Wagon Train.'

Carl stood breast high at the polished counter. It was still early so the bar was empty. He turned out the pockets of his crinkled Khaki shorts and piled the contents next to Gordon's clump of car keys before finally finding what he was after. Carl dealt a trio of family photographs out on the bar. 'To tell the truth, I'm worried about the political situation here. Things could turn nasty. Just like that.' He snapped his fingers.

16

'But then I've said it before.'

'You think?' Gordon wanted to raise the subject of the Foster interview and get his take on it.

'Beats me the company complacency. Total lack of awareness. They aren't following what's going on over the border. That's the real story out here. What I've picked up in the field is not pretty. There's a substantial anti-British feeling out at Mina Abdullah and Al-Shuaiba.'

In his work capacity Carl made regular trips out to the refineries and the power-generating stations which employed many foreign workers, mainly Palestinians and Yemenis.

'I've not picked up too much myself from my own Arab workers,' said Gordon, sliding a beer in Carl's direction.

'But wasn't it you who found the explosive device near the deep end of the pool?'

'It was only a fake,' said Gordon. 'Probably just kids having a laugh.'

'What if it hadn't been? There've been bombs planted in the city. I blame London. They were all about egging on the Iraqis at the Syrian border in '58. Where did that get them?'

'They didn't expect the outcome. No one did.'

'Allowed the opportunity for Brigadier Qasim to march through the capital and overthrow the pro-Western government there. He's a commie bastard, that guy.' Carl lit up a strong Turkish cigarette, which glowed red in the darkened bar.

'It's a t-t-tenuous situation where Kuwait's involved.'

'You've got Nasser who's been in Moscow lobbying the Soviets about the pesky United Arab League he's trying to set up.'

'I read somewhere Nasser denies being behind the coup.'

17

'He probably knew nothing about it at the time. But the outcome suits him just fine, doesn't it? Those Iraqi bastards executed the entire royal family. Burnt the embassy. Murdered the British defence attaché. And our lot did bugger all.'

'I don't think a Baghdad could happen here. Not for a minute.'

'Don't you?' Sandberg tapped his bottle on the counter and looked around the bar angrily. 'Well, I bloody do. I've been following it closely. You've got the Kuwaiti Socialist Youth Brigade waiting for their moment in the saddle. They are an offspring of the Iraqi Communist Party,' said Carl, leaning heavily on one elbow. 'They hate us all. Loathe the Brits. Yanks. The elite Kuwaitis. Royals.'

Gordon raised his eyebrows at the possibility that hostilities could break out so soon. He peeled the cellophane off a new packet of Camel. Carl passed Gordon his lighter. 'London will send troops before anything like Baghdad happens here.'

'It's not up to us British to bring them in.' Carl reached for an ashtray. 'It will be the ruling family who decides whether to invite in the army. And that's only until next year. Once the protection agreement ends, Kuwait's on its own. Though, let's not forget the Kuwaiti Resistance.' Thick grey ash had formed at the end of his cigarette ready to drop off. 'They are solid guys, pro-West and pro-royal. But a handful of resistance fighters is nothing. Not enough to defend us against a full Soviet-backed Iraq.'

'I agree. They would totally outnumber them.'

'But the Kuwaitis will not give up their land without a fight. I have a lot of respect for them. They'll fight for sure.'

'But what with? Toy aircraft?'

'Exactly. I think the Kuwaiti Air Force consists of just one plane or is it two? They have sixteen tanks and one battalion of men. Just fifteen hundred.'

The conversation moved on to Gordon's recent marriage. 'I'd better go shortly. I want to collect Anita while she's still up here at the club. Might as well.'

'Enjoying it, is she?'

'She keeps herself pretty busy, which is the best way.'

'Yes, I see her out and about quite a bit. Taking photos? Prettiest woman I've ever seen in Ahmadi. You're a lucky guy. Or unlucky, however you read it.'

Gordon ignored the last remark, aware his beautiful wife had more than a few admirers. But the comment had been friendly. Probably nothing more. Sandberg was no lady-killer.

The bar began filling up. Gordon scooped up his possessions and left Carl chatting with some Stetson-hatted Americans who'd just come in. Gordon wound his way through the convoluted corridor and out into the bright sunshine bathing the central expanse of the club. This area housed an Olympic-sized swimming pool.

He took his chlorine-testing kit out and dipped it into the water. The result was positive enough. The water was in good shape so he went in search of his wife. She wasn't on the terrace as expected. The sprawling complex contained many meeting rooms, restaurants, squash courts, tennis courts, snooker rooms, beauty salons, and a large underground library. The place was a labyrinth but he still expected to run into her somewhere. He carried out a methodical square search to no avail. Assuming they must have crossed somewhere, he gave up.

19

Feeling in his pocket for the car keys, Gordon brought out Carl's lighter. Realising he'd slipped it in by accident, he went back to the Blue Bar. But his drinking companion had already departed. It was time to head home.

Chapter 5

Gordon unlocked his car and slid in gingerly. The seat of the Saab 96 was almost hot enough to need a towel.

He wound down the window to let out the mid-afternoon heat and waited for the steering wheel to cool: a ritual practised every afternoon in the summer. He'd grown used to the searing temperatures. But Sandberg's view the political situation was also reaching a boiling point was more concerning than the climate.

Sandberg had left behind his wife and children in England. Gordon heard of a couple of other company employees also considering the same precaution and wanted to get their families out. Perhaps they were overreacting. Maybe not. There would be serious consequences for the Anglo-American community if Iraq invaded Kuwait. It could lead to a bloodbath for the foreign civilians.

The Ahmadi roads were laid out in an orderly US grid system orientated east west and north south. They carried numeric names such as 1st Street, 2nd Street, and so on. Main Street, which housed the upper echelon staff of the Kuwait Oil Company, ran across the top of the hill and was where the Carlisles lived. But nowhere was a million miles away in the tiny enclave of Ahmadi.

When Gordon arrived home just minutes later he was eager to discuss Carl's conversation with his wife, and it surprised him to find her still out.

Their three bedroomed bungalow, classified as a PS1, sat on a corner plot and had an identical layout to the others. Gardens varied greatly giving a degree of individuality. After five years of constant care, Gordon's one had matured sufficiently to have a tall eucalyptus tree and plentiful oleander bushes in the front. But to the side it was still undeveloped and had been left as desert. And out the back too was still just the inescapable sand so microscopic it found its way into every pore and onto every surface. In the rear there was a bare verandah where their Indian ayah, Florrie D'Souza, often squatted sifting through bowls of dry lentils. It also connected to the servant's room and toilet.

After going through the house for clues as to where his wife might have gone, Gordon checked the back driveway where Anita sometimes kept her car but there was no sign of the Austin A30. As a keen amateur photographer, her favourite subjects were the Arabs and their disappearing way of life and she could have been out anywhere taking pictures. But she'd specifically told Gordon she'd be at the club that afternoon.

There was no evidence of any preparations for supper either. He reluctantly concluded that she'd not been home most of the day. The Kenwood Chef food mixer was still covered, but the bulky copy of *Mrs Beeton* he'd bought for her birthday lay open next to the draining board. So plans for the next week's dinner party were at least underway in part, which pleased him out of all proportion to its importance.

Unlike most of the other Ahmadi wives, Anita Carlisle was

unconventional in her approach to marriage. She was single-minded in her determination to remain a free independent woman and not be just an appendage to her husband. She was her own person. Gordon found refreshing Anita's reluctance to conform to a kitchen wife model with a Belling and flouncy pinny.

Also her unflappability. When he'd proposed, she'd shrugged off the threats to the Middle East.

'We might have to leave as soon as we get there if it happens.'

'So?' she'd answered, unconcerned.

The neighbours took to her well enough. But they all had children, which set her apart. His wider circle of friends was a different story. While they accepted his wife on the surface, Gordon sensed there was a question mark attached. Anita didn't fit the mould. But Gordon didn't care. He reminded himself that afternoon, as he'd done on so many others over the past six months that he'd never been happier in his entire life.

The fly screen creaked behind him, then the door opened. Florrie sidestepped through, fastening her sari at her narrow waist.

'Sahib home early?'

He knew from the way she busied herself straightaway with the pots and pans she'd heard his car pull up. Poor Florrie, thought Gordon. Her immediate assumption was she should cut short her afternoon nap and apply herself in the kitchen.

'It's not time for you to cook yet, Florrie.'

She threw her hands up in the air in protest. 'I sleep too much, sir.'

'Very hot today.'

'Oh so bad.' She waved a hand in front of her small face.

'Too hot.'

'Do you know where the memsahib is?'

'I think she went out in the car. I was resting, sir,' she mumbled, holding a hair grip in her mouth, before using it to tuck a strand of dark grey hair back into the tight bun she always wore.

'Your day off tomorrow.'

'I will work, sir.'

'You should have a rest and enjoy yourself.'

'I'm an old woman now, sir. I am forty,' said the sweet servant from Bombay.

'Don't you get on with the other ayahs, Florrie?'

'No, sir.' She shook her head and tutted. 'They are different. No good. They are not kind.'

'How's the fan in your room working?'

'Very fast. I don't need it on so quick.'

'You should use it more in this heat, Florrie.' The servants had only ceiling fans in their rooms. 'And it keeps the flies down.'

Gordon poured himself a glass of cold water and gulped it down in one. He took off his spectacles, smeared them with detergent and then rinsed them under the kitchen tap. He polished the lenses with a drying up cloth until the glass shone.

En route to the lounge via the dining room, the phone went brring-brring.

Located on the shelf alongside where Anita normally sat, Gordon had to slip into her chair to answer. 'Seven one six one.'

The other end was silent.

'Is th-th-that you, darling?'

24

Nothing.

'Hello?'

Whoever was calling hung up. Gordon assumed it was a wrong number and replaced the receiver on its cradle.

Beside him was a neat pile of *The Kuwaiti*, the weekly company newsletter. Anita read the local news avidly. Next to this was a large black-and-white photograph she'd taken of women in burkas squatting together in a circle on the sand. On an airmail letter pad, he saw a scribbled phrase in her familiar scrawl. 'My Darling' was all she'd written, as if she'd been cut short or called away. This struck Gordon as rather odd.

He crossed the room and switched on the radiogram. The red light illuminated, showing that the long-wave band was active. But the set was as silent as the random call he'd just taken. He fiddled with the wires underneath the cabinet until a roar of static filled the room. The news still couldn't get through over the background noise.

He gave up on the wireless and picked up an LP by Sibelius. Gordon placed the record on the turntable and lowered the needle carefully. The name 'Ophelia Dickson' was written diagonally in the top right-hand corner of the cover. He read the description on the back. In the kitchen Florrie was busy peeling potatoes. He opened the fridge door and helped himself to a bottle of Carlsberg from the inside panel.

The sounds of *Finlandia* filled the room, and the cold beer lifted his spirits but where was his wife?

Chapter 6

The sound of a car engine broke through the orchestral sounds which filled the lounge. At least his wife was home safe. He smiled to himself, recognising with fondness the half-hearted door slam. Everyone has a pattern. And every little pattern attached to Anita Carlisle was fascinating to Gordon.

As he waited for her to come through the door, he recalled their first meeting at a London concert hall. How it had been fated all along. Him being there alone and her, the stranger seated alongside, also with a single ticket. From this chance encounter, their affair rocketed at a pace. Fast, furious, exciting. The whirlwind romance led straight to a quick marriage and her going out to Kuwait with him at the end of his leave.

Despite some creeping reservations about where she'd been, it was hard for Gordon to disguise the physical effect his beautiful wife always had on him. She made him light up.

He watched the woman he'd married glide gracefully into the room, taking in her wide-apart blue eyes as if for the first time. They grew even wider, surprised to see him there comfortably ensconced in an armchair by the window.

'Hello.'

'I wasn't expecting you home this early.'

Her coldish comment deflated Gordon.

She followed on with, 'Can we not turn that music down, please?'

Gordon quietly obliged, by lowering the volume.

There was a faint flicker of acknowledgement from Anita, but little else.

'I've parked behind you, I'm afraid.'

'I'll move the cars around later. Don't worry about that now.'

No explanation was offered as to her absence, which was another familiar pattern. Always playing the mystery card. He'd have to fathom out where she'd been himself.

'Just popped out, did you?'

'I was at the Hubara Club. I thought I said.'

'I went up there myself to look for you. Couldn't see you.'

'Maybe I'd left by then.'

'I've been back a while now.' He raised his wrist to check the time.

She smiled, but didn't respond.

'Was that for me?' He looked down at the unfinished note. Anita's eyes rested on it for a second and then shifted away.

'Obviously. Oh, I went to Spinneys afterwards. We needed more silver paper, but I left my purse in the car. By the time I remembered where I'd left it, it was too late. I gave up. This heat. I'll get it tomorrow.'

He hadn't thought of the supermarket, which was towards the bottom of the hill. It was a plausible explanation. 'Oh, that's annoying. Was it busy there?'

'Always is.'

'Can I fix you something?'

27

'If you're having a drink.'

'Anything in *The Kuwaiti*?' he asked warmly, returning from the kitchen with a gin in hand.

'I haven't read it yet.' She got up and crossed over to the radiogram before he had time to hand her the drink. 'I'm not too partial to this.'

'Change it for something else, more to your mood.'

She shuffled through the collection and selected a new one. A ballad from Nat King Cole's "Espagnol" finally crackled into life.

He handed her the Sibelius cover, and she slipped the rejected record back into its sleeve.

'Ophelia's?' She raised an eyebrow. 'Doesn't she want it back? If it's hers?' she asked.

'Probably. She l-l-lent it to me last year. The Dicksons have an extensive collection of Sibelius. If there's anything else of his you'd like to listen to, you could perhaps ask to borrow it.'

'It's not really my thing,' she said, which surprised him. After all, when they first met, it'd been at a Sibelius concert.

'I was going to invite them to our dinner party. What do you think?' He loosened his belt before sitting down again.

'Must we?'

'Not necessarily. If you don't want them, that's fine.'

'Do we have enough gin to cope? You know how much she drinks.'

'She d-d-does hit the bottle a bit.'

'A lot.'

'It's hard to judge her from that one occasion,' he said, referring to an evening when Ophelia had sat down in the punchbowl, mistaking it for a chair. 'She's not normally that bad.' He'd hoped Anita would take to the Dicksons as they

28

were long-time friends of his. But it was clear she hadn't so far.

'Sounds like you're keen for her to come.'

'What makes you say that?'

She shot him a quick, challenging glance. 'She's desperate for you to take her to bed again. It's written all over her face.'

'I should never have told you about that,' Gordon said and meant it. Somehow Anita had winkled it out of him. They'd had a brief affair but almost a year had passed since he'd ended it.

'I would have picked it, anyway.'

Gordon detected more than a hint of resistance to his suggestion that they invite the Dicksons. But was it jealousy? It'd never occurred Anita would consider her a rival. Just as it had never occurred Ophelia would be annoyed at his sudden marriage.

'You know it's not like that,' he chuckled, but when she didn't laugh with him, he changed the subject. 'There's a j-j-journalist in Ahmadi by the name of Pip Foster. He came to my office today. Nice guy,' he stammered. 'How are we doing for numbers?'

'Why?' She took a sip of her drink.

'He might want to meet a c-c-couple of others.'

'We can't have any more, Gordon.'

'Didn't you say The Hunts weren't coming?'

'Yes. But we've got the Goodwins now. We have so many reciprocations. Too many, in fact. The table won't take more than twelve.'

'Of course. Well, I'd better check our stocks. We're getting a delivery of two crates of Canada Dry and two of Coca Cola tomorrow. We've got plenty of Scotch. Drambuie. And gin, for that matter.'

'So you've got the drinks side of things covered.'

'You haven't told me what's on the menu. Maybe we should discuss that too?' he said.

'You're trying to get the subject away from Ophelia.'

They exchanged looks, her mouth firm, as if she was engaged in thought and in a particularly argumentative mood.

'What is all this?' he replied, rising to it.

'I'm only teasing.'

He felt himself flush at having been bated so easily. 'That's good.'

She gave a small sniff and opened a packet of cigarettes. 'Seriously. Thinking of the party, we're out of these too.'

'I'll put Benson and Hedges on the list.'

'What did the journalist want with you?' She asked, placing the last cigarette between her bright red lips.

'A look around the new hospital, mainly. Very charming chap.' Gordon tried to analyse Anita's expression as she leant back in her chair. Was there something he was missing which would explain her mood?

'You've been to the hairdressers?' Anita still hadn't curbed his curiosity about where she'd been all day.

'No. I was waiting until the dinner dance.'

He got up to refresh her drink. When he returned he found her thumbing through the pages of *The Kuwaiti*. 'I've joined the tennis club,' she announced, which led him to think perhaps that was the answer. He'd not thought to check for her at the tennis courts.

'Yes. You said you were going to inquire about membership, didn't you?'

'They have good trips abroad if you get into the team. I

think that's what I need.'

Gordon felt a chill in the pit of his stomach and looked down at his book to conceal the inner turmoil. But a new thought occurred, which he tried to block. Despite giving into her every whim, perhaps their relationship wasn't as solid as he hoped. More and more, she was looking for ways to get away from him and spend time alone. Or find excuses to duck away without giving any explanation. While freedom to do pretty much what she wanted had been one of the inducements to entice her to Kuwait in the first place, he now wished he'd not done it. She took it for granted and had started moving goalposts beyond what was acceptable.

The tennis team was the latest example, and it grated.

Chapter 7

Gordon pulled at the edges of his black satin bow tie. He examined his clean-shaven features in the bathroom mirror. It was six thirty on the Thursday evening.

Anita appeared in the doorway wearing a navy satin dress with a deep vee neck line which barely covered her breasts. She gave him a bemused look as he noisily slapped on some cologne. Her chilly manner following their tiff had evaporated, and she was back to her old teasing ways.

'Not too much. You will smell like a waiter.'

He turned and nuzzled into her hair. 'While you smell terrific.'

'L'Air du Temps,' she said.

'My favourite.'

'Will I do?' She asked, pulling away. Her left arm, akimbo, perched on her slim waist. She picked up a flat patent bag to match her outfit. He was as thrilled as ever before with her sense of style, her natural beauty, and her vivacious personality. But he kept this to himself. He didn't want her to tire of his extravagant compliments.

'Have I got everything? Spectacles, testicles, watch and wallet. Yes. Let's go.'

They drove to the club in the Saab and entered the reception arm in arm. Wending their way through the dense crowd, dodging waiters with trays held high, he proudly watched as heads turned in their direction. His new wife was a big hit.

The annual Golf Dance took place on the open-air patio next to the swimming pool. Catering had been hard at work. A sea of white tablecloths sat ready and waiting. Wrought-iron baskets made for a colourful scene, each filled with fresh flowers flown in from Beirut for the occasion. The table for eight was proudly hosted by their neighbours, all of whom had assembled in good time. They dutifully joined them. Others included the Parkers and a Canadian couple who drivelled on about their superior house on 7th Avenue.

Gordon got up on the pretence of needing the gents. He crossed to where his friends, Neville Beresford, the Chief Personnel Officer and Matthew Quinn, a senior pathologist, were deep in conversation as they downed their cocktails.

Quinn turned to greet him. 'Gordon. Join us.'

'I'm on the lookout for Carl if you see him,' he explained. 'I've got his lighter. He left it on the bar yesterday. Have you seen him at all?'

'No. Can't say we have. But we were just talking about him, actually.'

'As you know, we're neighbours now,' said Neville.

'Really?' Gordon then recalled Carl saying that he had recently moved house.

'Neville just told me that Carl left his family behind back home?' Matthew cupped his cigarette upside down in his hand.

'Yes. We d-d-discussed it the other day. He is unlikely to be here tonight.'

'Stuck the kids in school over there. So I hear,' said Matthew. 'Can't imagine they'll be back in a hurry.' It was also unspoken that Carl's wife hated the life in Ahmadi with its heavy drinking and endless parties culture.

'I'm thinking of sending ours home too,' said Neville.

The Anglo-American School only taught up to age thirteen. The decision as to where and when to 'send the children off' was an endless topic of conversation.

'But Jean's dead set against our two boarding so young,' Neville continued. 'What's your opinion, Gordon? On the Iraq situation?'

'As long as the S-S-Sabahs want to continue their current arrangement with Britain we'll be OK. There's nothing to be concerned about. Not as far as I can see.'

'But if they choose to break it off and instead join the United Arab Republic, then Westminster will probably send in the troops, won't they?' Matthew took a deep drag of his cigarette. 'Depose the Emir. Run Kuwait as a colony.'

'Let's hope it doesn't come to that,' said Gordon.

'Britain will not want to lose its most important source of Middle Eastern oil.' A perfect ring of smoke formed up past Matthew's starched collar and dispersed slowly in the light evening breeze.

'And the ruling family will not want to risk losing their autonomy, will they?' added Neville, who always acquainted himself well on world affairs.

'If they feel threatened, they can ask for our military support. It's the deal, after all, isn't it?' said Matthew rhetorically.

Gordon caught the eye of a roving waiter whose wobbling tray he had narrowly avoided earlier. This time, he helped himself from the array of pre-prepared drinks. 'Until next year.'

Neville swirled the amber Scotch around in his glass. 'Everyone's relying on British troops to come in and save the situation. I'm not too happy about that. We should be more self-reliant.'

'But it would be a last resort, wouldn't it, bringing in the army? Solely up to the Emir.' Matthew took another quick puff.

'Well, let's t-t-toast the present situation,' said Gordon, 'And hope it lasts.'

'Yes. Good show.' Matthew made a toast. 'Here's to things settling down.' They chinked glasses and smiled in unison buoyed with sudden optimism.

Gordon and Matthew both had offices in the new hospital, so they discussed the improved facilities.

'A few items still left to finish.' Matthew's eyes twinkled, referring to the multiple unfinished power sockets and badly hung doors. He raised his tumbler in the direction of his wife, who was at their table looking for him and showing every sign of getting a bit agitated. She ordered him back with a peremptory wave of her arm.

'Oops. Better go back to the ladies.' He gave a good-humoured chortle.

Neville took a last swig of his drink. 'Time to trip the light fandango.'

'Yes, I suppose we'd all better,' Gordon agreed.

After dinner, the assembled band struck up, and dancing began. But before Gordon could get to Anita, someone she'd met on one of her independent evenings out whisked her off for a trot around the dance floor. He was the leading light in a band of amateur thespians who performed at the Kuwait

35

Little Theatre.

'He played the waiter in The White Horse Inn,' she said when she returned hot and flushed to the table. 'And his wife played the owner.'

'Was it any good?'

'It was very funny. Unintentionally so. We should go together some time. If you can resist laughing out loud during the performance. People are never so trivial as when they take themselves seriously.'

'Perhaps you should join that club too.'

She ignored the jibe, but her mood dropped at the suggestion. 'They need men, mostly.'

'Sorry. I didn't mean it like that.'

'No?'

'Amateur operetta is not my thing,' he said.

She lit a cigarette, still visibly offended.

Gordon leant forward and removed it. 'Leave that. It's my turn.'

He took hold of Anita's hand and escorted her on to the tiled patio under the balmy black skies. They moved deeper into the dance floor and the swirling couples. She made a point of dancing well away from his size eleven feet. 'I know you are going to land on me sooner or later.' She gave him a look filled with sexual innuendo.

Light as a feather in his arms Gordon guided her through a couple of clumsy twirls. Eventually the band took a break. The crackle of a record player needle, followed by the familiar sound of Ray Conniff blaring out, set a far breezier, lighter tone to the dance. After that, the music switched to bop and jive. The laughter got louder and more raucous as the volume ramped up. They jigged around. Exhausted by the effort and silly laughter, they finally sat back at their table,

Anita excused herself. 'I'm off to the powder room.'

As Gordon watched his wife weave her way through the crowd, he spotted John and Ophelia Dickson. He'd not seen them before, so assumed they'd just arrived. Their guest was the journalist Pip Foster who was looking in Anita's direction, his eyes fixed on the way her bottom swayed under the tight blue fabric as she crossed the floor.

Until that point in the evening, Gordon had forgotten all about The Telegraph writer and the damn article he was writing.

Chapter 8

The two women in Gordon's life, if you could count Ophelia as one, were chalk and cheese. Anita was petite, fully formed and a closed book. Ophelia, by her own account, a tall skinny rake, who loved putting people down in public. 'Subtle as a Soviet tank' is how her husband once described her.

As far as Gordon was concerned, Ophelia had zero love history with him. The couple had been friends for years. He was the available bachelor always included in their dinner invitations.

Ophelia had attempted to initiate sex with Gordon several times. Usually when she suspected her husband was having it off with someone behind her back. One evening, after John Dickson slipped away from their own party with a newly arrived nursing sister, she succeeded.

They promised never to mention the one-night-stand to anyone. And they both stuck to their little pact. But Gordon's arrival back from London with a new wife in tow, got to her. Ophelia promptly forgot all about their agreement.

On three separate occasions, Ophelia tried to engineer a meeting with Gordon alone. Each time he resisted and began to dread her company if John wasn't present.

The Dicksons went to every social gathering, so Gordon expected to bump into them at the golf dance. And had worked out a strategy which included inviting them to dinner as a couple to demonstrate to Ophelia his full commitment to his marriage. But Anita's standoff approach had thrown a bit of a spanner in the works. Now he thought best to avoid the couple completely.

He was thinking through the situation when Anita returned from the ladies' and tapped him on the shoulder. She announced she wanted one more dance and then leave.

Movement at the Dickson's table indicated they were about to go too. He'd seen Ophelia making parting gestures. So he was delighted to take his wife back out on to the floor and avoid any awkwardness before they left.

Gordon breathed a little easier. As they circled past the Dickson's table he noticed with relief they had left. But he was wrong. After the following twirl, he found himself bang next to Ophelia on the floor and she had partnered up with Pip Foster.

'Darling,' she crooned, pressing for a partner swap.

'Shall we?' Foster instantly seized on the opportunity to hold Anita's body close to his own. Gordon had no choice but to hand her over.

'He's so charming. Don't you think?' Ophelia clutched hold of his splayed fingers and gave them a tight squeeze. 'You've met him, haven't you? He said so.'

'He came to my office earlier in the week.'

'Could charm monkeys out of the twees,' she slurred. 'He'll be working on her next. You know that, don't you?'

'How are you anyway, Fifi?' he asked, using her nickname to conceal his annoyance at being trapped in the situation.

Grateful at least for a partner who was almost his own height, he managed a light smile.

'Oh, I'm just brilliant,' she spluttered with drunken sarcasm. 'In fact, never been better, have I?'

'You're looking lovely.'

'Listen to you with your compliments. We don't want your wife to hear something like that, do we?' She tilted her face up to his ear.

'I don't think she'd read it that way.'

'No, of course she wouldn't.'

'Sorry?' he was finding it hard to make out her words over the noise of the band.

'Oh, never mind.'

'Stop messing with me.' Ophelia looked drunkenly into his eyes. 'How do you expect I'm doing? With you avoiding me.'

'I'm not avoiding you.' He felt a tinge of apprehension, wary of a scene developing right in the middle of the dance floor.

'Yes, you are. Didn't you get my letter?'

'What letter?'

'What's the use?' She sighed.

'I think you're a bit tipsy.'

'Pickled. Stewed. Blame it on the booze.'

'It's been a good evening, hasn't it?' Gordon picked his words cautiously. 'Have you been doing much pottery?'

'Am I potty, did you ask?'

He grinned and swayed with her to the music.

'Where did you meet her?'

'Malcolm Sargent concert at The Royal A-A-Albert Hall.'

'How very proper, darling. What was it?'

He bent closer to hear. 'S-S-Symphony Orchestra.'

'What was it that made you marry her?'

'She's a lovely woman.'

'Oh, I know she looks lovely.'

'She is lovely. I proposed straight off. Well, almost.'

'So you love her, do you? Really?'

'Very much,' he replied with a half-smile.

The next bit was completely unexpected. 'I would have left John for you, you know?'

'Would you?' Shocked, he looked away, not knowing how to react.

'Yes.'

'I don't think so, Ophelia.'

'You only had to say.'

'What was that?' He genuinely couldn't hear.

'I would have divorced John if you'd asked me,' she yelled, oblivious to listening ears.

'It was never like that. You know it wasn't.'

'But it could have been.'

'Come on, now. You don't mean that.'

They swayed back and forth to the music. Her movements and speech were slow and jerky.

'Hold me, Gordon,' she said into his ear.

Gordon really didn't want to make a spectacle of themselves. Particularly at the Hubara Club. He cared about Ophelia enough to protect her from the humiliation. And he had Anita to consider. She'd warned him about Ophelia, after all.

'When can I see you?'

'I don't think that's a good idea.'

'I have to talk to you, Gordon.'

Some couples waltzed close by and eavesdropped as best they could. Every word and nuance were being lapped up, joined together and dissected. There was a lot of barely

41

concealed grins.

One dance ended and another began, a foxtrot followed by a boogie. But there was no disengaging from Ophelia. She wouldn't let him go. Not until he agreed to see her on her own. Which he eventually did out of desperation.

Her weight grew heavier in his arms. As he manoeuvred her back to her husband seated quietly blowing smoke rings from a fat cigar, she was ready to disengage and on the point of collapse.

'Thanks, old chap,' John said, putting aside his smoke and rising to help hold her vertical. 'Might get you home, darling,'

Gordon walked quickly back to the Goodwins' table where Anita was sitting alone. He leant on the back of a chair, searching for his wife's reaction. The entire affair had been beyond embarrassing.

She propped her head up with one clenched fist, silent and resentful.

'Enjoying yourself?' she asked.

'P-P-Perhaps we should s-s-say our farewells and make our escape.' Gordon adjusted his spectacles nervously.

They said their goodbyes and thanks to the hosts and headed off. Pip Foster stood waiting to intercept them by the exit doors. Gordon saw him quite openly look down at his wife's barely covered breasts. Anita noticed and stared back coldly.

Pip flushed with a mixture of irritation and embarrassment as she stormed off into the night towards their car.

'Thank you, Pip, for holding the door open for us,' Gordon said, covering for his wife's apparent rudeness. This gave Foster the opportunity Gordon had hoped to sidestep.

'I was waiting to catch you. Don't suppose you've got any

free time for me tomorrow, have you, old boy? Bit of pressure from the office to get something back to them pronto.'

Chapter 9

Gordon couldn't keep up with his wife. She had shot off ahead and stood waiting by their locked Saab when he got there.

'Are you OK, darling?'

'Sure. Why wouldn't I be?'

'I apologise. He was the journalist I told you about. Wanted us to meet up again tomorrow. I didn't mean to keep you waiting.'

He unlocked her car door and held it open as she clambered in. Crossing over in front of the bonnet, he climbed into the driver's seat. Anita sat staring out the window sulking.

'What is it?'

'Nothing.'

'You were a bit rude to him, you know.' It was a side of her he hadn't seen before. Brusk, off-hand, unsubtle.

'Why do you say that?'

'The way you brushed him off. Did anything happen out there?'

'What are you driving at?'

'Did he make a pass at you? Or something?'

She didn't answer.

'You were dancing with him, weren't you?'

'I had no option, did I?' she said icily.

'I suppose not. One of those partner swaps. They can be deadly. I'm so sorry. But I couldn't get away.'

'Oh, I could see that.'

He adjusted his glasses in the darkness. 'I was d-d-doing my best to get away from Ophelia.'

'Six dances?'

'Believe me. It wasn't my idea. She was so tight she could hardly stand. I had to be a gentleman.'

'Oh, you had to be, did you?'

'Couldn't just dump her on the dance floor, could I?' He let out a forced giggle at the thought.

'You should have done,' she said.

'I thought you'd see the funny side of things.'

'Well, I suppose it is amusing for other people. You two were the main entertainment.'

They sat in silence.

He twisted the key in the ignition. 'How did you find Pip Foster?'

'Why?'

'D-d-did you need to be that rude?' It was his second attempt. Having coughed briefly into life, the engine spluttered and died. 'He seemed rather put out by you rushing off.'

'He did, did he?'

Gordon sat with one hand on the key, wondering what to say next.

'I just want to get home. I've had enough for one night. Looks like you have too.'

He started the engine again. He'd had too much to drink, but knew he could still drive if he took things slowly.

Several other cars had started up and were driving off. They had to queue to leave the car park.

'Did you enjoy yourself?'

'It was quite a pleasant evening.'

They came up to the roundabout, and she gave a noisy yawn.

'I thought the band was pretty good, didn't you?'

'Yes.' She wiped her brow. 'I'm not feeling too great. Can we get home any quicker?'

He stretched his free hand across and felt her forehead.

'Perhaps some of the food didn't agree with you. Mass catering can be quite dangerous. Particularly in this heat. Stuff goes off.'

'Oh, I don't know.'

'You didn't drink too much, did you?'

Anita fell silent again.

'OK. Hang on in there. We'll get you home in no time and I'll tuck you into bed.'

As they turned into Main Street, the car mounted the kerb before regaining the road with a thump. This jerked Gordon back into alert mode. They reached home almost without further mishap apart from scraping the left side of the thatch fence, which partitioned the drives between the houses. Having to reverse to free the car, he was forced to acknowledge he was fully pissed.

It was standard practice for Gordon to get out first, then open the car door for his wife. But on this occasion she clambered out before he got there.

'I'll unlock the front door for you,' he protested, but she'd already found a key and was out of ear shot. He staggered in, locked the door behind him, and followed on. Anita was in their bedroom, struggling to get out of her tight clothes.

'P-P-Perhaps you should drink a glass of water. I'll get one.'

46

'No. I just want to lie down.'

She unzipped her dress and let it fall to the carpet. He leant down, picked it up and draped it over the back of a chair. He was used to operating drunk, but knew his wife wasn't, and not in the mood to make conversation.

'Let's get you horizontal, shall we?'

She sat on the bed to unhook the stockings from her suspender belt, but fumbled with the clips.

'Let me,' he said.

He gently pushed her back against the sheets. It wasn't like Anita to get that paralytic.

'Oh God, the room is spinning.'

'Get these stockings off if we can. You'll be more comfortable.'

She lifted her hips as he peeled down her nylons.

'If we could just get that tight corset off, you'll sleep better, darling.'

'I need to be sick.'

He rushed off to the kitchen to fetch a bowl. When he returned, she'd wriggled out of the underwear and managed to get between the sheets. She had turned over but Gordon noticed a tear running down from one eye and across the bridge of her nose.

'It's OK, darling. You sleep now. I'll be in shortly.'

He flicked off the overhead light, so the room was pitch black. At least she doesn't have an early start, he thought.

Gordon made his way out to the kitchen and made a pot of coffee. He was drunk but not ready for bed. He moved to the lounge so he could read a book and switched on the standard lamp. He untied his bow tie and tossed it aside. The relief was immediate, but still he couldn't concentrate.

Instead, he lit a cheroot and wrote a mental list of where he would take the journalist the following day. He'd not expected another interview to crop up at such short notice and was behind with his monthly report. The full day would be taken up by tedious questions. Plus a tour of unlikely fleshpots of Ahmadi all of it with a thumping great hangover.

Gordon tried to think it all through. Perhaps he could drive Foster down the coast. Maybe see the jetty. Or take in the Arab village of Fahaheel, where donkeys roamed the unpaved streets amidst the Cadillacs. But somehow he sensed that wouldn't cut it. The journalist seemed keener on the banal than the bizarre. Anglo-American community activities. The golf club, bowling alley and shopping facilities. In his befuddled state, Gordon couldn't work out why.

And now there was the Anita issue to complicate matters. She'd given Foster a look to kill, warning him off. But Gordon wondered what they'd been talked about on the dance floor together. He'd been too preoccupied at the time to overhear anything. Had Foster groped his wife? Or propositioned her? Something had caused her angry reaction to him when they left the club.

He would never know unless he asked. And Gordon's pride wouldn't allow him to do that a second time.

Chapter 10

Jean Beresford watered her flowerbed of nasturtiums every morning during summer, bang on the dot of six thirty. Certainly the best time of day. Before it grew too hot.

Neville, her husband, left for work promptly at seven.

'Hurry up,' she called out to her children, Sylvie and Stewart. 'You'll miss the bus.'

'Give them back,' her daughter whined. 'Mummy? He's got my five stones.'

'Do it. Give them back to your sister, Stewart.'

'I was only playing with them,' her son said, shoving a small satin bag in Sylvie's direction.

Jean saw them through the front gate at ten past seven. The yellow 'North' bus to school was as regular as clockwork. Her neighbour Carl Sandberg reversed down his drive at seven fifteen and headed off to do whatever he did in his office. You didn't need mantelpiece clocks in Ahmadi to know the time. Things ran to rigid routines.

Mary, their ayah, crept unobtrusively down the corridor balancing a full basket of laundry on her hip. The morning was calm and still fresh. Perfect. Jean loved home decorating in the peace and quiet just after the children left for school.

She began on the delicate work of pleating and pinning a red lampshade. The phone broke into her pleasure stream.

'Hi. Is that Jean Beresford?' The caller, with a pleasant Irish accent cleared her throat.

'Yes,' she said. 'Who's this please?'

'It's Theresa Lloyd here. Meg's mother. From school.'

'Oh, hello Theresa. We've met once, haven't we?'

'But not spoken before.'

'Not properly.'

'And with our girls in the same class.'

'Are they?'

'Your Sylvie's a lovely girl.'

'Thank you.'

'Since Sylvie rejoined the school, they've become good friends.'

'Yes, she's been in England for a year. We went over to start building a house.'

'Sylvie was in another set before, wasn't she?'

'Yes. She was friends with the Roberts' girl. But they went back to Guernsey.'

'And groups change, don't they?' There was a pause. 'The reason I'm calling, would Sylvie be allowed to stay at a sleepover? Meg's having a slumber night. And she wants to invite her.'

'Oh, I see.'

'She's been nagging me for ages to have one. You know what they're like at this age, don't you? Ahead of their time.'

Jean didn't know what 'they were like' at all. She didn't much appreciate the inference that her daughter was grouped with a bunch of precocious girls but agreed all the same.

'They like to consider themselves teenagers before their

50

time,' Theresa said.

'Do you think so?'

'I do. Can't wait to grow up, can they? I can't see what the rush is myself. But, hey ho.'

'I suppose so.'

'Anyway, Meg keeps asking me if I've rung you?'

'Does she?'

'So I thought I'd better get on and do it today. I got your number out of the book.'

'Sylvie is already on the bus. So I can't ask her yet, I'm afraid.'

'Look, I use the word "party". But it won't be, really. Perhaps just four or five.'

Jean Beresford had never even heard of such a thing as a slumber party. It was obviously an American idea and, as such, she automatically disapproved. But she'd never say that either.

'Well, it's very kind of you to ask her.' She hesitated.

'Not at all.'

'But I'll have to run it past her father before agreeing.'

'Of course.' Cynthia's voice brightened up. 'I was thinking Thursday.'

'Is it for a birthday or anything special?'

'No. Nothing like that.'

'Right.'

'One warning. Vince and I are going to the cinema that night. So they'll be home alone. But our ayah will be there. And we'll be back at ten o'clock. Straight after the film ends.'

'Oh.'

'Are you OK with that?'

'I would have to ask Neville. But probably that will be OK.'

51

'We've left them before and it's been fine. They've been well behaved. So it's not the first time we've done it.'

'What does she have to wear?'

'Just normal clothes. Bring her pyjamas. Meg wants a midnight feast. She keeps on about it.'

Jean reluctantly agreed in principle, aware her shy bespectacled ten-year-old had never been anywhere before for a full night on her own. But when the children came in at eleven thirty and Sylvie Beresford heard about the date she gasped at the idea.

'I don't want to go there, Mummy.'

'I've already said yes. It's on Thursday.'

Sylvie burst into tears. 'Please don't make me.'

Jean flew into a mini rage. Now she'd have to call Meg's mother and think up some excuse to get out of it. So embarrassing. 'Why ever not?'

'Meg is always calling me "four eyes" because I wear glasses. And trying to make me look stupid.'

'Don't be so silly.'

'At times she's really horrible. Really, really so.'

'I thought you said once she was a nice girl.'

'Well, she isn't.'

'You spend too much time on your own reading books.'

'I've got other friends. Nicer than Meg.'

'It'll help you to make some new ones, though.'

'Not her.'

'You said once you played with her at break.'

'I did because I like Lynn. But Lynn doesn't play with Meg anymore. And Lynn won't play with me if I'm friends with Meg.'

'You're going. And that's it.'

'Why do I have to?'

'Because Daddy and I might go out that night. That's why.'

'Then can I stay with Godfrey?' Stewart was instantly on to an opportunity to go across the road.

'We'll see.'

'Yeah!' He pulled a triumphant face and jumped up and down.

'You're stupid,' said Sylvie to her brother. Now she had no way out.

'And you're a cretin.'

Neville came through the door at twenty to twelve, straight into the bickering quarrel. 'What's going on?'

Jean wished her husband wouldn't come in grinning so broadly when she was trying to impose discipline on the children. She had a genuine dilemma with the invitation and Neville's trivialising it all was not helpful.

Over a lunch of cold chicken, boiled potatoes and canned peas, he listened attentively to them each in turn. Ever the diplomat he absorbed the social aspects carefully.

'Meg's always talking about boys and things.' Sylvie tailed off at the end and played about with her food.

Neville adopted a thoughtful expression. His pale green eyes radiated a natural sympathy for his daughter. 'A lot of the children are far more mature than her, Jean. What do we know about the family?'

'I've already said yes to Meg's mother, and that's it.' Jean's voice raised in protest.

'Fire one!' Stewart launched a silver napkin ring across the polished table at his sister, who sat with her arms firmly crossed in a deep sulk. The ring flew off the side of the table, dropped and rolled. 'Aw! You're supposed to fire it back!'

53

Stewart got down from the chair and recovered it from the far corner of the room.

'Will you get back up this minute!' Jean shrieked.

'Yes,' said Neville, 'We're in the middle of lunch. Do as your mother says.'

'You're driving me up the wall, both of you.' Jean aimed the words at her children. 'And hold your knife and fork properly, Stewart. Or there's no boat club this weekend. No water skiing.'

Stewart dropped his lip. They all fell silent.

'What are you planning for this afternoon?' Neville Beresford asked his wife anxious to lower the temperature around the table.

'I'm meeting Pam up at the club. Hear all the gossip about last night, if you know what I mean.' She flashed across a knowing look in his direction.

'You going to the pool? Can I come?' Stewart saw his chance.

'Only if you're good.'

Sylvie's face lit up at the prospect, the looming sleepover pushed aside for the moment. 'Can I come too?' She liked playing with Pam's daughter, Helen.

'I'll wait until the bus comes at three thirty. Then we'll all go up together. Maybe Daddy can join us when he finishes work at half past four. Darling?'

'If you wish. Fold up your napkins, children,' said Neville Beresford, wiping his hands as he spoke. 'And you may get down if you have finished. If you'll excuse me, Jean, I'll just lie down for fifteen minutes before going back to the office.'

It was a normal Beresford day like so many others in the sleepy company town.

54

Chapter 11

What's going on out at Magwa these days?' the newspaper journalist asked as they drove along 6th Avenue.

Gordon Carlisle felt a sudden wariness. 'Magwa?' He took his eyes off the road to look over at his passenger.

The tour had already been quite extensive. They'd even done the rifle range and the experimental farm. Now Pip Foster was throwing up new, more borderline demands. No-go areas. Places which were really out of bounds.

'There's nothing much to see there.' Gordon hesitated. Before Southwell, there'd been a medical facility in North Ahmadi just off the 7th ring road. 'It's where the old hospital used to be.'

'An old clinic?'

'Started out as a few tents and two clay pavilions. Four wards. I think they could only cope with eight patients back then.'

'I was rather hoping you would drive me there.'

Gordon didn't like Foster's tone too much at all, too direct. But then he was a journalist. 'We have a small industrial plant out there to run tests on new vaccines, but it is very hush-hush, I'm afraid. Not somewhere I can take you.'

The next was a stunner. Pip pulled out a visiting card and handed it across to Gordon. 'Maybe this will explain.'

Gordon snatched a look and took in at once the die-stamped foreign office logo. 'I see.'

'I wear two hats, if you hadn't already guessed,' said Foster, repocketing the identity card.

'That explains why Magwa.'

Now it all made sense. So he was an MI6 man and already knew about the storeroom and testing centre out at Magwa.

Gordon slowed the car and brought it to a stop. Some of the background to their earlier conversation came to mind such as Foster's knowledge of facts not generally known about his past.

Gordon, who prided himself on his perspicacity with people, had not picked Foster as an agent. He asked himself why had he been so slow to get the message? As a journalist for a respected newspaper, Foster had the perfect cover. It gave access to a wide range of sources all good for information to pass on to the British Secret Service.

His interest in Magwa had been obvious all along. Defence ministers in London knew about the anthrax testing. And it was to be expected there'd be a follow-up on his report what with tensions ratcheting up the border issue between Iraq and Kuwait.

'Sorry about the subterfuge,' said Foster, as Gordon performed a swift three-point turn.

Driving on to Magwa, they talked about Gordon's project in more depth and how anthrax was endemic in the Middle East.

'It's because of the goat herds, mostly,' Gordon explained. 'They pick it up from the soil while grazing. The s-s-spores can lie dormant for years. From time to time Arab goat tenders become infected through a cut or a scratch and if they don't have access to antibiotics they can die quite quickly. Anthrax isn't a big killer of people in itself, though.'

'Unless it's weaponised.'

'Yes. Then it's potentially a m-m-massive threat,' Gordon conceded.

'Could be all part of the Soviet's Operation Oasis. The spread of communist ideology across the Middle East.'

'That's a p-p-possibility. Delivered by the trillions as an aerosol, there's no s-s-smell and it's invisible. If anthrax gets into the lungs in those high proportions, it is deadly. Perhaps kill ninety per cent of those infected.'

On the journey to the lab Gordon filled Pip in on the background to the Bedouin who'd died. On questioning the tribe they'd traced out the exact path the nomadic family had taken when they'd entered Kuwaiti territory.

'Mansour and I found the four-room structure which the Bedouin described to us and it appeared to be a onetime Soviet experimental complex. As you know, they're backing the Iraqis in all this.'

'Is the building still there?'

'Not anymore. My assistant checked it out the day after we found the bodies. He s-s-said the building had been reduced to rubble.'

'A former chemical storage unit?'

'Yes. There's a possibility the Soviets murdered them to shut them up about the facility before demolishing it to hide the evidence.'

Approaching the former hospital, they passed an open jeep with what looked like at first glance a machine gun mounted on the back.

'Pest control,' said Gordon with a grin. 'Their unit is right next door to our testing centre. We do regular spraying to keep the insects down. And we operate anti-locust expeditions from here too. '

'Is that necessary?'

'A swarm can pack between 40 and 80 million locusts into less than half a square mile.'

'Does that happen very often?'

'Usually every seven years and not normally more fre-quently. But this year was different. We came across a body of young hoppers which needed to be wiped out.'

'The Iraqis aren't the only threat of invasion?'

Gordon laughed. 'Small but s-s-savage.'

'How big were the ones you found?'

Gordon steered with just his left hand. 'The ones at the early stage were only half an inch long.' He demonstrated the dimension with his right thumb and forefinger. 'But we found some in the fourth stage of skin change.' He extended his spare fingers. 'These were a full three inches in length. Big buggers.'

'They go through five growth spurts, I believe.'

'By then they're hard to catch because they move lightning fast.'

'Unlike the Iraqis. Do you mind if I smoke in the car?' Foster took out a cigarette and Gordon nodded automatically. 'It's why we lay poison bait,' he continued. 'The men spread it out across the advancing swarm. The locust must love the taste. Within thirty minutes, they succumb but don't always die.'

Foster gave a sceptical sigh. 'I thought the Arabs ate them?' He lit the cigarette and took a couple of quick draws.

'That's indeed a problem we have. Not just a delicacy, locusts and grasshoppers are the only halal insects and an excellent s-s-source of protein. So the locals collect them in buckets. We put out advisories the pesticides contain phosphorous and are toxic. But they still eat them.'

The laboratory building was set behind the original operating theatre and well-hidden from public view by a row of tamarisk trees. As Foster rammed his cigarette into the overly compact car ashtray, Carlisle attended to the unlocking of the facility and then waved Foster in.

The distinctive odour of the wooden cabinets mixed with chemicals was familiar to Gordon but Pip Foster paused and sniffed cautiously.

Gordon picked up on it. 'Don't worry. We lock away the anthrax specimens back there.' He nodded towards the padlocked storeroom.

There was nothing much else to show. The room contained a couple of refrigerators and an oven to heat soil samples. The counter top was covered with glass flasks, Bunsen burners, flagons, and sample jars.

'Who else knows about this place?'

'Just Mansour and Najib, who help me run it. The insecticide unit next door is a good cover for our chemical tests. Plus, we keep Gammexane back there. It's a powerful pesticide. The team mix it with bran to make the locust poison. We've got organophosphate, carbamate, and pyrethroid. All deadly poisons.'

Gordon explained that the team also had a couple of guards who patrolled at certain times. At that point, a battered Ford pulled up upside. The door opened and a good-looking young Arab in his late twenties strolled in.

'Ah, here's Najib now,' said Gordon. 'Perhaps leave us for the moment. We will be out of here quite soon.'

'I'll come back this afternoon,' said the Palestinian in an almost faultless English accent, eyeing Pip Foster with an expression of curiosity mixed with slight concern.

Gordon opened a drawer and took out a set of photographs taken when they had come across the desert facility. 'There wasn't a lot of evidence lying about other than scraps of paper. The place had been stripped clean.'

'What are you doing here about the anthrax?'

'This st-st-study gives us a molecular fingerprint. If another outbreak occurs with this particular strain, we've evidence of a deliberately designed biological compound.'

'With chemicals manufactured out in the desert?' Foster leant back against the cabinet. 'If the Soviets have armed the Iraqis with bioweapons, perhaps they plan to use them if the invasion falters or fails.'

'Releasing just a bag of sugar's worth of spores over the Hubara Club during a sw-sw-swimming gala would be enough to infect the whole Anglo-American community. And if the microbes are resistant to antibiotics, it'd be lethal. By the time the British army arrive, most of us would be dead, that is certain.'

Chapter 12

The short walk in the overpowering heat to the upper pool terrace at the Hubara Club had been enough to leave Jean Beresford gasping for air. At just past three thirty in the afternoon it would be impossible for her to lie out in the full sun with her friend Pam Quinn.

Their children followed on behind, dawdling and chatting.

Jean put her beach bag down under a Cinzano umbrella. 'Are you sunning today or not, Pam? I never know with you.'

'You should do by now. I'm always topping up.'

Pam flapped her towel vigorously startling her daughter, Helen, out of her caught-in-a-dream world. 'Run along, you two.' She shooed Helen and Sylvie in the direction of the pool. 'Go off. We grown-ups want to talk.'

While she was the same age as Jean's daughter, Helen was in the class below at school. Pam called Sylvie a clever clogs.

The two girls walked down the steps to join Stewart who was already in the water doing duck dives.

'We'll give you kids a shout when the cokes arrive,' Pam called after them.

'Don't talk to me about Sylvie. She's sulking,' said Jean when the children were out of earshot.

'Why's that?'

'She's been invited to play with a girl she doesn't like. I told her in no such uncertain terms. "You can't just say no." She has to try to get along.'

'Good for you.'

Jean was in a stream. 'It's all very well Sylvie playing with Helen, but she also needs to get on better with the girls in her actual class.'

'I agree. Good for them to play with different types of people.'

'I don't know how you can take all this sun.' Jean patted her lacquered hairstyle, still sticky from the club dance.

'It's easy. Just watch me.' Pam wore a too bright orange two-piece. The bikini was new, and she didn't mind it bleaching out a bit.

Jean looked down at her small breasts, already turning pink even inside the padded swimsuit. She wondered how on earth heavily-busted Pam got away with what she wore in front of men, never mind the sun aspect.

'I know it's ageing, Jean. But you're younger than me. You don't need to care.'

'I'm thirty-three though, Pam. Can you believe that?'

'You worry too much about things.' Jean's friend had dark brown eyes, which she always closed before shaking her head to stress a point. 'I haven't got your colouring,' said Jean, rubbing in Coppertone tanning lotion. 'I burn to a frazzle if I bake too long. I don't know how you do it.'

'Because I have skin like buffalo hide, that's why.' Pam pulled her generous mouth into a bright, false smile revealing a set of glaringly white teeth. 'And I hate being pale,' she said. 'It doesn't suit me. If you think I'm tanned, take a look at Nola. She's as black as the ace of spades!'

Jean had little to do with Nola, Pam's tennis partner. What Pam and Nola got up to after their mixed double matches was anyone's guess. As a result, Jean and her husband Neville had dubbed them "Les Girls".

Eventually, the subject moved on from tanning regimes to discussing the fiasco at the Golf dance.

'Poor Gordon. It looked like he was trying to avoid "O.D." all night.' Jean gave a mischievous grin and shook her head from side to side.

'Who's that?'

'O - feel - y - a.'

'You don't have to "poor Gordon" him. He can take care of himself.'

'Oh, I don't know. He's only just got married. And Ophelia looked to me as if she was trying to cause trouble.' Jean leant back in the wicker chair and crossed her slender legs. 'I wondered if something was going on between them. Though I shouldn't gossip, should I?'

'Of course there was. Surely you know that.' Pam gave her friend a disbelieving look.

'Do you really think so? I can't imagine Gordon doing that.'

'He's a dark horse. Everyone says so.'

'Honestly, I didn't know where to look.' Jean's eyes sparkled with excitement. 'It was such a spectacle.'

'Everybody was watching it, weren't they?'

'She practically collapsed, didn't she? I thought, "wait for it", said Jean, reliving the moment.

'It's not the first time Ophelia's behaved that way in public.' Pam lay back in the sun, chatting on with her eyes closed.

'But not with Gordon.' Jean fingered her delicate chin and ducked her head from under the fringes of the umbrella to see who was about.

'No, not with him, Jean.' Pam pulled herself up on an elbow. 'But she's often paralytic.' She closed her eyes and wiggled her head from side to side, feigning drunkenness.

Conversation moved on swiftly to how they'd always thought of Gordon as a confirmed bachelor. Someone who would never marry.

'Didn't so-and-so like him? The red-headed girl. I can't think of her name.'

'Ruby Taylor? Dental nurse?'

'Ruby Taylor. That's it. My memory. Honestly.' Jean gave a tut of self-derision.

'Gordon never liked her, though. Everyone could see that. But he's had dozens of affairs.' Pam closed her eyes and shook her head again.

'I don't know exactly what to make of new wifey just yet.' Pam rolled over to bake her back even browner. 'She's not his type. What's she doing with him?'

Jean's mouth turned down in disagreement. 'Well, I don't know Pam. I think differently. Just by looking at them together, you can see he's keener on her than she is on him.'

'Which is why he likes her, probably.' Pam turned onto her front again and spread her legs wide apart.

'Really?'

'Men. Men only want what they can't get.' Pam lifted her head to make sure her favourite saying had been taken on board.

'And, if what you say is right. That he's played the field. Maybe came across someone who didn't come across so easily.'

Pam laughed out loud at Jean's word play. 'She won't stick

with him. Mark my words. You'll see.'

'Oh, I don't know about that.' Jean began to feel uncomfortable at the girlie predictions they were making.

'She's got a wandering eye. Already.'

'Well, I don't know whether they'll have any children, do you?'

'I doubt it. But who knows?'

'He's in his early thirties now. He has to be.'

Pam sat up and looked around as if about to impart a state secret. She lowered her voice. 'I get the impression she's older than him.'

'Do you?'

Pam nodded her head. 'Definitely.'

'But someone I know in England just had her first baby at thirty-eight. So you can never tell, can you?'

'Far too old for him, I think.' Pam wrinkled up her nose.

'I can't imagine a performance like the one last night will help the marriage much.'

'On the contrary.' Pam squinted up at Jean with her dark eyes. 'It's what he needs. Gordon's too soft for a man.'

'He's got lovely manners though, hasn't he?' said Jean, rising to Gordon's defence.

'He's like a little puppy dog around her!'

They sat in silence for a few minutes.

'It'll be interesting to see what happens at their dinner party, won't it?' Jean pulled a face.

'We were wondering ourselves if they would invite the Dicksons after all that.'

'Depends if they'd already asked them.'

'But they've always been close to Gordon.' Pam slapped another handful of suntan cream on her thighs. 'Now we

65

know why, don't we?'

'I don't think it's fair to draw too much from what happened last night. Blame it on the turps,' said Jean.

'She doesn't know her limit,' said Pam. 'Not that I blame her. What with that oaf of a husband John running after other women all the time.'

Jean put on a serious expression. 'She's so stylish. Classical music and the like. I think the parents have money. Maybe John feels inferior. You knew she went to a fancy finishing school in Switzerland, did you? What I heard.'

'He's just a big brute and a bully. Anyway, enough about them. Let's cool off, shall we?' said Pam, tucking her thick black hair into her white latex swimming cap.

Chapter 13

They left the Magwa complex and headed south. Gordon offered to drop Pip Foster back at the Ahmadi Guest House where he was staying.

'I rather fancy a swim. You couldn't drop me at the club on your way through, could you? Is that all right, old boy?'

'I'll have to sign you in. Anyway, there's no problem.'

'Splendid,' Pip said, lighting up another cigarette.

'One thing. What exactly will you do with the information I've given you on the testing centre?'

'I have a debriefing session planned for when I get back to Beirut. It will be useful for the office to have an update on Magwa.'

'We can't do much. Only we'll keep those samples just in case there's another outbreak.'

As they arced around the roundabout which fronted the Hubara Club, Foster sprang him with something completely out of the blue. 'Have you ever considered working for the Service yourself?'

'I can't say I have. I've not been approached before.'

'You could be of great use to us.'

'As I s-s-stated in my report, I'll keep monitoring anything of an anthrax nature.'

'There is more you could do.'

'In what way?'

'We need to know names. Just who's pro and who's not here in Kuwait.'

'The Ahmadi community are all of like minds. Obviously they are pro. Everyone is concerned about a potential invasion.'

'Is there much discussion about it?'

'Constantly among the expats.'

'How about among the locals? The other Arabs? Can you help there? We don't have much to go on.'

Gordon knew there were influencers at work spreading anti-British sentiment to once loyal Kuwaitis. 'How do you mean?'

'There's talk in Beirut of Soviet agents recruiting spies and informants. An undercover force which will emerge if there's an invasion. Local officials, school teachers, public service workers in Kuwait City. What about here in Ahmadi?'

Gordon parked up, and they sat there for a while. He told Pip how he assessed the situation, what he knew. How some expat Palestinians never lost an opportunity to attack Britain. As a result, there'd been fights even between his own workers. 'They can be a problem. Their roundabout agenda, of course, is Palestine. They s-s-spread the message that the KOC operation is just another example of British imperialism at work.'

'We need to identify exactly who are the trouble makers.' Pip took a final draw on his cigarette before tugging open the stiff ashtray. 'It's bloody hard for us to get intelligence from here. You speak Arabic, don't you?'

'Shwaya shwaya,' he replied.

'And you've got a close relationship with the locals.'

Gordon couldn't name there and then members of any potential guerrilla force. But anyway he also had no interest whatsoever in formalising a relationship with the British Secret Service and let Pip know it.

'Fair enough. But if you do hear of anyone.'

Gordon nodded. 'I'll give it some thought.'

One person stood out as a potential. Carl Sandberg.

So an hour later Gordon drove over to see him on the off-chance and found him wiping down the barbecue at the front of his bungalow.

'Come along in, Gordon. Let's get out of the sun.' Carl was pleased to see him. Hearing of the mission first-hand from his old friend made him more than willing to help. 'I'm your guy. Tell me more about it.'

'Operation Vantage is the British code name for London's plan to defend Kuwait against any invasion. They can't keep troops on standby in the vicinity because they simply don't have the resources, as you were saying in the Blue Bar the other day.'

'What about the Americans? Did this fellow consider using any of them?'

'Only willing t-t-to be involved in the discreetest of fashion.'

'Take a pew, Gordon.' Carl flipped the top off a 7 Up and handed it over. Having just inspected a tank farm, he was still in shorts and sand boots. 'Sure I can't give you a beer?'

'Lemonade is fine.' Gordon preferred to keep his head clear when it mattered. As he took the open bottle, a strong plume of vapour shot out and up his nose. He gulped down the ice-cold drink.

'MI6 has sources within the Iraqi army. They need to be

confident they are getting genuine stuff from there.'

'To corroborate what they've heard.' Carl swigged his beer.

'Whitehall won't sanction high altitude photo surveillance yet. They have to be a hundred per cent certain Brigadier Qasim plans a move. Or things could sp-sp-spiral. They're very concerned about Khrushchev's response to it all too.'

'I will put you in touch with people who can check it out, if you like.'

'That's more than helpful.'

'Gordon. How did you get involved?'

'I chanced across a possible Soviet chemical complex in the desert.' And with that, Gordon elaborated on what he'd already told Carl and included the full story of the murdered Bedouin.

'Jeez,' Carl said and whistled. 'That sounds serious.'

'Nothing might happen,' said Gordon. 'We know that. Qasim's speech was possibly pure propaganda. They haven't mobilised, after all.'

'Not raised the readiness level of either their air force or tank units yet?'

'No. Nor moved Iraqi troops down to the capital Baghdad. But apparently there is an army battalion in the south. If Qasim wants to surprise Kuwait, he could cross with those in no time at all.'

'And if they do, it'll be a quick dash from Basra. We're only forty miles from the border, for Pete's sake.' Carl lit a cigarette and inclined his head up to allow the smoke to curl away.

'If,' said Gordon. He fished in his pocket and pulled out Carl's lighter. 'Before I forget.'

'Thanks. Stupid of me leaving it there. Intelligence from this side of the frontier? That's what's needed, you say? Like this, for example?'

Carl handed Gordon a leaflet lying on the sideboard. 'I got this from a worker who I know is undercover Kuwaiti Resistance. When he finds this sort of thing, he brings it to me. There's plenty being distributed. It's in Arabic but you're fluent. Brainwashing. A rallying call to join this underground movement.'

Gordon ran his eyes over the poorly produced handout.

Carl cocked one leg against the kitchen cabinet and crossed his arms. 'In this they call for help to depose the British and overthrow the Emir.'

'This is exactly what Pip Foster was on about.'

'Accusing the Brits and Yanks of stripping the country of oil until it runs dry.' He continued, 'Hate the royal family with their Cadillac and concubine culture.'

'They see it as un-un-Islamic.'

'The problem is this. The Emir of Kuwait is one of the wealthiest men in the world. But the ordinary Kuwaitis? What have they gained from the liquid gold? Just lots of labourers coming in. Overcrowding. Inflation. Ingredients for a perfect storm.' Carl paced in a thoughtful circle.

'As you s-s-say, there's bound to be a buildup of resentment among the locals.'

Carl jumped to his feet and waved the leaflet about. 'Someone I know can tell me who is behind this.'

'You think so?'

'Yes. The labourers working out at the gas separation plants. I'll give you the names in a minute. There are rumours they are agitators. According to my source, who works with them, they are UAR men but are handled by the Soviets.' He opened a file, quickly copied out a list of names and handed it to

Gordon.

'I'm not sure if this is true, mind,' he raised a hand urging caution, 'but one handler goes by the name of Agent Alex. I'll try to find out who it is before I see you next.'

Gordon drove back to the office to use the telephone there rather than make the call from his bungalow. It didn't seem right to land Anita into what might be a messy situation. And, officially or unofficially, acting as an informant for the British government required the utmost discretion.

He called the Guest House and left a message for Pip, who he reckoned might still be at the club, then he phoned Anita and told her he'd be home late.

The viper slithered slowly around its cage. The faint scuttling of the jerboa was the only sound as Gordon painstakingly wrote out the list of names to keep as a record.

The shrill sound of the phone shattered the stillness of the office.

'I h-h-have some information for you, Pip,' Gordon said. 'Perhaps I can drop over now.'

He believed that by passing on the names of Iraqi agents as well as pro-West locals with ears to the ground would end any involvement with MI6.

Chapter 14

Gordon was determined not to let Ophelia's silly scene at the Hubara Club undermine his relationship with Anita or worry her that Pip Foster worked for MI6. Particularly as she appeared to have some sort of grudge against him. He decided to avoid both subjects.

When he got home, she was curled up in her favourite armchair. Anita nodded briefly as he entered the room.

'S-S-Sorry I'm late.'

'No need to apologise.' But she still raised her eyebrows in a questioning way.

'I don't s-s-suppose you've eaten yet?' He placed the keys in their usual place on top of the radiogram.

'No. I wanted to wait for you.'

'There's some cold meat in the fridge, isn't there? That'll suit me, if you are OK with it.'

She looked him straight in the face as she pulled at some loose threads on the yellow slipcover. 'So where were you, then?'

'I had something to attend to.'

'Oh?'

'Nothing important.' He realised she was waiting for more. 'A situation developed at work.'

'What kind of situation?' She gave a quizzical smile.

'Some disagreement amongst the men. Nothing you'd be interested in. Shall I fix us a bite, then?'

'No. I'll do it.' Anita uncurled herself and swung her suntanned legs on to the floor. 'You relax.'

Gordon dropped a stack of 45s on the spindle of the record player and started them off. He could hear Anita fiddling about with saucepan lids.

'I'll just go and freshen up, darling,' he called out.

Gordon quickly removed his office clothes, took a quick cool shower and brushed his hair fastidiously. Dressed in shorts and a sports shirt he shuffled back down the hallway in the Arab sandals which he wore around the house. Anita had laid out the supper ready.

'That's better.' He gathered her in his arms and held her close.

'When will this heat end? It's so hot today, isn't it?' she said pulling away.

'Did you get out of the house at all?' Gordon took his place at the table and began forking out sliced meat from a platter of salami and liver sausage.

'Are you really interested in whether I did or didn't? Just to let you know, I sent the Dicksons an invitation to our dinner party.'

'Why did you do th-th-that?'

'Because you asked me. Don't you remember?'

'That was days ago. You weren't too keen on the idea then. So I thought we'd agreed not to.'

'I assumed that's what you wanted. They're your "friends" after all.'

'We can't have another s-s-scene like the one on the dance

74

floor.'

She said nothing and began on her supper.

'It's not me I'm thinking of.' Gordon put down his knife and fork. 'It's you, darling.'

'Well, I've done it now,' she said.

He gave a deep sigh. Then shrugged his shoulders.

'I can't go back on it, can I?'

'And? Are they c-c-coming?'

Anita flushed. 'They won't have got it yet.'

'I wish you'd checked with me before you did that.'

'Why? As you said, The Hunts are busy. We have plenty of space. As you pointed out.'

'I should have listened to you about her. I think perhaps she was-s-s a bit in love with me after all. And to reassure you, I certainly didn't encourage anything last night.'

There was a long silence. 'Anyway, they might not come.'

'Well, it's fine with me either way if you're OK with it. She was very drunk. I don't think it'll happen again.'

'Do you have any more secrets you wish to share with me while we are on the subject?' Her voice held a sliver of menace he'd never noticed before.

Gordon put his knife and fork together in an act of closure, ignoring her icy stare. 'Only those in your own interest.'

'Which are?'

'Those which threaten our way of life and perhaps even our lives.' He faced her squarely again.

'Oh? Like who you spend your time with after the office?' Anita said with a sceptical curl of the lip. 'How does that work with our marriage?'

Her words took him aback. 'Our marriage is not under threat.'

'No?' She shot another defiant glance.

'You need to know where I was. Really?'

'Why not? If you have nothing to hide.'

Gordon's intuition told him not to follow on the line of questioning; not tell her about Sandberg or Foster. But she was his wife. Someone from whom one shouldn't have secrets. Images of her boarding a plane sprang up in his mind. What if he lost her? Did she realise how much she meant to him? How she had lit up his routine life?

She got up and pushed back her chair ready to leave the table. The moment to explain was about to disappear. Perhaps a half way answer would suffice. 'You have every right to know where I was.'

He reckoned a part explanation would cover him in case Operation Vantage kicked off. A partial truth might just bring them closer.

'I uncovered an anthrax outbreak.'

'You told me when we first met.'

Anita sat down again at the table and rested her head on an elbow. Deep shadows formed in the fading light as she listened to his explanation; how a Soviet plot to support a failed Iraqi invasion with chemical weapons was now a distinct possibility.

He told her about the Arab deaths and Whitehall and Carl Sandberg and the Kuwait Resistance. He edited Pip Foster out completely.

She took a long, relaxed breath and covered her mouth as he spelt out how, under no circumstances, would he ever put her life at risk. 'If a Middle Eastern war breaks out, I'll put you on the first flight out of here.'

Her eyes moistened slightly and he was overwhelmed with

the desire to protect her. He stretched out his hand. 'You're the only woman I've ever l-l-loved.'

She squeezed it, then got up as an excuse to pull it away. 'Is "Carl Sandberg" with British Intelligence by any chance?'

'Not officially. Just helping me with an investigation.'

'So that's why you keep that gun in the cupboard? Just to be ready?' There was laughter in her eyes as she cleared his plate. 'Well, darling. Thank you for saving me from the Soviet peril! My knight in shining armour!' she said with light sarcasm.

It was obvious she hadn't believed a damn word of what he had told her and wanted him to know it. She put her hand on his arm, and he pulled back, unable to control his irritation.

'But I'm very touched anyway,' she followed up with as she walked the plates out to the kitchen. And Gordon couldn't help feeling deeply resentful at her attitude.

Chapter 15

Anita Carlisle had a real passion for photography, which Gordon was delighted about. It gave her an interest of her own, which filled in the day when he wasn't around.

He'd bought her the little black Austin A30, so she was car independent. Unless it was off the road, she used that to nip about finding subject matter for photos to fill the frames lining the bedroom walls.

She was also attracted to the Women's Liberation Movement, which didn't bother him in the slightest. He wasn't interested in having a wife just look after him. Anyway, Anita was too spirited and sexy. Would never be just a traditional stay-at-home housewife.

Occasionally, her left-wing views put her apart from the more conventional wives. One other factor which set her apart was a lack of interest in children. She didn't want a baby and be tied down. He even sided with her to a degree, but for different reasons. The recent nuclear scares concerned him. Cooperation between the West and the Soviets had come to an abrupt halt. Gordon worried, with both superpowers testing new weapons, the threat of mass destruction was real enough. Talk of fallout shelters and radiation concerns dominated conversations in the Protectorate. Did you really want to bring children into that world, he mused? Was it fair on them?

In Britain and America, survival stores had mushroomed selling everything from air blowers, filters, flashlights, protection suits, first aid kits, and bottled water. People watched civil defence films urging them to wall-off their basement areas and stock up on packaged meals.

Gordon had expected Anita's left-wing views to soften over time and a part of him hoped she'd change her mind about having a family. So far, there was little sign. If anything, he'd noticed the opposite.

Last week they went to see On the Beach at the cinema. While the rest of the company wives lapped up the romantic drama between Ava Gardner and Gregory Peck, Anita was more interested in the film's political message. As far as she was concerned, Hollywood was a male dominated society which demeaned women and promoted Western war culture.

'The American film industry is contributing to this mass panic with the likes of nuclear war doomsday films ramping up international tension,' she said.

At first Gordon had been interested in her liberal viewpoint. But the day after the discussion around Carl Sandberg, he no longer found their debates quite so entertaining.

'So, Mr James Bond. What daring mission are you up to this morning?' she teased the next day.

He bristled. 'Why do you say that?'

'You men live on a different planet,' she said, pushing him just that bit further. 'It's all because Ian Fleming is coming here. You playing at secret agents.'

Gordon wondered if Pip Foster had mentioned his 'James

Bond of the Desert' quip to Anita on the dance floor.

'That's a bit below the belt, don't you think?'

'Gordon. You'll have to concoct better stories if you want to cover your little dalliances,' she goaded.

'If you thought there was a d-d-dalliance, why did you invite Ophelia and John?'

'I want to see how you behave when she is here.'

'I hope you're not serious.' He did his best to suppress a growing anger.

'I thought you could take a joke. Obviously not.'

He tried to see it that way, keen to avoid a fight. So for the next few days he steered clear of contentious subjects and tried to keep things on even ground.

He went out of his way to compliment her on the pictures which she was assembling for her book.

'I'll call it, "From a Feminist Perspective". Good title?'

'Are you sure I can't get you to photograph my lady lizards?'

'Come on, now.' She didn't pick up on the humour. 'Lizards are territorial creatures,' she said, back on her hobby horse. 'Males fighting other males. You said so yourself.'

Finally, he rose to the provocation and lightly fought back.

'I don't think the local women here completely shrouded in black are too fine an example of the liberated female, though, are they?'

'You know so little about it, Gordon.'

'Women are seen as chattels to Arab men.'

'There's not one country in which there's complete equality. You used to agree with me.'

'Except for Soviet Russia and the communes of Israel,' he said with a half-smile.

'Please don't be so patronising.'

'I apologise. Men tend to have a wicked sense of fun. I'm only teasing you as you do me. I'm proud that you have your own opinions. But I worry sometimes.'

'Why?'

'People here aren't all that broad minded.'

'So?'

'I want them to like you. See you as I do.'

'Of course,' she said, in an appeasing tone.

'If you choose to be entertaining, you can be the life and soul. If it helps, I think your work is original,' he said, to mollify her and they kissed. 'You know that.'

The following day they were invited out on a launch trip to Kubbar Island. It departed from the Yacht Club at Salmiya. There were two other expat families aboard. Anita had taken the hint. She kept political views to herself and concentrated on her photography. At lunchtime the twelve of them ate cold chicken and drank chilled beer from a huge ice-packed freezer on deck. The water was blue and deep, full of jelly fish and sea urchins which bobbed to the surface around them as they swam ashore. The sea glittered a bright silver in the sunlight. Back on the boat they could see, with the help of Gordon's binoculars, a pair of turtles mating clumsily in the distance. Everyone got along perfectly all day.

That evening, they went together to a performance at the Kuwait Little Theatre and life resumed its earlier patterns. They swam in the pool at the Hubara Club after work, played music at home and even acquired a second-hand swing seat for the patio. Their disagreements were put behind them.

Gordon still felt something was different, despite life being semi-normal. Anita appeared on edge and he felt watched all the time. On one occasion, he found her searching through his cupboard. On another, he interrupted her rifling through the glove box of the Saab.

'What are you looking for, darling?'

'I thought I left a lipstick there.'

Whatever had led to such a complete change in Anita's personality, it was not going to be resolved easily. Perhaps the marriage was still too new, and Gordon overly sensitive to her many shifts in behaviour.

'Are you pleased you married me?' he asked one night out of the blue. They were in the kitchen together at the time. She was rearranging the shelves, and he was busy cleaning out the water filter on the fridge.

'Why wouldn't I be?' she said. But the ambiguous answer hurt. It wasn't the tone he wanted to hear and he regretted asking in the first place.

Chapter 16

Source 687 loved the cinema. In particular, Egyptian films. As he waited in the truck, he dwelt back on his favourite.

The heroine had been a peasant girl who took revenge on the engineer who'd seduced her sister and resulted in her "honour" killing by their uncle.

How he'd loved that movie.

Oh to be at the indoor cinema eating popcorn right now rather than sitting there keeping an eye on the exit to the Hubara Club. Hanging around for the British colonial traitor. Waiting to take revenge on someone who'd tricked the true occupiers of the Arabian Desert.

Despite the temperature, Source 687 wore his dishdasha and red check keffiyeh, so he didn't have to hide his face every time someone passed. He preferred the traditional loose clothes to the Western style. Arab dress allowed air to circulate freely around the body and so reduced perspiration. The white robe was not his normal attire. Western trousers and a collared shirt were necessary for his day job.

687 had sworn an oath on the Quran to fulfil the mission. As an undercover agent for Brigadier Qasim, it was his sacred vow.

Any day now the invasion would begin and Kuwait would join its rightful country Iraq, and he was proud that he had become a part of this historic moment.

Source 687 was a true comrade and loyal to the higher Arab cause. He'd recruited twenty followers who'd pledged to spy on Kuwaiti military movements. These devoted Arabs were courageous, and hated the West and all it stood for. He collated all the pieces of information they gathered and passed them on to the Palestinians in the Iraqi Army, forced by Israel to flee their homes in Haifa and Jaffa ten years back. He also relayed on what he had to Agent Alex, who in turn sent it on to KGB operatives in Beirut, a city crawling with intelligence agents from all the major powers. The Soviets were friends and allies to the Palestinians and supported the struggle to return all of Arabia to the true owners, the Arab race.

He checked his watch. How long had he wasted now? Two hours or more. But he couldn't leave. Not yet. Or the informer he was about to eliminate might give things away to the British intelligence service. If so, certainly the Kuwaiti Military Police would be notified, who'd round them all up. Not a pleasant prospect. To end up shackled, tortured, and forced to stand in stress positions for hours at a time. Beaten repeatedly at the whim of the guards.

Fellow Palestinians were often beaten up as it was. Even failure to display a valid car registration earned a whipping.

As political agitators, several of 687's comrades had had their eyes gouged out as a warning to others. This British denouncer deserved to die. Source 687 visualised the execution with relish.

Murmuring the words from the rallying call strengthened his will. 'We will make the princes slaves and the slaves princes! Kuwait Oil belongs to the Arabs and not to the ruling family. Nor to the British under any circumstances.'

He had to protect his companions above all else. Many of them were ordinary middle-aged men who saw themselves as dedicated nationalists fighting for a great cause. If these brave fathers and brothers were prepared to fight using a few stolen weapons and home-made bombs, he would lead by example.

They looked to 687 for leadership. Many, like himself, worked in air-conditioned offices for a foreign boss. Others had penetrated right into the Kuwaiti royal households.

Some worked as field engineers. They knew the layout of the oil rigs and how the admin functioned. When the time came, they'd act. Blow the wells sky high using their technical knowledge to great advantage. However, even highly trained people needed specific instructions, which Source 687 had delivered. Such as how to place the explosive charges in direct contact with the wells and in the exact position as shown in top-secret communications. The quantity not less than 30 lbs per well. The demolition wires laid to a place sufficiently remote and so forth.

'Each group of wires must be connected to a single circuit. Note the direction of the prevailing wind. Blow wells furthest downwind first and then work forward into wind.' He'd read it so often he knew it by heart.

There were the leaflets written in Arabic which warned of the colonials' devious and exploitative way of working. How they'd robbed them of oil and would continue to do so. Source 687 sighed with quiet pride. He'd distributed hundreds of pamphlets and not come close to being caught as yet.

But tonight, the agent was an assassin-in-waiting and could

barely control his trembling hands as he gripped the steering wheel. If only his target would hurry up! What if the man didn't leave the Hubara Club until closing? What was taking so long? Drinking alcohol and gambling as usual, no doubt.

Time dragged. Reaching into a small sack he brought out a cheap plastic flask filled with fresh lime juice, which had already lost its chill. After a quick swig he replaced the cap, shook it, and took a second gulp.

He opened the glove box, felt around, and pulled out a knife. Unsheathing the long blade, he twisted it back and forward, going over again what he had to do.

Earlier in the day, Agent 687 had been inside the Hubara Club servicing the pool filtration equipment. So there was a real risk he might be recognised. He opened the car door and let some fresh air into the stifling cab.

To pass the time, he drifted into one of his fantasies that he was a famous actor, and was about to meet one of the great Egyptian movie makers. His favourite was Youssef Chahine. He knew a lot of stars, like Soad Hosni and Hussein Riad. Maybe he'd become a big name himself one day. Hadn't his friends dubbed him "Omar Sharif" after they went to see one of the films he had managed to get a small part in?

He went to the cinema as often as he could. On one occasion he'd seen his favourite entertainer. In the film, Ismail Yassine played the part of a hairdresser to a big star. How Source 687 wished he could make people laugh like that. Where did the comedian get his start? He remembered so well the newsreel that presented the film and how the audience erupted, chanting out, 'Nasser! Nasser! Nasser!'

What a night that was! He thought the roof would lift. Complete support from everyone for the United Arab Republic and Nasser himself. So much so, the Kuwaiti authorities shut down UAR youth clubs the next day. Did they really feel so threatened by a few young men joining the clubs?

The night sky blackened. How had this traitor blown the cover they'd spent years building?

What more does the enemy know about us? How many and who we are?

His body glistened with sweat. Twisting and turning in the driver seat, he almost missed his target leaving the club.

687 would hit the oppressors hard. Even if it meant punishing people he'd known for years. Hands wet and shaking, he fiddled several times with the ignition key before the engine sprang into life. Now was his moment.

Chapter 17

Carl Sandberg had just clocked up his twelfth year working for the oil company. His department managed the process of producing crude from all the Kuwaiti fields and was responsible for managing personnel at gathering centres where the gas was separated out from the heavy crude. Also, the supervision of workers on the tank farms. He loved what he did and knew his job well and certainly didn't complain about the very high tax free salary with all the extras such as the generous biannual leave entitlement. Suddenly, he was on the verge of tossing it all in.

As he drove out of the car park of the Hubara Club and headed north towards 1st Street, he wondered just how he'd arrived at that point. Here he was contemplating a career change and an immediate exodus from a country he loved so much.

Overhead the stars shone brightly out of the velvet tropical sky over Ahmadi. Verandah lights glowed through gaps in the thatched fencing as he sped by. Very little traffic moved in the opposite direction. He should have been relaxed, but instead he felt uptight and irritable.

Sandberg had long prided himself on his relations with foreign workers in the field. That day it had certainly produced unexpected results.

He'd done as asked by Gordon Carlisle. As the expression went, he was "in like Flynn". Having raised the issue of troublemakers when no one listened, it'd been a relief to have someone at last share his concerns.

When the oil field was discovered, unskilled labourers flooded into Kuwait and now made up nearly half of the workforce. Many had joined his own department. Had no one realised the risks associated with that other than the loyal Kuwaiti Resistance members? That day he'd continued on with the given task as promised, adding more suspects to the list of those "hostile to their British employers".

Pondering his decision to leave the country Carl swung left heading for the roundabout. After all, he was being drawn into the dangerous mess of Kuwaiti politics. Now he was being asked to pass on the names of undercover pro-Western informants as well. That Carlisle had close connections with MI6 had not come as a complete surprise. With his unconventional lifestyle and diverse range of abilities and skills, Gordon had acquired a reputation among those who didn't know him better, as a bit of an enigma.

Carl Sandberg trusted Gordon. They went back years. He'd had little compunction about feeding him intelligence but what would happen to those on the hostile list? Likely, they would lose their jobs. The data would be checked, and double checked. Carl was sure of that. Their colleagues might have set them up on purpose out of personal ambition. Eliminating competition by fair means or foul was common when well-paid work was at stake.

Maybe the workers he'd identified were indeed undercover agents for Iraq, intent on killing British colonials and their families. In which case it was essential he turn them in. More likely however, was that they were simply former members of the United Arab Republic youth clubs before they were banned and deemed "terrorist" organisations.

Sandberg had made tough decisions before, which affected his employees' futures. It was part and parcel of responsibility. He could be hard-boiled and ruthless. It didn't bother him in the slightest.

But today he faced a more challenging call. Today Carl had been given the name of another suspected Soviet agent, code named Alex, operating at the very heart of the Anglo-American community. At first, he'd scoffed at the idea. Derided it as snide and ludicrous.

The tip-off about Agent Alex filled him with a range of complex emotions. Had he become drawn into some counter espionage operation? What would happen if someone had set him up? The fall out would be terrible and he knew he would be held accountable?

Carl knew there was one way out of the quandary. It was plain and simple. Ignore what he'd been told. Do what his sensible wife had wanted for him most of their married life. Resign from the company. Hand in his notice. Leave Kuwait and return to England. Run a nice country pub back in Wigan. Bloody tempting. A brilliant one had just come on the Northern property market close to the Haydock Racecourse. Become a landlord and start over in a completely different way.

But he knew it was wrong somehow, the coward's way out. That's why he'd tried to drown his sorrows all night long in the Blue Bar. He'd been in there longer than usual, staving off the dreaded moment before heading home to make the crucial phone call. He was on his way now though and wanted to get it over with.

As he approached the street where he lived, he slowed right down and turned right. Home and secure at last.

A set of lights appeared in the rear-view mirror of his Humber. Distracted, and half drunk he nearly missed a young girl stumbling along the side of the road. He recognised his neighbour's child, Sylvie well enough. It seemed unusually late for her to be out walking alone.

Approaching his drive, he changed down to second gear. As he swung the heavy Humber into the strip, which ran up to the garage, Carl noticed Sylvie's house next door was in darkness. He decided to check up on the girl, who appeared to be heading back to an empty home. But his thoughts became distracted by the lights behind him. He couldn't make out whether it was a car or a truck. Only that the vehicle had pulled on to the sand at the foot of the driveway. What was it doing there?

A man wearing full Arab dress got out and walked up the drive towards him.

Bloody hell. Another damn taxicab doesn't know where it's going, Sandberg thought. And at this time of night. The driver's dress itself was one reason women rarely used local taxis. Trussed up so tight you could barely see the face, he looked naturally threatening. Who would get into a car with him at night and not be afraid?

'You've got the wrong address. No one has called you from here.'

Carl Sandberg wasn't in the mood for a chit chat.

Then he had second thoughts. Sylvie had stopped and stood by the front fence. Even though they weren't home, the

Beresfords could have phoned for a car. But it wasn't safe for kids to use taxis, anyway. Surely Neville and Jean would never allow their child to use one on her own. What the hell was going on?

The driver walked quickly up the drive towards Carl.

'Wait. I'll put the overheads on,' Carl announced. 'It's not here you want. Who are you looking for? Perhaps the next house?' He repeated everything in fluent Arabic.

Carl Sandberg unlocked the front door and flicked on the outside light switch before turning round to deal with the Arab.

Just maybe the taxi driver was there for another reason, he thought. The build of the body under the dishdasha reminded him of a worker he'd crossed paths with several times. 'Don't I know you from somewhere?'

Carl didn't even see the knife coming until just before the long blade entered an inch below his rib cage and felt no pain as he fell backwards over the Rattan chair standing by the front door. The assailant slashed across Carl's throat opening up the jugular arteries. Two more stabbing thrusts and the latest MI6 recruit lay dead beside his barbecue on the patio.

Chapter 18

Jean Beresford got the fright of her life. One minute she was sitting quietly watching Kismet at the Hubara Club outdoor cinema, the next second she was being rushed out of the place by Theresa Lloyd.

'Don't worry. She's fine. But Sylvie's not at our house anymore.'

Jean instantly feared the worse. 'What's happened?'

'Everything is OK. But it seems something the girls did at the slumber party upset her. And she up and left.'

'What?'

'That's exactly how I reacted.'

The two women tiptoed on as fast as they could to the back of the open-air complex.

'She walked home.' Theresa whispered.

'How could she do such a thing?' Jean Beresford felt her neck tense with the embarrassment of it all.

'Meg rang me in tears saying "Sylvie's gone," and I nearly fainted.' Theresa clutched her hands to her chest. 'They were playing a game with the lights out. Sylvie was on the top bunk. Meg and Lynn were pinching her or something like that. Sylvie got upset. She got down, put her clothes on and said "I'm going home". And that was it.'

Jean leant back against the tall fence, taking it all in.

'It's all right, Jean. Don't worry. I found her.'

'Where is she?'

'She walked all the way home.'

'Walked?'

'It must have taken her a while.'

'Yes, you're miles from us. But to think she did it on her own and in the dark.'

'The girls spent quite a while looking for her in our garden. Couldn't believe she'd really left. I went straight home as soon as I heard. Thank God they rang me when they did.'

'Oh, my goodness.' Jean's ears reddened. What would people think?

'Apparently she was hiding around the back where your ayah lives. Couldn't get into the house, poor little thing.'

'No. We locked up when we left.'

'You have to hand it to her, though. Finding her way from our place without really knowing where to go and at night too.'

'Our ayah's off for the evening, as well.'

'So she said. Found her hiding in the servant's toilet. I called her name and out she came. As white as a sheet, she was,'

'I'm sorry about all this, Theresa.'

'Oh, don't be. But, as hard as I tried, I couldn't get her to come back with me. She said she wanted to stay there. The little darling was in floods. She knew you were at the cinema. I thought I should come straight over and tell you.'

'Thank you very much. I apologise for putting you to so much trouble.'

'Tell you what. You give me your key. I'll go back and let her in. I'll sit with her until you and Neville come home.'

Jean Beresford was livid with her daughter. The fuss Sylvie had made over some stupid thing. What had she told her? Try to get on. It's only for one night.

Theresa jangled her car keys. 'Seems a pity to spoil your evening.'

But of course, Jean couldn't let Theresa do that. What would it look like? The Beresfords out watching a film while some other mother was left to babysit their daughter. Everyone would talk, say she was a neglectful parent.

'Let me think this through and talk to Neville.' Jean went back to her seat to tell him what happened and found him dipping into the bag of Maltesers. He jumped up at the news.

'I'll go. You stay and watch the film.'

'No, I'll go,' she whispered. 'Theresa's waiting.'

The theme song "Stranger in Paradise" blasted out from the huge speakers framing the screen. With all the to-ing and fro-ing people had picked up something was amiss. Jean didn't blame them for making shooshing noises what with all the bobbing up and down.

Driving Jean back from the club the two women began to self-recriminate. Theresa said, 'I see this as my fault, in a way, Jean. Had I been there, I could have intervened.'

'Not at all. Sylvie's old enough to behave properly.'

'Look, Jean. She was crying her eyes out.'

Still worked up, fuming at the whole drama of the affair, Jean fumbled with her car door. 'You go on with your evening. I'll take care of this.'

Theresa reached over to help open it for her 'Are you sure, Jean?'

'Absolutely. I'm so sorry about this.'

'These things happen. Well, if you're certain, I'll get back to my own lot then.'

'I'll be having a few words, I can assure you.'

'Don't be too hard on her. It was probably Meg mucking around. Perhaps Sylvie didn't understand it was just her way of having fun.'

They said their goodbyes, and Theresa drove off.

Sylvie stood waiting on the front verandah, a tiny forlorn figure.

'You've ruined our evening. Whatever were you thinking of?'

'I'm sorry, Mummy.'

Once in, Jean switched on the soft lamps.

Sylvie sat down and crumpled up in a chair her face buried in both hands. Jean could see she'd been crying a lot.

'You're not sitting there now. I can tell you that. Look at the time. Go on and get ready for bed. I don't want to talk about any of this right now.'

The girl looked up at her mother and welled up again.

'I never wanted to go.'

'I said I don't want to talk about it. It's time you grew up. You can't go around willy nilly expecting to do what you want the whole time. I've had enough of you. I told you to go there and get along with them.'

'But -'

'Don't you "but" me. I am so angry with you. What on earth will people think of you running away like that in the middle of the night? I'm ashamed of you. Getting Mrs Lloyd back from their evening out. Having her have to drive round here and find you and then come up to the club and dig us out of the cinema. So embarrassing.'

'I never wanted to go there in the first place. You know that, mummy.'

Jean became even angrier. 'You didn't want to go there? Who do you think you are? You are totally and utterly spoiled. Spoiled rotten. You can't go through life just doing what suits you all the time. "I don't want to do this" and "I don't want to do that". I am sick of hearing it, Sylvie. You will find the world does not revolve around you. Sometimes we have to do things we don't want to.'

Jean couldn't stop herself. 'Your brother is two years younger than you. He doesn't act like that. Like a baby. Why is it always you causing all this trouble in the family?'

'I'm sorry. Please don't be cross.'

Jean glared at her daughter. 'Go to your room. Get ready for bed.' She lit a cigarette and tried to control her temper. She hated scenes like these. What a way to end an evening. The last thing she expected.

The bedroom door opened, and Sylvie reappeared at the doorway in her pyjamas. 'Mummy?' she asked timidly.

'What is it?' Jean inhaled deeply.

'They were fighting.'

'I've said I'm not going to talk about it now. It's late. You've got a school day tomorrow. Let's not go over this again. Go on and get some sleep.'

'Can I leave my door open?'

'OK.'

'Thank you.'

'I'll be right here if you need me,' she said, softening a little.

Sylvie retreated into her room. Jean sat at the dining room table to send a few lines to her own mother in England. She wrote, 'Dear Mum, I don't know what to do with Sylvie. She was such an easy child. But she's at that awkward age, isn't she? Late developers often have difficulties. I am hoping we are not going to have troubles with her.'

When Neville came home he had a totally different take on it all.

'She can't go wandering around Ahmadi after dark like that. Not at her age. She doesn't have any idea the trouble she could bring on herself.'

Chapter 19

The day before their dinner party, Gordon Carlisle suggested to Anita he might get hold of Pip Foster.

Bringing him along might diffuse things between the Dicksons and his wife. Safety in numbers. Balance the odds. They'd half promised it before Foster left the Guest House. He'd not been in touch since Gordon had passed on Carl's list of names. 'Any problems with that?' he asked.

'No,' she said, in a half-hearted way.

'Nothing happened with Pip at the dance, did it, darling? He didn't try anything on by any chance?' he asked, as he recalled her strange reaction towards the journalist.

'I can't remember much of that night,' she added rather coolly, giving no direction as to her inner feelings.

'I'll phone him from the office and invite him then. Wh-wh-what are you up to today?' he asked.

'I'm going to the market. Audrey mentioned Union Traders have got some new toys in from Chad Valley. She wants to get some before they sell out. And I said I'd go along.' Anita had gone shopping with their neighbour on other occasions.

Gordon left for work as usual at seven, arriving fifteen minutes later. First up on the agenda was a quarter to eight meeting outside the office with the maintenance crew when he gave directions as to which area to cover for insect control. All this was standard stuff. That morning they were one short. Mansour was at the clinic getting treatment for a sprained wrist, but Najib assured his boss they had recruited recently and were still well covered in the staff department.

Gordon waited for a reasonable hour before calling the Guest House to speak to Pip Foster. No luck. The journalist had already left.

There was a quiet knock at eleven and Matthew Quinn's face appeared at the door. He looked overly anxious.

'Wondered if you'd heard about Carl?'

'Come in, Matthew.'

'The latest?'

'Anything in particular?' There were always stories circulating about him. Sandberg wasn't everyone's cup of tea.

'I'm afraid he's been killed.'

'Carl dead? It can't be.' Gordon drew in a sharp breath.

'Yeah. It's a shock, isn't it? You hadn't heard?'

'No.'

'Yesterday.'

'C-c-car accident?'

Matthew solemnly shook his head.

'Heart attack or something?' Gordon jumped from one likely cause to another. 'So common in a man of Carl's age.'

'Nothing like that, from what I heard.' Matthew paused. 'Seems he was in some sort of fight. Found stabbed to death.'

Both men fell silent for a moment.

'Where was this?'

'At his own home.'

Gordon sat there stunned. Matthew looked down at the floor at a loss as to what to say. 'Just processing it myself.'

'Any further details?' Gordon asked.

'They've ordered an autopsy. Chilling isn't it?'

'So out of the blue.'

Matthew nodded slowly. 'Yeah.'

'Who found him?'

'The sweeper, you know his male domestic, saw him lying on the front verandah. Multiple wounds to the body.'

'Good God.'

'Word is the police think it was the sweeper who did it. Pretty convinced of it.'

'Really?'

'Sorry. I've got to go. Just thought I'd let you know.'

'Thank you.'

'We're seeing you tomorrow, aren't we?'

'That's right.'

'I'll keep you updated on the QT,' said Matthew, as he pulled the door closed.

Gordon paced the room. He recalled a conversation about the charismatic Indian sweeper who'd served the Sandberg family for the past three years because his own ayah Florrie had recommended him.

Carl had been grateful for the referral and taken him on. However, the man had been prone to mood swings and erratic behaviour. On one occasion they caught him wearing Carl's dinner jacket. On another, he'd decimated Carl's display of miniatures by opening the bottles and drinking the alcohol. Arguments grew more frequent from what Gordon had heard. But nothing of a violent nature. And now this.

It was definitely time to take any outbreaks of anti-British sentiment as a threat, Gordon reasoned. You can't tell what's around the corner.

He drove home for lunch desperate to share the news with Anita but she was out again. Assuming she was still shopping, he helped himself to some ham and cheese and laid down on the bed, the steady hum of the air conditioning providing a soothing background to his thoughts. The brutal death had shocked Gordon to the core.

Back at the office, Pip Foster rang.

'You left a message about a party? Or was it the other matter?'

'There's been an awful turn of events.'

'Sandberg?'

'You know about it?'

'I've just heard from Kuwait City. They have to contact the family before we can write anything.'

'I hadn't thought of that aspect.'

'His sweeper, they say? Is that true?'

'I d-d-don't have the facts.'

'Rather timely we got the list of names when we did, don't you think?' said Foster. 'Carl was an old friend of yours too, wasn't he?'

'Yes, indeed.'

'I got the message about dinner. I am terribly sorry, but I can't make it tomorrow. Moving back into the city this afternoon. But thanks all the same.'

The news seemed to make the rest of the day pass slower than normal, but at last he was home and still anxious to tell Anita the news before she heard from someone else.

'It's a shame I didn't get to know him better,' she said, raising her eyebrows.

'I'm sorry about that too,'

Gordon recalled she'd referred to him, derisively as "MI6"

but he decided not to go down that path. Instead, he admitted Carl was sometimes a belligerent drunk who must have had pretty serious issues with his servant for things to go this far.

'He had a family back home, didn't he?' She sighed sympathetically.

'Perhaps it was just as well they weren't here.' Gordon wondered why Carl hadn't fired the man earlier if he'd been that concerned about his mental state. It'd ended up costing him his life. 'All the same,' he said. 'I think we'd better be aware of tensions in the community. I'm unhappy about you going out alone as much as you do. Just in case.'

'You are so sweet and protective,' she said, but her eyes held a mocking edge. 'Besides we don't have a male servant. We have Florrie.'

Sunset was not until after six thirty and so they sat out on the front patio. Gordon made Anita a Tom Collins cocktail of gin, lemon juice, and sugar and himself a rum and Coca Cola. He sat quietly smoking a cheroot in the gloom and listened to the sound of the crickets.

'Are you still happy to go ahead with the dinner tomorrow? By the way, Pip Foster can't join us. Nothing to do with how you treated him, I'm sure,' hoping to raise a smile.

'You called him?'

'Yes. He suggested "another time". He's just moving back to the City. But if you want to, we could postpone under the circumstances, out of respect for Carl.'

'If you feel we should. But it's up to you.'

'I don't like cancelling things.'

'I can't see what difference it would make, myself,' she said.

There was no doubt about it. His wife was a woman he couldn't read easily. He expected Anita to say she'd like to postpone. 'You've made me the happiest man in the world. You know that, don't you?' He took her hand.

She drew her fingers away slowly, so as not to offend. 'What can we do with this garden?'

'Whatever you want,' he answered. 'It's rather a trial-and-error approach out here finding what will survive such a tough environment.'

'I can see that.' She looked up at the bright desert moon.

'Speak to Jean Beresford about it tomorrow. She's a k-k-keen gardener. Won a competition. And she knows how to get hold of KOC plants cheaply. It'll take her mind off things.'

'What things?'

'Well, Carl. They were Carl's next door neighbours.'

Chapter 20

Every time the phone rang in the office the following day, it was from someone "breaking the sad news" about Carl Sandberg.

'Just wondered if you'd heard?' asked the secretary from the Ahmadi Motoring Club.

'Yes, I had.'

'I thought you would've done. Tragic, isn't it? Poor Carl.'

'It's shocking,' Gordon replied. 'Matthew Quinn was the one who told me.'

'Stabbed, wasn't he?'

'It appears so. Right on his own front verandah.'

Similar calls came in from just about anyone who'd known him.

'What with poor Jenny and the kids over in the UK,' said Roger Graham, who captained the local rugby team to which Carl had belonged. The sharp, gritty desert sand gave a very hard surface and caused many injuries. It was hard-going even for a seasoned player. But Carl was tough. 'Probably as well they weren't back here under the circumstances.'

'Perhaps it was.'

'Do we know exactly what happened?'

Gordon passed on all he'd picked up from Matthew and

others. The assailant had ambushed Carl on his return home and knifed him to death on his own doorstep.

'Are they a hundred per cent sure it was the sweeper?' Graham asked.

'They had various issues going back over the previous months. So he's the chief suspect at the moment, as I understand it.'

'Why did Carl keep him on then? He didn't care about giving people the boot, did he? He was fairly thick-skinned our Carl. It doesn't add up to me.'

'Well, you know how these things can develop.'

'Erm, I'm not too sure,' Roger said, unconvinced. 'It could've been someone else. He was very vocal about the Kuwait state of affairs. A bit too open in public for his own good.'

'I doubt that would have been enough to cause it,' Gordon murmured.

'Several people are thinking about doing like he did. Sending their families home. What do you think, Gordon?'

'Personally, I don't believe we're at that crossroads yet.'

'Weren't you and Carl talking about it in the Blue Bar just last week?'

So Roger was one among others who'd overheard Gordon and Carl's conversation about the security measures being planned against anti-Western agitators. There was no point in denying it. 'Let's hope there wasn't a connection. It spells trouble,' Roger said, ending the conversation on a sobering note.

Gordon raised the subject of the killing with Najib when he returned from a stock take out at the Magwa stores.

'This is not good. Many people in Kuwait hate the white boss now. I am very sorry if he was your friend.'

'You locked up securely out there after you?'

'Yes, Sir.'

'Have you finished your report on the suppression spray programme?'

'It is my next job,' Najib replied, gathering up a substantial pad and some carbon paper. 'I'll write it up now in the truck so I won't disturb you.'

'Sit at my desk, Najib. You can't write properly balancing things on your knees in a hot pickup truck.'

'Thank you, Sir.'

'Where is Mansour?' asked Gordon.

'He is still all bandaged up because he fell from the truck yesterday,' he explained.

'Yes, so you mentioned. Send him my best regards,' said Gordon, complimenting himself how, unlike Carl, he had such excellent relationships with his own Arab staff.

After lunch, Gordon walked over to the other side of the new, ultra-modern hospital for a scheduled meeting to discuss the programme on the inoculation campaign against cholera.

'Shocking to hear about the killing,' said the pleasant nursing sister from Edinburgh. 'I didn't know the man. I've heard kindly words spoken about him though. And he had young children too, I believe?'

'He's been in Kuwait since 1948.'

'Well, that makes me sound like a real newcomer.'

'I've been here that long myself.' He wondered where all the years had gone.

'We've only been here for five. People say things have changed a lot since the fifties.'

'The way of living is a lot less stable than it was.'

'Let's hope this ghastly murder doesn't make everyone think

bad things about all their Palestinian and Indian staff,' she said.

Gordon left the office earlier than usual and drove to the local bank to draw out some rupees before crossing to the supermarket to pick up fresh lemons. The place was full of bustling shoppers.

He recognised a couple of the wives. The women gossiped as they pushed their half empty trolleys up and down the aisles. He picked up the sibilant words as they discussed "servants" and "sweeper". The grapevine was working overtime as the news spread of the gruesome attack.

Gordon could hear every word. 'Well, I one hundred per cent trust my ayah. Mind you, we had a gardener once who was very difficult indeed.'

'I've not had any trouble with any of our servants,' said one.

'It depends on how you treat them,' said the other. 'Maybe they had words.'

'That's not enough to do that to him.'

'I expect it will all be in *The Kuwaiti* tomorrow.'

People who had liked Carl had nice things to say. He was always a willing pair of hands if anyone needed practical help. He volunteered at the local swimming gala if they were short of someone to record times and so on. And before the dog catchers shot a straying pet, he would intervene and get it back to its owners.

But Carl had been deeply troubled about potential terrorism. Gordon felt deep down that could have been behind it somehow.

Not only had Carl sounded the alarm about anti-Western unrest, he'd been one of the first to actually act on it. Convinced a war might erupt at any time he had kept his family back in the UK. It seemed ironic that someone who'd harboured such large security concerns should become the victim of a random murder.

Before going to Kuwait, Carl had seen service in Special Operations in World War II. He'd been fluent in Arabic, was quick on his feet, and could survive independently in the desert for days on end. But Carl was known for his fiery temper and was quick to take offence. Still, that a mentally ill domestic servant could have killed him in a psychotic outburst seemed odd. There had to be more to it.

Gordon drove home slowly in a pensive mood. As he swung the wheel, he thought through a potential twist. Had Carl uncovered something on the task Gordon had set him which ended up costing him his life? Had he found out too much? Perhaps even identified a Soviet operative leaking detailed information on British preparations for the defence of Kuwait?

This would give the killing a much more sinister implication if it was true. But Pip Foster's reaction to the news cast doubt on the theory. It seemed unlikely the killing was related to undercover work.

Gordon put it out of his mind for the moment. He didn't want to jeopardise the new relationship he'd built with Anita. And on a lighter level, they had a dinner party to throw. It was at times like these that everyone needed their spirits lifting.

He pulled up at the house and checked his watch. There was just time for a quick shower and shave. He took for granted Anita and Florrie would have completed all of the preparations.

Chapter 21

When Gordon walked in the front door, he found Florrie in tears. There had been no preparations made whatsoever for the dinner party.

Gordon was a bit of a fusspot. He became quite pedantic about making sure everything was done to a high standard and ready long before guests arrive. Clearly, nothing was. Anita wandered the hall in a semi-daze, as if she'd just woken up from a long druggy sleep.

'Let's clear the lounge together, shall we?' he suggested, a trifle curtly. They moved the chairs against the walls. 'Do you want that thing on to give the room a vibe?' He pointed at the fake electric fire with its plastic logs.

Florrie, who should have had all this completed, now busied herself in the kitchen catching up on cooking rice and reheating saucepans.

When Gordon checked on progress he found her dabbing her eyes with the end of her sari.

'What's the matter, Florrie?' Gordon asked.

'Nothing, sir. There's so much to do.'

'You've prepared all the food in advance, at least. It looks superb.'

'Yes, sir. But not the room. You should not have to do that.'

'Were you out, Florrie?'

'Yes, sir. I am sorry, sir.'

'What's the problem then exactly?'

'Nothing, sir. I don't want to trouble you and memsahib with my life.'

'What is wrong? Do you need help with something? You have to tell us,' Gordon insisted.

Her small face crumpled. 'You are good to me. I don't want to leave this house.'

He wondered if Anita had blown Florrie up over things not being ready for the dinner and not let him in on it.

'There's no reason for that. Whatever makes you think we need you to leave us?'

Eventually, he got it out of her. 'My cousin, sir. His nephew. He is a bad boy. They say he killed a sahib.'

'Do you mean Mr Sandberg?' Gordon concluded that Florrie's recommendation must have got back to the police somehow.

'I don't know his name, sir. The man who was killed.'

'So that's where you were?'

'Yes, sir. The police came here for me. I had to go with them. I'm sorry, sir.'

'Have you seen your relative, Florrie?'

'No, sir. All the ayahs are talking about me. Talk, talk.'

Gordon went out to find Anita. He explained what the problem was. How Florrie had been brought into the investigation. 'It seems the sweeper Florrie recommended is a distant nephew. She never told me that. He's accused of the k-k-killing and she's worried we'll get rid of her. I've assured her we wouldn't judge her because of his actions.'

'Of course not,' Anita said.

'Did you have words with her earlier?'

'No.'

'Well, now at least we know the problem. Anyway, should we set the table, perhaps? Let her get on with the curry?'

Everything was quickly set up in the dining room. Linen. Utensils. But Anita's mind still wasn't on the job. It was as if, distracted by the Florrie situation and with the clock ticking she had become overwhelmed with everything.

He poured pistachios into a shallow bowl and watched his wife dart from one room to another, as if not knowing what to do next.

People ran to their own timetables. Anita had hers. But perhaps the murder had shaken her more deeply than Gordon realised. Or was he to blame? Had he said something that offended her in some way?

'Are you feeling OK, darling?'

'Sure. Of course.'

But her face wore a strained expression. Maybe she'd been waiting for Florrie to start on the lounge. Or had fallen asleep and hadn't noticed the time.

'Did you have a lie down this afternoon?'

'Why do you want to know that?' Anita's face seemed paler than normal.

Gordon pulled bottles of whiskey, gin and vodka out of the sideboard and clanked them on the top. 'Is there beer in the fridge?' he asked with a certain irritable edge.

'Yes. It's full,' she snapped back.

Gordon knew he could be a nit-picker on occasions. He liked everything just so, and recognised this in himself. There was no reason to visit his perfectionist tendencies on his wife, was there? She seemed unusually edgy and nervous, so he softened his tone.

'Where shall we put these?' he asked gently, seeking her involvement with the nuts and cigarettes.

She pointed at the side table. 'Over there is the best place.'

'Do you want any more help with the main layout before I sort the music?' he asked. 'We're twelve, aren't we?'

'Probably,' she said, evening up the white table cloth, so it was level on both sides. They worked together in silence.

Gordon suggested they let Florrie off for the evening. 'In case there's talk about what happened to Carl. Which there's sure to be. We now know what she's crying about. Best she doesn't hear anything to upset her feelings.'

'Now that's a good idea,' Anita agreed.

'If you feel we can cope. I'll do most of the heavy lifting. Everything's ready to bring out.' They were serving beef and chicken curries with mulligatawny soup to start.

They stood back and surveyed the setting. 'How's the time?'

'We-we-we've got plenty now. Are you going to have your bath?'

'I've had it already. I left the water for you. But I still need to change.'

The Hughes couple, a biochemist and his wife, were the first to arrive. Next Charles Parker walked in, both hands behind his back accompanied by Audrey, wearing a pink satin cocktail dress.

'Where's Anita?' she asked.

'Just getting herself ready. Did you find the toy c-c-cars you were looking for? I know they sell out as soon as they come in, don't they?'

Audrey appeared puzzled for a moment. 'Am I missing something?' she asked.

'I thought you went to the shops yesterday.'

His neighbour cocked her head, puzzled briefly, before taking the cigarette Gordon offered. But before he could follow up on his question, Anita appeared. She looked stunning in a bright crimson dress. The doorbell sounded again as the Quinns and Beresfords arrived.

'Sorry we are a few minutes late,' Jean said apologetically. 'The children needed to be settled before we came out. We've left our ayah inside with them and she's got the phone number here. Just in case.'

Jean wore her favourite gold bracelets, which clanged whenever she started talking too fast, moving her hands around as she got excited. 'You know we are right next door to the Sandberg's house?' she announced to one and all. She couldn't wait to let everyone know. 'We shouldn't bring up this dreadful affair at a social occasion though, should we? We agreed not to talk about it.'

But at dinner, it was all they did discuss. Men talked to each other. The women nattered to the other women. Carl's appalling death was the only topic of interest.

Two conversations on the subject split the table. The men went into all the minutiae, all the whys and wherefores. Hadn't he had problems with his sweeper before? What did Matthew know about the autopsy?

The female take on it was more family orientated. Why they mustn't discuss the matter with their children, so as not to frighten them. Kids had enough to worry about. What with dope and grass and weed.

There was a minor topic which got the ladies attention. Pam Quinn asked why were there still two places vacant? Who was missing? The Dicksons. And didn't everyone think it a bit "off" of them? It was very rude. Just not to show up without at least an apology.

Chapter 22

Gordon picked up the empty glasses, stacked them in the kitchen and waited for Anita to finish up in the bathroom. And in the flimsy see through negligee she was a picture of perfection in every way.

Gordon went over and stood in the doorway looking at her reflection in the mirror as she wiped off every tiny trace of evening makeup before applying Pond's cold cream liberally. Without make up she was even more beautiful, her corn-coloured hair framing the pale translucent features.

'I'm surprised by John and Ophelia. Not showing, I mean.'

'Really?'

'Well, it's not normal behaviour. Not for here,' he said. 'Didn't even bother giving a call.'

'Maybe they had an argument. Perhaps with good reason.' She raised her eyebrows. He knew she was referring indirectly to his drunken behaviour the week before at the club.

'Or coming so close after Carl's death? Perhaps John was drawn into the follow-up.'

'We made a joint decision to go ahead, didn't we?' She threw him a challenging look.

'Under the circumstances, I consider it was a reasonable one. You, of course, were the hostess with the mostest.'

'I was trying to cool the rhetoric. Get away from all that war talk.' She tossed a cotton wool wad into the bin with a deft hand.

'What do you mean?'

'All that conjecture, you know. Do you think it will actually happen?'

'Neville seems to be taking matters pretty seriously. It sounds as if he's done a good job with getting the VW Beetle ready. If they do have to escape.' He unbuttoned his shirt, slipped it off and threw it straight into the laundry basket.

'What about you? What do you think?'

'We haven't discussed what we would do, have we?'

'What if the Iraqi stuff is just a storm in a teacup?'

'Yes. There might be nothing to worry about.'

She looked back into the mirror. 'My hair needs a cut.'

'It depends on how much the Soviets get behind Iraq. Encourage them to invade. No doubt they have their ears to the ground and it would be a feather in their cap to drive us British out of the region.'

'It would be a piece of cake to do that.'

This took Gordon aback. 'Not necessarily.'

'You said yourself Kuwait does not belong to Britain.'

'I said that we should respect their customs. We are visitors.'

'Not invaders.'

'The British? Invaders? Never.' Anita's attitude pushed him to a defensive response.

'It depends how you look at it,' she added provocatively.

'We know Arabisation is on its way in one form or another. What c-c-comes with it is anyone's guess.'

'That will upset the bourgeoisie, won't it?'

'Put an end to some things here undoubtedly.'

'A lot of things.'

'Oh, I don't think the expats are too bad.'

'No? The Jeans with her hairdresser and tailor. The Audreys with Victoria sandwich cakes and embroidery. The Ophelia's...' she began and stopped mid-sentence.

'But other than the Dicksons not showing, I thought it all went off rather swingingly, don't you?' He watched silently as she checked for any skin blemishes in the mirror, searching for at least a flicker of agreement in her eyes.

When it did come, it was half-hearted at best. 'Yes. Everyone seemed fine. The table cloth looks beyond redemption, though.'

'Sign of a good party,' he said.

'Jean did a proper job of slopping food on it.'

'She gets rather excitable when she's telling a s-s-story.'

'Turmeric will not come out. Never. It's the worst stain of all on damask.'

'We can buy another cloth.'

'Let the laundry have a go, anyway.'

'I'd f-f-forgotten to remind you they lived right next door to Carl,' he said, slipping off one of the slender straps of her negligee and massaging her shoulders lightly with his fingertips. Anita shivered at the touch.

'So?' Anita arched her back enjoying the massage, as Gordon ran his hands over her skin,

'You didn't say anything about my meeting up with him, did you, darling? It doesn't matter if you did.'

Anita frowned and stiffened under his touch. 'Of course not. But what if I did? Is it a secret?'

'It's probably best kept to ourselves. If the matter comes up again.'

'I can't see how it will.'

'Well, you know, chatting with Jean. These things can slip out so easily.'

'Well, I'm not likely to be chatting too much one to one with Jean Beresford, am I?'

'I th-th-thought you got along all right with her.'

'Well, yes. In small doses. But we're very different. She has children and I don't.'

'Interesting though what Jean said about Sylvie, their daughter. That she thought she saw something the other night. At the Sandbergs' house.'

'That's the little girl with glasses, isn't it? She's supposed to be quite bright, I think. Perhaps takes after her father.'

'Well, yes. Neville's got a brain on him.'

'That explains it.' Anita removed her gold earrings and laid them on the bathroom shelf. 'Don't let me lose them, will you? I'm going to bed now.'

'Me too,' he said, nuzzling into her neck.

'Wish we could get rid of that thing,' she said pointing to the Arab rug, which she thoroughly disliked.

Gordon pushed her down, and she landed on the oversized soft toy dog Florrie always positioned there after making the bed. He pulled it away and threw it across the room. Anita gave a little giggle.

'Wish we could get rid of that bloody thing more. It's always in the damn way,' he said. 'What the hell is it?'

'It's for your pyjamas, if you want to know.' He lifted up her nightie. 'Not that you concern yourself with what happens to them after you drop them on the carpet.'

'The last thing I need right now are pyjamas,' he said, taking her in his arms.

119

They made love in a direct, functional way, devoid of much emotional connection and Gordon fell immediately into a deep sleep after he withdrew.

At four Gordon woke with a start, his mind crisp and clear. There were too many things which didn't add up about Carl's death. And that went for the present background situation in Kuwait. All last night's guests were concerned, frightened they would be sitting ducks if things turned out bad.

What would happen to the ex-pat community if war broke out? How would they all get evacuated? Lying awake Gordon felt real fear for the first time. Outnumbered, a target, and options for evacuation limited, it would be bedlam.

He got out of bed, went out to the kitchen and poured himself a glass of water from the pitcher in the fridge. He knew he would feel rough later unless he got some more sleep but he couldn't clear something on his mind. Anita's reaction to the Dickson's no show troubled him.

Having invited them against his wishes, why hadn't she seemed more put out at their non-appearance? Had they been in touch with her in the interim to decline the invitation? If so, why hadn't she mentioned it? Also, why had she been so devious, saying that she'd been out shopping with Audrey Parker when she hadn't at all?

There were many other unexplained issues which needed answers too. Another weird thing he couldn't work out. Why did Pip Foster seem so casual about Carl's murder? Did John Dickson, who'd introduced them, know Foster was working with British Intelligence?

Exhausted, Gordon knew he was overthinking it all and climbed into bed. But not before he checked inside the wardrobe cupboard that his Colt 45 was just where he'd left it last time he checked.

Reassured, he ran his hand over the cold metal grip of the revolver. The weapon was an insurance policy. He hoped it wouldn't be the case, but if things turned sour, he could be forced to use it.

Chapter 23

Ten-year-old Sylvie Beresford woke up slowly from a terrifying nightmare. Although her eyes were wide open she couldn't see more than two inches in front of her in the hot black bedroom.

It seemed as though everything around her was turning in slow motion and that there were weird beings in the room.

Sylvie lay curled up unable to move any part of her body. Was she awake? Or dead? She was able to think and work out her thoughts. So she had to be alive.

But paralysed and powerless she saw a large, ghostly figure fly out through her closed cupboard door. The figure drifted around the room almost zooming in and out in size before approaching Sylvie lying motionless and petrified. The presence stayed for a time silently by her bedside. Her heart pounded but her whole body was numb, all control lost. Had this "thing" given her drugs or something?

'Please let this be over soon,' she prayed and opened her mouth to scream, but nothing came out as though her lips were frozen rigid. She wanted to raise her hands to shield herself, but was unable to move. What would become of her now she was so totally defenceless? The shadowy figure, now right there beside her, stared into her face, close as close could be. Right there.

She shut her eyes. Surely it could hear the thump, thump, thump of her terrified heart? If Sylvie stayed absolutely still, perhaps the thing would go back to wherever it had come from.

Sensing a change Sylvie dared to open her eyes to find the presence shrivelling, changing and fading. As it wasted away, her foot twitched. What was happening? She could move again. First her right leg, then her left. She lifted one arm a tiny weeny bit and her upper body came back to life.

But Sylvie daren't sleep because the horrors might start all over again. She had to be brave. She needed to wake up completely. The terrifying being had gone altogether and disappeared.

Little prickling sensations on her cheeks. Tickling, stinging. How Sylvie desperately wanted to be able to scratch her face. But if she did, what would happen? Something might grab her hand if she took it out from under the sheets.

Sylvie blinked, trying to work out the lay of the room in the darkness. There was a strange object on the windowsill. The form and shape confused her. What could it be? It looked like a tiny man crouching on the window ledge.

She pulled one hand out slowly from under the sheet and rubbed her cheek. Bliss! The small man on the sill remained where he was, hadn't moved at all. Even when she twisted her neck, the spooky outline stayed rigid. She screwed up her eyes in the darkness. Where were her glasses?

Stretching out a hand she found her spectacles on the bedside table and moved them towards her inch by inch, so the "thing" wouldn't see. Ducking under the sheets, she put on the glasses.

Now she could see clearly, Sylvie realised the fuzzy outline was only the edge of a toy basket. So the "thing" was nothing. She was at home and safe inside her own bedroom. That was something. Not like the night of the dreadful sleep-over, still so fresh in her memory. How her friends Meg and Lynn had called her a dope and a baby for not wanting to play monsters in the dark. How could she be a wimp? She'd made her way back from 7th avenue all alone, hadn't she? They couldn't find their way home on their own.

At first she'd been scared stiff. She considered turning around and going back. But by then Sylvie was more than half way and so kept going. But could she even find her home street? She'd only ever walked one way from her house to the Club with Stewart in broad daylight. Never by herself let alone at night.

She remembered the thrilling feeling she felt as she reached Main Street. She was only scared of what her mother would say. Nothing else. And she knew she'd be OK when she saw Mr Sandberg drive by. But when she'd gone to ask him for help, she saw him fighting with an Arab in front of his house.

She had screamed as the man ran past her and raised a hand warning her to be quiet. She'd run on home terrified. Prayed to God he wouldn't follow, just like she'd prayed to God to get rid of the ghost. Only when she heard his truck start up, did she breathe a sigh of relief.

She couldn't forget the fear that he might be after her. Nor the sting from the Oleander bushes as the leaves thwacked her in the face. Their sweet smell. She remembered at one stage dropping to her knees and crawling across the sand. Recalled how she found it strange. How the same sand near the hedge was as cold at night as it was boiling hot in the day.

She hid in Mary's toilet, desperate for her to come back after her night off. How long was she there? It had seemed like hours.

Sylvie turned over under the sheet and wondered where Mary was. Then she remembered. Her parents were with Mr and Mrs Carlisle at the dinner party. Mary was babysitting, probably asleep in a chair in the lounge.

Sylvie drifted off into a restless sleep for an hour or more before the noise of the front door woke her. Sylvie had wanted so much to hear that noise.

She heard her mother and father stumble in, their barely stifled laughter and the banging and crashing into things in the hall. 'Making a racket,' as her mother would say. But Sylvie didn't care. She knew she was out of danger.

'You can go to bed now, Mary,' she overheard the words in her mother's comforting voice.

'Mummy?' she called out quietly.

She read the noises. Followed the footsteps. Knew their pattern.

'Mummy?'

There was the sound of a toilet flushing.

'Mummy!' she cried out. Then screamed out again. 'Mummy!'.

The door swung open and her mother strode into the room.

'Why aren't you asleep at this hour? What on earth are you doing with your glasses on?'

Sylvie took them off and her whole body racked with sobs.

Her mother leant over and pressed a cold hand to her daughter's brow.

'Is she still awake?' her father's voice sounded lightly amused.

'Is she still awake? Yes. Lying here refusing to sleep until Mummy and Daddy are back.'

'I wasn't,' she said.

'Is she all right?' Her father slurred his words.

'You've got a bit of a temperature, haven't you? Let Daddy look at you.'

She nodded into her pillow.

'I might get Alan to look at her, darling. She could be coming down with something.'

Her father agreed. 'She's a trifle hot. Yes. I can feel that.'

'Having nightmares, are you darling?' Her mother's voice soothed away Sylvie's fears.

'Yes,' she answered weakly.

'Are you having bad dreams, little one?' asked her father as if she was still three.

He stroked her hair gently.

She tried to sit up a bit, but the sheets were too tight with her mother sitting on the bed.

'Is it the girls at school? Is it because you got them into trouble?'

She shook her head firmly. Not that they weren't a part of it, Sylvie thought. They were. Sneaking off without her, to say bad words out aloud.

'I'm scared he'll come after me.'

'Who'll come after you?' her mother smiled.

'The man from next door.'

'Darling. He can't do that. He's gone to the angels.'

'No. Not Mr Sandberg. The man who did it. '

'He won't. How can he? He's locked up. There's no way he can hurt you. Come on. Get some sleep. Daddy and I are back. You're safe and sound. Maybe stay off school tomorrow

126

if you're still not feeling well.'

'Was it nice?' Sylvie asked.

'Yes.'

'Who was there?' She loved hearing about her parent's parties.

'Never mind that now. I'll tell you all about it in the morning.'

Chapter 24

At the heavy knock on his office door Gordon Carlisle swung slowly around in his swivel chair, still nursing a serious hangover. 'Come in, come in' he stammered.

Najib ushered in John Dickson and then vanished back into his own office as quickly as he had appeared.

It'll be the explanation for why they missed the dinner party. Gordon had been half expecting a call.

Dickson wore an open shirt and informal trousers, hadn't shaved and there was little sign of his customary good-humoured self. He buried both hands firmly in his pockets. John looked as if he was about to explode.

'John. Good of you to drop in. Take a pew.'

Dickson stared at Gordon in silence.

'How can I help? So s-s-sorry not to see you last night. Anita said she sent you an invitation. Didn't you get it?'

He nodded. 'We got it.'

'That's good to hear. Did you have a problem?'

John's face turned even redder and started twitching with rage. 'What are you playing at?'

'I'm not with you,' said Gordon, rising to his feet.

Dickson walked across to the viper cage and looked as

though he was about to put his boxer-size fist through the glass.

'Why do you keep these things? Eh? Are you some kind of psycho? Do you have a snake fetish or something?'

'I think you'd better tell me what's going on, John. Has something happened?'

Dickson spun around. 'Why my wife and not someone else's?'

'Ophelia?'

'What exactly did you do to her? Tell me now.' Gordon had never seen his friend in such a state, his face a mixture of anger and exhaustion.

'Wh-wh-what's she been saying?'

'I should knock your fucking block off,' John tugged at his unshaven chin.

Gordon waved in the direction of the uncomfortable steel chair. 'Sit down and we can talk about what's eating you.'

It occurred to Gordon the Dicksons must have had a fight over him. Something to do with her antics at the golf shindig, even though the dance had been over a week ago.

'She'd had a lot to drink that night. Don't take it out on her though.'

Flecks of spittle flew out as John spat out the words. 'Me? Me take it out on her?'

'There's nothing between us if this is what it's about. You're some of my oldest friends. You know that.'

John pointed to the scorpion cages. 'Got many of these too, have you?'

'I've got a meeting to go to, John. Maybe we could continue this conversation later, in private.'

'I knew you'd try to slide off the hook.' He clenched his

hands angrily.

'I'm not doing anything of the sort,' Gordon demurred.

'You're a prick. But you know that. I've spent the last few hours wondering whether to put a bullet in your skull.'

Gordon felt a flush of adrenalin. It was all going a bit beyond a joke.

'There has to be some real reason f-f-for feeling that way. What the hell's going on?'

John Dickson threw himself into the chair. 'I shouldn't have said that.'

'It's obvious you're upset about something, for c-c-certain.' Gordon swivelled round left and right. 'Get it all off your chest please.'

John pulled out his wallet and took out a small folded note.

'What is that?' Gordon immediately thought that Ophelia must have been up to some sort of drama.

'You should read it. Seeing she meant it for you.' He slammed the note down on the desk in front of Gordon. John stared at Gordon as he read the words in Ophelia's scrawly handwriting.

'Darling G. When can we see each other alone? We have to talk. Please don't ignore this one too. You promised, remember? I am desperately jealous, but that's another matter. I will always love you, whatever. Ophelia.'

'I've never seen this before. I promise.'

'No?'

'Where did you get it?'

'It was in her hand, old boy. In her hand.' The muscles of his neck stood out like knotted cords.

'Th-th-there's nothing behind it. I don't know why she's written this.'

'Attempted suicide is not nothing.'

The shock rippled through Gordon's nervous system.

'Suicide? Surely not. Are you serious?'

John took the note back and painstakingly refolded it along the original creases. The two men sat in silence for a moment. 'I knew about you two. But you didn't need to destroy my life completely.'

'I had no idea, John. Really, I didn't. When did this happen?'

'I found her after work last night.' His reddened eyes filled with tears. 'She was going to get her hair done at two. I phoned at four. There was no reply. I assumed she was at the salon.' His voice cracked.

'Where was she?'

He shook his head, bracing his hands on the armrests of the chair.

'I haven't checked whether she went there or not. But I had a late meeting, so I didn't get home until six.'

'So sorry, John. Will she be OK?'

John shook his head slowly from side to side.

'I'm lost for words.' Gordon couldn't find anything more to add.

'What the hell did you ever say to her?' John spat out and rocked back. 'Or did you just cut her off?'

'Do you really believe we were having an affair?'

'So it never happened?' John's lips trembled in disbelief.

Gordon avoided the question. It had. If only once. But this wasn't the time to talk about a one-night stand.

John Dickson pulled himself up from the chair and looked down at the floor.

'What did she take, John? Is she going to pull through?'

John walked slowly towards the door. 'They're flying her

back to London later.' He left the office, slamming the door shut with such force that the noise sent the jerboa scurrying off into the corner.

Gordon sat absorbing the news. The brutal way in which his friend had delivered it all left Gordon feeling deflated and defocused.

What had made her act that way? He knew Ophelia suffered from attacks of anxiety and had been on Meprobamate for her neurotic misery. But then, so many were popping pills. It wasn't a big deal. Gordon briefly recalled a conversation he'd had with her once about dependence on prescription drugs in an attempt to warn her off them.

'I can't stop popping them. Never will.'

'But how many Miltown you taking, Fifi?'

'One every breakfast.'

'But why?' he'd asked.

'Everything. You can't imagine what a state I get into.'

'You shouldn't be downing pills unless you really need them.'

'Just going to the damn supermarket gets to me, darling. All the decisions.'

'That's r-r-ridiculous.'

'I take another before lunch too. That way I can bear listening to John as he drones on about me without having to say anything back. I down one to make me sleep too. They're wonderful.'

On that hot summer day Gordon's comfortable and predictable world had been badly shaken once again.

Chapter 25

Gordon drove home straightaway to break the news about Ophelia. He didn't think it was something to be shared over the phone and expected Anita to be upset about it.

The rush of air conditioning as he opened the front door was welcoming, but Anita's greeting less so.

'Back early?' She sat in her favourite armchair wearing a shapeless shift dress, no shoes and a nondescript expression he couldn't work out exactly.

'I've just heard s-s-something rather awful, darling. Thought you should know. So I came home specially.'

Her face clouded over. 'Ophelia Dickson killed herself over you, so they say.'

He didn't count on her already knowing everything.

'You've heard? How come?' Gordon couldn't understand her insouciance.

She pointed over at the phone. 'John rang here looking for you. For once he wasn't on his high horse. In tears, in fact.' She studied the nails of her left hand.

'What did he say?'

'Very little. And to you?'

'That's why they didn't show last night.'

'Well, obviously.'

She looked around the room which was still in full dinner party mode. Chairs against the wall, ashtrays full. 'We need to put things straight again,' she said. 'I don't know where Florrie is.' Anita scooped up a few of last night's peanuts and put them in her mouth. 'I'd better get to it.'

'It's fine as it is for the time being. Surely?' he said truthfully. It seemed the wrong time to worry about that.

'Well, possibly for you.' Being so tall, Gordon had admitted that he preferred less clutter about the place. Fewer small tables to stumble over. 'Where do you think she's gone?' Anita raised a curved eyebrow in Gordon's direction, then got up and straightened out her dress.

'Who?'

'Florrie. I've not seen hide nor hair of her this morning. Help is never there when you need it. Anyway, I can do it myself.'

'Florrie's usually very reliable. There'll be a good reason.'

'No doubt.'

'Going back to Ophelia, I was wondering what more John told you. I didn't learn too much from him myself.'

She walked slowly across the room and stared out the window. Gordon wanted to join her but couldn't miss the frostiness.

'Did John say what she did exactly?' he asked.

'We didn't go into the ins and outs.'

'Of course not.' He put the car keys on the radiogram and went over and stood close to her. 'She was taking a lot of sedatives.'

'Was she?'

'I was wondering how we could find out what happened

discreetly.'

'Why do you need to know?'

'It would be helpful, if only out of natural curiosity.'

'I'd rather not, actually.' She shivered and crossed her arms, the usual body language of a retreat into her inner self.

'Someone at the hospital might be able to give me more information.'

She nodded. 'OK. Do as you think.'

Through her curt responses, it was obvious his wife wanted to end any further discussion on the whole subject. All the same Gordon had to mention the suicide note. 'She left a letter. Did John tell you that?'

She shot him a look. 'Yes. But must we talk about this? I don't feel like it. Not now.'

'Of course. I understand,' but he continued on anyway. 'She was clearly going through an emotional crisis. I j-j-just want you to know I did nothing to encourage it.'

'You've said that before.'

'I know. But this has been a terrible shock.'

'I'm quite sure of that.' She let out a short, bitter laugh.

'And obviously, it's certainly not your fault.'

'Thank you,' she said sarcastically. 'In the patriarchal society we live both men and women are victims.'

She turned and faced Gordon. 'In fact, more men commit suicide than women in an hierarchical system. Did you know that?'

Gordon turned his head away to hide the irritation and gave a deep sigh. But Anita continued on nevertheless.

'Big boys like John Dickson don't cry. That's what makes him such an objectionable bully. A way to take out his frustrations on others.'

'I don't think you can blame John for what happened.'

'No? Women like Ophelia have to be young and pretty. And once they're not, they feel their life's over. John's attitude might well have been a factor.'

Gordon distanced himself from his wife's unexpected rant, not knowing where it was leading and went out to make some coffee in the kitchen. People react to extreme situations in different ways. That he understood well enough and it had all been so unexpected.

The dirty dinner party plates lay stacked in the sink, untouched from the night before. Gordon wondered whether Anita's churlish response was in some way connected to Florrie's absence. She was a bit of a neat freak. It was out of character for her to allow kitchen mess to pile up.

As he waited for the water to boil, another thought dawned. How well did he really know his own wife and her past? Perhaps someone close to her had killed themselves and she'd never mentioned it. The Ophelia incident might have opened old wounds. He'd never asked much about her life before their marriage. What had Ophelia herself put to him that night? 'What do you know about her?' Perhaps his unquestioning love had blinded him to sides of her personality that he hadn't wanted to delve into too much. Spoil something which was so good and whole in itself.

Bearing two steaming mugs of coffee Gordon placed one next to her and sat back in his chair in the opposite corner. He decided it was best to leave the subject alone for now, as she'd suggested. Perhaps Anita needed time to process things and gain her own perspective on it all. That he should respect.

Gordon attempted to lighten the mood. 'I had a bit of a head this morning. Mixing drinks. Did you?'

'I wasn't too bad,' she replied, and a small smile crept across her face, the same smile she wore when they made love. Beautiful, inviting, but still distant and enigmatic. She looked down at the coffee, didn't touch it and picked up a cigarette. 'I had a throat like parchment when I woke this morning.'

'Should you be smoking then?'

'You think I shouldn't, do you? Is that what you think?'

'Well, I get put off cigarettes in this full heat.' He took a sip of coffee.

Anita rose from her chair. 'You sound like you need another drink?'

'That's the last thing, and for you too I imagine.'

Anita strode across to the sideboard and poured herself a large neat gin. 'Cheers, darling!' She raised the glass in Gordon's direction with another tight-lipped smile.

Gordon didn't rise to the provocation and tried to work out what game she was playing. 'I think I'll go back to the office. Just give a call if you need me. Don't sit here dwelling on things. You should leave the house for a bit. Go for a swim or something. Florrie can handle all this.'

Chapter 26

Back at the office, Gordon watched Sammy the snake sliding around its enclosure, flicking his tongue about to left and right. He had to get Mansour to feed him later. After all, the caged creature depended on them for survival.

Gordon sat at his desk but couldn't settle into work, couldn't stop thinking about Ophelia's bizarre over-dependence on him. Why hadn't he seen it before? But what good would that have done, anyway?

His own wife's detached reaction to the suicide troubled him. It was like passive aggressive and he felt a sense of emptiness and disappointment. But was it fair to judge Anita in that way? What had he expected? Floods of tears over someone she obviously considered a rival.

He needed to find out more about Ophelia's background, if only out of compassion. Plus, the Dicksons were friends of long standing. Perhaps somebody in the Intensive Care Unit he knew would be able to shed more light on it all. Had John's wife been so completely hooked on sedatives that she'd overdosed?

But what if he bumped into John Dickson?

He might take an actual swing at me this time.

There was no point in raising the passions even further. Gordon was still stunned by the accusation he'd been the trigger which had brought Ophelia to want to kill herself. Had it not been what she said to him at the dance and the suicide letter, Gordon would never have suspected he'd been a factor.

It could be seen as interfering if he got too involved and perhaps make things worse. Gordon had to put his thinking cap on and work out a strategy.

With windows glittering under the morning sun, the new hospital complex looked a damn sight better than the old Nissen Hut. Gordon chewed on a toothpick and tried to get his brain in gear. Absentmindedly he picked up a dead fly on the windowsill and dropped it into Sammy's cage.

A visit to his friend Matthew Quinn might be a smart move. The Path Lab would know what actually happened.

He turned up the air conditioner before leaving and checked on the animals. Now Mansour's injury was better, Gordon would get him to give all the cages a thorough clean.

Half an hour later Gordon found Matthew in his office standing by a filing cabinet, wearing his customary white coat and reading a report from one of his trainees. He was alone, which was ideal under the circumstances.

'Matthew. Got a minute?'

'Sure. Come in, Gordon.' Matthew looked unduly troubled.

'H-h-have you heard about Ophelia?'

'Ah.' Matthew shifted his gaze. 'Yeah. Awful.'

'Right.'

'Tragic for John, isn't it?'

'Just wondered what you knew about the background.'

Matthew turned slowly to face him. 'Gordon. I only know

139

what I've heard from Geoff. He was on shift last night. We were at yours, as you know.' He dropped a report down on top of the filing cabinet. 'Do you want to sit down?'

Gordon declined. Something didn't seem right. 'Is she going to be OK?'

'It doesn't sound too good to me.' Matthew shoved both hands into the pockets of his white coat.

Gordon sensed Matthew's discomfiture.

'Can you tell me anything else you know? I've only had sketchy details so far.'

'It's a difficult one, Gordon.' There was a long silent pause. 'You'd be better off speaking to John.'

'Well, he's already been to see me.'

'He has?'

'But he didn't go into anything much. He was pretty upset.'

'Yeah. It's hard to know what to do, isn't it?' Matthew was fumbling for words.

'It may help if you can tell me anything. I don't know what to do next about John.'

'I know he wants everything kept on the QT.'

'You said it doesn't sound too good. Is she going to pull through?'

Matthew shrugged in his usual compassionate manner and took out a packet of cigarettes. 'Do you want one of these? I'm trying to cut down. It's not working though.'

'Do you know if she left a note?' Gordon placed a Peter Stuyvesant between his lips. 'Perhaps she was having a mood swing.'

'Yes.' Matthew paused. 'I heard something about it.' He gave a worried look.

'We had a one-night stand. I never for a second thought

Ophelia took it so seriously.'

Matthew smiled and shook his head.

'John was playing around,' Gordon continued in a defensive tone. 'I doubt if anyone knew. It wasn't a big deal at all. Just one of those things that happen.'

'Ophelia was very fragile though, wasn't she? Heavy drinking didn't help either probably.'

'She seemed to have built s-s-something quite casual between us into a major event. Women get emotionally involved so quickly, don't they?' Gordon sought a sympathetic response from his friend but only got a neutral one.

'They can do. Yes.' Matthew inhaled deeply and tapped ash into an ashtray. 'Have you seen these? Got the Southwell Hospital logo on them. Not a great incentive to help stop smoking, is it?'

He's trying to change the subject, but why?

'She took an overdose, didn't she?'

Matthew sniffed and gave Gordon a puzzled look. 'You don't know?'

'No. John never said. I didn't think it was right to ask.'

'I see.'

'What did she take exactly, Matthew?'

'It seems she took organophosphate pesticide.' Matthew looked down at his shoes for a time. 'Basically poison.'

'I d-d-didn't know that. No idea. I thought perhaps sleeping pills.'

'Apparently not.'

Gordon leant against the wall of the office. Now at least he'd got some hard information. Poisoning was the last thing he'd expected.

'Wonder how she got hold of it.'

'Who would know?' Gordon replied.

'Well, I suppose if anyone did, it'd be you. Seeing as the stuff is used here mainly in locust suppression. You keep it in the stores out at Magwa, don't you?'

Gordon felt himself grow cold. 'There are substantial quantities out there, true, but they are kept under lock and key.'

'Did you give Ophelia some by any chance for any reason?'

'Me? Why would I do that?' He was horror struck at the inference

'For the plants?' Matthew said, trying to cover quickly. 'You know what I mean. It works on weeds too. I had some off you when we were planting out our back yard.'

Gordon's mind raced through past incidences when he might have given out, somehow, the organophosphate. The Dicksons had a flourishing desert garden. Perhaps he'd passed them some from the small supply of the pesticide he kept at home and forgotten it.

'I don't honestly remember.'

'It's just a thought,' said Matthew.

Gordon thanked him for clarifying the position, stubbed out the almost untouched cigarette and made a move. It was clear now why Matthew had been reluctant to discuss the situation. Things were being said behind his back and Matthew felt awkward about it.

He drove out on 8th Avenue and turned left on to Avenue 6 West. In the small enclave it took just eight minutes to get to the Magwa Road. Kuwait remained sweltering well into autumn, and the heat fogged Gordon's brain, making it hard to think clearly.

On top of the weather, the shock events of the last few days meant he couldn't seem to rationalise as normal. But the implications were horrific. Not only had he caused Ophelia's mental breakdown but also supplied her with the tools to kill herself. Did anyone really believe that he killed her intentionally?

Gordon drove on until he got to the Magwa stores. He had to check that the stocks were secure. Everything appeared to be normal and safely under lock and key. He let out a huge sigh of relief. At least that unknown could be put to bed.

Chapter 27

During the drive back to Ahmadi, Gordon's mind was in a high state of bewilderment and confusion. He was being alienated by everyone and everything which were familiar to him. Even the desert seemed more eerily hostile and threatening than usual.

More than ever he needed the comfort of his wife. He called by the shops and hunted out a box of chocolates with the picture of a Swiss chalet on the lid. Corny and trite, but passable.

Florrie opened the front door of the house as he crossed the verandah. She took in the gift and read the situation instantly. The master and mistress must have had a tiff and he wants to make it up.

The ayah's usual impassive expression was distorted by worry and Gordon's heart went out to her. That her relative had been questioned over the murder had grave implications for her simple life.

'Those are nice, sir, the chocolates.'

'Where is Memsahib, Florrie?'

'She's gone, sir.' Florrie waved airily over her shoulder in a generally northerly direction.

'Gone where? Salamiyah?' The Salamiyah Road was an

area crammed full of tailors, shoemakers, textile makers from Pakistan, the Lebanon and even the Far East. Anita had made several trips there from the time when Gordon first introduced her to the district.

'No. Gone sir.' She wobbled her head from side to side in typical Indian fashion, and raised her dainty fingers.

The lead of the vacuum cleaner lay traipsed across the room.

'I don't understand.'

'She took her things, sir.'

Florrie tossed her sari over her shoulders and ambled back inside to continue with her daily duties by plugging in the vacuum cleaner.

Gordon went straightaway to the bedroom. *There must be some misunderstanding.* But Florrie was right. He couldn't tell exactly which ones, but several of her clothes were missing from the wardrobe.

On the top shelf of the airing cupboard where they kept suitcases, one was missing too. Gordon was aware that Florrie deliberately kept herself back in the lounge, tutting and making little flicking noises with the duster. Leaving him to absorb the implications in private.

'Did she leave a note for me, Florrie?' he called out.

'She left a phone number. I don't know anything else, sir.'

Gordon had heard about another wife in Ahmadi who'd inexplicably up and left, but the husband turned out to be a wife beater. At least I'm not that, he thought. Nor had they had any significant rows during their eight-month marriage. There had to be a simple explanation for it all. Perhaps Anita had received bad news from home in the UK and hadn't shared it with him.

Gordon poured himself a drink before trying the number

she'd left with Florrie. Twice it rang off the hook. The third time she picked up.

'Wh-wh-what is this all about?' he asked in his calmest voice. 'Are you OK?'

'I'm sorry. I should have told you. I'm house sitting a flat in the singles quarter of Oleander Court for a bit. That's all.'

'This was pl-pl-planned, was it?' Again he felt resentment at her casual selfishness.

'Not exactly planned. I wanted to work on my photography. I can black out the spare room there. Save you barging in and destroying all my negatives.' She gave a nervous giggle.

At first Anita had shared a darkroom with another amateur photographer. It meant using the facilities when he didn't need them and she'd complained of feeling like an intruder all the time.

'Well, if that's what you want, but I don't understand why it's suddenly so important.'

'It's for the best at the moment.' To Gordon she sounded unconcerned that the decision had been made as if it had no bearing on their married lives together.

'When did Florrie c-c-come in to clean up after the party?'

'Just after you left. It's nothing to do with that, though,' she said.

'You'll need money. I will get some to you.'

'That is very kind,' she said.

'Are you going back to England then? I can organise that for you,' he said, trying to keep the depth of emotion he felt out of his voice.

'There's no need for that just yet,' she said flatly.

Anita apologised briefly and hung up, ending with a kitten-ish promise to speak again soon.

Gordon sat down, stunned. Florrie looked over at her master.

'Would Sahib like something?' Her look was a mixture of painful perplexity and partial understanding.

'No, thank you Florrie. Isn't it your evening off tonight?'

'Yes, sir.'

Gordon lit a cheroot deep in thought. Angrily he kicked away a pair of his wife's high heels left behind in her hurried departure.

I'll scratch out a brief note of sympathy to John Dickson now I know what happened to Ophelia, he decided. But what to say?

At 7 pm Florrie excused herself to go off duty. Gordon filled the bath and balanced a glass of whisky on the edge of the tub before lowering himself into the lukewarm water. He closed his eyes and ran through the series of events, and the horrors of the last few days. How Carl Sandberg's murder had happened so soon after their meeting about Operation Vantage. Of Ophelia's poisoning and the note John had shown him in the office that morning. And Anita's attitude on learning about it and her ridiculous accusation 'that woman killed herself over you'.

All this raised the barely suppressed demons in Gordon. He'd been a sensitive child. Class mates at school had jumped on to his speech impediment and poor eyesight. They mocked his finicky nature. Called him a spastic, a cissy, a weirdo. By his teens the stammer had become more pronounced. He'd reacted to every childish insult in the wrong way. Instead of confronting the bullies, he'd become withdrawn. During a particularly bad period, he even planned to exit it all by jumping off a bridge and ending the pain. Sixteen-year-old stuff.

After the war Gordon had several friends commit suicide. Either stuck their heads in a gas oven, or hung themselves. No women he knew had been driven to such lengths.

How about Anita? What was her mental state? And had she left him for good? He attempted to analyse why their relationship had deteriorated so rapidly. The dramatic change had really only come about over the last few days.

When his wife first arrived, she wanted to experience everything together as a couple. They'd made trips to Fahaheel and Kuwait City. Keen to soak up the colour of real Kuwait, she'd photographed the port and the ancient buildings in the old quarter while he'd acted as a guide. Then she started going out on her own. He understood her unwillingness to be confined to just the time when he wasn't at the office so he'd bought her a car to give some independence. But she started going out without telling him where she'd been or when she'd be back.

Perhaps a short breathing space would be good for their marriage. A temporary separation might even strengthen the bond. But then he remembered the unfinished note he'd seen when he'd missed bumping into her at the Hubara Club. Who was 'My Darling?' He believed her and assumed she'd intended the message for him. But perhaps it was all very simple. That Anita was having an affair on the side.

Chapter 28

Brigadier General Mustafa al-Ramiz al-Sabah sat enjoying the outside shade of the cafe on Abdulmunim Riyadh Street. The traffic streamed by, disturbing the peace. But inside, the air was thick with tobacco smoke. Which was worse, he asked himself? That or the traffic fumes?

Prince Mustafa was a member of the Kuwait royal family. He'd inherited the coffee-coloured skin from his father, a minister in the Government. But the dark curly hair came from his mother and the engaging brown eyes from both.

As a member of the ruling class, he'd travelled more than his Aide-de-camp, Captain Jamal al-Zafairi. Mustafa spoke good English, but his deputy did not. Naturally, they conversed in Arabic.

'I don't know of anywhere drivers honk their horns as much as here.' Rather than find the cacophony obnoxious and the driving insane, he felt comfortable and at home. That was how it was in Kuwait.

'You can change one horn for another,' his officer said. He was an expert in such trivial motor matters. 'Just mount the new one and wire it up. Some of them sound crazy.'

Prince Mustafa was one of the first Kuwaitis to receive a commission from Sandhurst in Berkshire. As such, he'd been tasked with setting up a platoon of crack commando specialists to protect Kuwait from an invasion by Iraq. Plans were already underway to create the elite fighting force, designed to make shock raids behind enemy lines.

'Well, my force won't be attacking with blaring horns, I assure you,' said the prince a touch pompously. 'We will be the finest in the Middle East. I will train them in the desert to fight under the harshest of conditions. We will overcome anything they throw at us.'

They had been discussing the recent death of an oil company employee. Had the killing been a terrorist act? A sign of anti-white tension? Or a straightforward murder.

What could be behind it if it was political, Mustafa mused as he leant back in his chair?

His sombre mood lifted when the cafe owner, a heavyset Arab in full dishdasha set down two tiny cups of strong coffee and a bowl piled high with pistachios.

'Your Highness, my house is your house,' said the owner. Hussein obsequiously placed a hand on his heart and gave a deep bow. This was only expected because Brigadier General Mustafa was a very special customer.

Prince Mustafa was accustomed to the grovelling style. It was part of cafe life. The owner would have crawled on broken glass if necessary to keep the high-ranking customer coming to his place.

The prince picked up a pistachio and prised it open. 'I am addicted to these.' He waved a chef's kiss with one hand.

'They are very good for the health. And the ladies,' Hussein smiled suggestively in reference to the aphrodisiacal side effects.

Prince Mustafa ignored the vulgarity and resumed their

discussion. 'This is the problem,' he said to his officer and pointed to a compact transistor radio standing in the middle of an adjacent table. 'Get it for me,' he ordered.

The officer brought it over and handed it to his master. The small radio was the latest thing for all the young men walking the streets.

'They carry these sets everywhere. They are light enough to have by their sides.' The prince tapped the radio to emphasise his point. 'Ball games are fine but the Palestinians listen to the Voice of the Arabs.'

'It has a wide reach, sir,' agreed his assistant.

'These powerful transistors are manufactured in the Eastern Bloc somewhere, but the station is in Cairo and is pro-revolutionary. The disc jockeys are all terrorists, each and every one of them.'

Well aware of his superior's suspicious attitude towards the Palestinians, the officer flicked on the set. A mournful but popular melody sung by a local chanteuse poured out of the small speakers.

'No, no. Give it to me.' Mustafa snatched the wireless and rotated the frequency knob through the range. When he couldn't locate the station, he clicked it off angrily. 'Later, it will be on. Because the audience listens in all night. All the way from Cairo. Everything they hear they think is fact. No matter what the man says, they believe it is the truth. Even when they are lies. All lies.'

'You're right, sir.'

'Nasser is clever. And has a golden smile.' Mustafa imitated him, showing off his own gold tooth before taking a sip of coffee. 'The radio. He knows how powerful the air waves can be as a weapon. And Ahmed Said, the commentator?

Everyone recognises his voice. Everyone.'

'Certainly. He is more famous than Nasser himself.'

'How many radios are there in Kuwait? Far too many.'

He beckoned to Hussein hovering nearby, ready to refresh the coffee at the lift of a finger. 'Come here. How many of these Ahmed Said boxes are there here in Kuwait?'

The owner hesitated, uncertain of which tack to take before taking the plunge. 'Every cafe has one, my Prince. Maybe two. A transistor radio draws men off the streets for me.'

Owners welcomed the extra custom that went with it.

'What do you think, Hussein? Who is behind these infernal broadcasts?'

Hussein shrugged and spread his hands palms up disassociating himself from any such knowledge. 'Who knows, my Prince? But I will be delighted if you would accept some dates baksheesh in honour of your visit.' He backed away and disappeared into the safety of the inner cafe area.

'The radio station itself may not be all that large in itself. Perhaps they operate out of one room somewhere in the Cairo suburbs,' his aide offered.

'The average listener doesn't know that,' said Mustafa. 'These nincompoops do not imagine that the Voice of the Arabs studio could be just a scruffy office with four chairs and a table. They think the commentary comes from this powerful leader sitting in a palace or a huge government building somewhere. Someone to look up to who is speaking to them as if they are a dear, dear friend. So they believe the bilge they receive over this.' He picked up the transistor and shook it. 'Every single night they hear how bad the British are. How they control the Gulf. The station puts out this message to these gullible fools.'

'I have heard for myself, sir.'

'So you can see how bad this is for Kuwait?'

'Yes, sir.'

'They keep telling them the same thing. They are Arabs. Brothers. Many can't read or write. That's why they listen to the radio. That's why they are turned on when they hear this stuff, the nonsense about freedom and independence. Like they are turned on by women.' He dived into the pistachios.

'I know, sir. It is new, and it is exciting.'

'Exciting?' Mustafa leaned forward in his chair and clenched his fists. 'It winds them up. They are being told to fight. The Palestinians believe what they are being told. Of course they do. They hear it repeated over and over. The same message.'

'It's true, sir. Time after time.'

'It gives them a direction, don't you see? Stirs them up.'

The dates arrived, and they both examined them with interest. The Prince selected the best one and popped it into his mouth.

'The radios are indeed a problem,' said the officer, wondering if he dared to take one of similar size.

'Take all these Palestinians in their refugee camps. What do they have? This radio puts ideas into their silly heads.' He shook his head wearily and waved his arm as if shooing away all the difficulties of the Middle East in one gesture. 'Many are fifth columnists. Even those from good homes. They have lived amongst us in Kuwait for years. But they still back Iraq. They are a security risk and hate the as-Sabahs almost as much as they hate the British.'

'I understand your concern, sir.'

'We must look more into this murder. Carl Sandberg. It is

153

my idea the man was a specific target. I don't believe he was murdered by the sweeper. Not for one minute. Why? The servant was an Indian. He also has a water tight alibi from what I've been told. That person could not have killed him. I am certain of it.'

Chapter 29

Florrie was busy whipping up a fresh batch of powdered milk with the hand mixer when Gordon got up the next day. Wearing one of her best and brightest saris, she placed a hand to her breast and bowed when Gordon walked into the kitchen.

'Sahib. Sahib. Thank you, Sahib.'

'Whatever for, Florrie?'

'They have released my relative. So, so happy, sir. I heard this from another ayah. He was with a lady. Raj has an alibi.'

Gordon thought for a moment. 'That's great news for you, Florrie.' But added a cautious rider. 'Let's hope he's in the clear.' It was common practice for Kuwait police to release but then rearrest the same suspects days later. Maybe she shouldn't celebrate too soon. 'But I had nothing to do with getting him released, Florrie.'

'I know, sir. But you were very kind to me.' She tapped her forehead with her left hand. 'So much worry.'

'I understand, Florrie.'

'Thank you, sir.'

'There's so little to do here, Florrie. Why not take the day off?' He didn't need to explain. Neither of them mentioned Anita's abrupt departure as though it all had been factored in.

155

But then as Florrie tucked in the end of her sari, she said, 'I will stay just in case Memsahib comes back and needs anything.'

She finished the mix. The watery concoction which substituted for the real thing was still bubbling as Florrie placed the glass pitcher firmly on the fridge shelf.

'I don't imagine Mrs Carlisle will be around for a few days. There won't be much work for you to do.' Gordon took a sip of the tasteless tea set out for him more out of politeness than need.

'But Sahib will be home for lunch?' she asked. And when Gordon returned at his regular hour, Florrie was waiting outside the front door looking very agitated.

'The police came here to see you, sir.' She blinked in the bright sunshine.

'What did they want, Florrie?'

'I don't know, sir. I hope nothing bad.'

'Did they say whether they would come back?'

'No, sir. I am very worried. Very worried.' Florrie gave little tuts and buried her head in her hands.

'I'm sure there's nothing for you to worry about,' said Gordon, but worried, despite himself, about his wife. Had something happened to her?

'And they didn't leave a contact number?'

'No, sir. They were looking all over the garden. I did not let them inside the house, sir. I did not know what to do.'

'I expect they'll be back. Don't distress yourself unnecessarily if they do.'

Gordon ate the dry pork chop, which she'd fried, together with some tinned sweet corn. He ran through the whole scenario in his mind. Perhaps the sweeper had given a false alibi, and the lie had somehow implicated Florrie. He could imagine his ayah's distress as the police pulled apart the candy pink Oleander bushes and tramped about on what was left of the sun-scorched lawn. Perhaps they were searching for evidence, such as the murder weapon, but why here? Did they still suspect Florrie's nephew, after all?

When Gordon got back home at four thirty he found Brigadier General Mustafa waiting in a military jeep accompanied by two black-and-white police cars with Arabic scrawl across their doors. Gordon assumed they were the same officers Florrie had been so concerned about.

'How can I help you, Brigadier?' Gordon read the stars and crossed rifles denoting the rank and elevated status of his visitor.

The Brigadier didn't beat about the bush. 'We are here about the death of Mr Sandberg.'

'Our ayah told us you had released her relative. Is that not the case?'

'Yes. It seems he was not responsible for the killing.'

They went inside the house, where Florrie stood shaking with fear, terrified she was the reason for their visit.

Gordon pointed to Florrie. 'This doesn't involve her, does it?'

'No, of course not.'

'Florrie, wait out the back. I-I-I'll take care of this.'

'Thank you, sir.'

'I am very fond of the English countryside,' said Mustafa, taking advantage of the proffered chair. 'And I like London in the rain.'

They exchanged further pleasantries, drank Coke, and sat in awkward silence for a few minutes.

Eventually Mustafa got to the point. 'You are wondering why I'm here, no doubt. It's very unusual for any British people to be killed so unconventionally. So we wish to know everything, you understand.'

'A very shocking thing, without a doubt, Brigadier.'

'The mind boggles. Is that not what you say in England?' He raised his eyebrows in a questioning and dry way. 'It's just that we found your name written on the front of a newspaper in Mr Sandberg's house. Can I ask you how it got there?'

'Of course. I lent him a copy of an article he was interested in reading.'

'So you met with him? When was that?'

'A few days back. I can work out the exact time if you want me to.'

'Do you know who killed him?'

'I h-h-have no idea.'

'You have no opinions on the matter?'

'He may have upset someone, perhaps. Or it was a random attack.' The very same question had passed through Gordon's mind when he learnt they had released the sweeper.

'Mr Carlisle. Are you one of London's men out here?'

Gordon knew he was referring to MI6. 'I-I-I don't know why you would ask that.'

'When my police entered the house, they found certain documents. For example, a list of names.'

'What has that to do with me?'

'Do you know anything about this list? We know some people on it are pro-Iraqi. Palestinian agitators. There are many of these subversive groups operating in Kuwait. As you probably know, they have let off explosives in the City, mostly. Saboteurs working on behalf of the Iraqi secret

158

services from within my own country.' He raised his bushy eyebrows waiting for a response.

'I know Carl was a strong supporter of what he called the Kuwaiti Resistance.'

'A supporter or an opponent?' He threw a suspicious glance in Gordon's direction before downing his glass in one. 'Thank you for the Coke.'

'Why would you th-th-think him an opponent of the state? Nothing could be f-f-further from the truth.'

'How would he know about these men on the list?'

'Maybe from his contacts. Many workers here don't dislike the British. They have good jobs and prospects. More than willing to report troublemakers just to keep in employment.'

'Can I ask you why you went to see him?' Mustafa swung his legs back and forth.

'To return a lighter of his.'

'Cigarette lighter? Is that when you gave him the paper?'

'Yes, it was.'

'Do you meet with him often?'

'Wh-wh-where is this going, Brigadier?'

'We are concerned about you.' There was the slightest hint of menace in his voice.

'Me?'

'Yes.'

'Perhaps he was killed by someone with a grudge. From within his own department?' Gordon suggested helpfully.

'Or more likely Palestinian? Someone loyal to the cause of Arab nationalism. Maybe the beginning of a campaign against you British and the Americans?'

'There are many of them amongst the workers, I understand,' said Gordon.

'The revolutionary groups are ready to help any invading force. They keep well-hidden and have double identities. Mr Sandberg had access to all the plans and layouts of the oil wells, didn't he?'

'Of course.'

'Such drawings would be useful to Iraq if obtained say by a Soviet agent working for them with their own USSR agenda.'

'Are you really suggesting Carl Sandberg was opposed to British interests?'

'Or he knew someone who was. Do you have any Palestinians working for you yourself, Mr Carlisle?'

'Yes, of course.'

'Then you must be very careful.'

'One moment please.' Mustafa got up and crossed to the door and made a noisy display of yelling in Arabic to his accompanying officer to join him inside.

'Oh, and the leaflets. Inciting men to the cause of overthrowing the Kuwaiti royal family. Do you know anything about those?'

'Yes. Mr Sandberg showed them to me when I was over.'

'He didn't write them?' He smiled dangerously exposing the gold incisor.

'Of course not.'

Responding to his commander's order the brigadier's ADC rushed through the front door with a fat file, which he dumped on the table in front of his boss. Filled with photos of stolen cars he began to thumb through them rapidly.

'He knows everything about cars,' said the Brigadier proudly. 'That? A Chevrolet. Another Chevrolet,'

'Impala,' corrected the car enthusiast. 'Pontiac, Chrysler New Yorker. An Opel.' He stopped thumbing when he turned up the grainy photo he'd been looking for.

'Here is one like yours,' said Brigadier Mustafa . 'A Saab 96?'

'Yes, it could be,' Gordon agreed.

'That car was spotted at the petrol station opposite the headquarters of the fire brigade at Salmiya. Where they found some of the propaganda leaflets.'

'There must be lots of similar cars to mine.'

'Many the same, I agree. And you haven't reported yours stolen?'

'No.'

'Very well,' said the Brigadier. 'But I must inform you we're working on all this. And we may be back in touch.'

They said polite goodbyes and the small convoy of police vehicles drove off, leaving Gordon to recap alone, and reflect on the wringer he'd just been put through.

He sat down over a cold beer. What had the Brigadier been driving at? There was the ludicrous suggestion that Carl had been an undercover Soviet agent passing stuff to the Iraqi secret service. And that he, Gordon Carlisle, had discovered Sandberg was working for the KGB and had been involved in his friend's murder in some way.

Chapter 30

Sylvie once used to love the heavy heat of Kuwait. But now it gave her nightmares. Always the same one where she was buried in burning hot sand up to her neck.

She began to amble towards the pool, but the concrete hurt the under soles of her feet and forced her to run. Sylvie knew she looked silly. Her heart pounded with the embarrassment. She was painfully, overwhelmingly aware she was being watched by half the world.

There was a forced hush from the children on the terraces, then low droning noises. Sylvie knew without looking they must be whispering about her. Making gestures that she was crazy.

She'd not been to school for two days. And there they were. A set from her class sitting altogether in a huddle, talking and sniggering about her from behind cupped hands.

She dived into the water, which felt freezing against her sunburnt skin and gasped at the unexpected iciness and tightness in her chest.

Using breast strokes Sylvie reached the edge of the pool and hung on the side to catch her breath. One by one, her class group moved down to join in. A girl called Lorna swam up and hooked herself to the edge alongside.

'Where have you been? We've all wondered. Everyone wants to know.'

'Just sick. But I'm better now.'

'You can come and sit with us if you like. Do you want to?' Lorna raked back her dripping hair with one hand.

Sylvie's heart flipped with excitement to be invited like that. But as she splashed her way toward the steps, she shivered and a cold feeling ran through her body. She saw a club worker standing by the diving board. He looked just like the man she had seen the night Mr Sandberg was killed. He wore different clothes though. She couldn't be sure.

Sylvie took a quick breath and duck dived. She was determined not to break the surface until long after he'd gone away. But she hated being under water for too long.

And when she broke the surface at the pool edge, he was right there crouching down looking at her.

She pushed herself off from the side and swam as fast as she could to the steps and ran up to join her mother.

'I know I saw him,' she whispered to her mother as she dried off with the towel.

'Come on now.'

'I'm sure, mummy. Well, nearly sure.'

Her mother looked around, but said she couldn't see anyone fitting the description. 'It's good those children asked you to join them. Go on. Go over and make friends.'

'You won't go home without me, will you?'

'Of course not, silly billy. Go off and enjoy yourself.'

'Mummy, I feel he is watching me.'

'That's just because you're self-conscious. No one's looking at you. You are imagining it.'

163

The following day was equally bad. No one believed her anymore. At the Anglo-American School, they were preparing for the eleven-plus exam. The class groaned and moaned as if it was the worst thing ever.

The test was in three parts. Arithmetic and problem solving, English comprehension and an essay, plus one on general knowledge. Today was only practice, to give them an idea of what to expect.

The teacher, Miss Angwin, handed out a question paper. 'Now remember to write neatly. This is a very important try out for the examination.'

As the teacher placed the sheets upside down in front of her, Sylvie looked around the room.

'Put that down now, Robert.' Miss Angwin glared at a boy who'd been banging his ruler crazily on the desk. 'It's not a drumstick.'

When she finished handing out all the papers, Miss Angwin reseated herself primly at the table. 'OK, children. Turn over. You can begin now.'

Sylvie found the sums easy. 'Subtract two-thirds of 834 from 23 times 185.'

Afterwards, they all went outside and stood around chatting and comparing notes. The girl who put on mime shows in her back garden was trying to sell home-made tickets. Two other girls amused themselves by tossing a beanbag to one another. The day was nicely warm and windy.

Sylvie took out her cat's cradle and looked around for a potential partner, but no one was interested. She would have to join in, even if it was Meg Lloyd's group.

Meg's set sat in a row on the edge of a small wall. Same place each day. They all looked miserable after the ordeal they'd been put through.

'Why were you off school again yesterday?' Lynn asked with a smirk.

'I didn't feel well,' Sylvie replied for the umpteenth time.

Lynn started giggling. But Sylvie would not give up this time. Not having anyone to talk to at break was horrible.

'What answer did you give for the first sum?' she asked, forcing her way into the conversation.

'I can't do pounds, shillings, and pence,' said Meg's friend, sucking the end of her plait. Suck, suck. A disgusting habit Sylvie's mother said when she'd seen it for herself.

'I hate arithmetic.' Meg was not the slightest bit interested in learning anything.

'When are you taking your real exam?' Sylvie asked. 'I've already done mine.'

'No you haven't.'

'Yes, I have.'

'No, not this one. The proper one?'

'I took it in England.'

'You can't have because you're not old enough,' Meg Lloyd dominated the group in most areas despite not really being at all academic.

'I was in the year above for my age.'

'What did you do then?'

'I can tell you all about it. You have to write a composition about-'

'Are you coming to the swings?' interrupted Meg, turning to Lynn and rushing off mid-sentence. Meg preferred to stand up rather than sit when she swung, and that way soared through the air to a great height, so her skirt blew up, showing her knickers.

That afternoon, the teacher held their lesson in the assembly hall. 'Take a musical instrument from the trunk and then go and sit down,' she commanded, pointing to the box of recorders, tambourines, and triangles. They had begun practising for the annual Christmas concert even though it was still yonks away.

Waiting to start the practice Sylvie looked out the window into the grounds. She thought she saw the man again, wearing a long white shirt and the same checkered headdress from that terrifying night. Then, when they crossed the tarmac to the main building the man was watering the flowerbed and she realised it was someone altogether different. Perhaps she was thinking too much, as her mother said.

Anxious to impress the group, Sylvie told Meg about the pool incident all the same. 'I think I saw the man who killed our neighbour. He was at the club yesterday.' Sylvie regretted it the moment the words were out of her mouth. Having squeezed back into the group at the music class, they turned on her again.

'Why do you keep making things up?' Meg looked pleased with herself for getting all the others to giggle and nudge one another.

'Like what?'

'Like that. And your dad's car and stuff.'

Sylvie's eyes filled with tears. All memories of the sleepover came back with a rush. How they had ganged up, bullying her and calling her a liar just because she told them that her family were planning to escape if there was an invasion. How her father had adapted their VW Beetle and taken the front seat out to make more room.

'But it's all true.'

Sylvie decided that from then on she would keep any secrets to herself and to herself alone.

Chapter 31

Jean watched affectionately as her husband worked on the car. She was very proud of him. Neville Beresford was a hard worker and a wonderful protector of the family. Who else had such a practical escape plan, doesn't just talk about it but gets on with it, Jean thought proudly.

'We're very lucky,' Neville said when she boasted to him about their water tight marriage. Particularly when many of the other women in Ahmadi seemed so unhappy. Did nothing but complain endlessly about their husbands.

'Do you really think it could happen?' Jean patted her hair lightly.

'Let's hope not. However, it always pays to be prepared.'

Jean stood, arms crossed, as Neville continued to strip out the small area underneath the bonnet of the VW.

'Are you planning to fit me in there?'

He looked over at her through adoring, hooded eyes. 'I bloody well might unless you get me a cold Carlsberg.'

Jean reappeared with a tray of drinks, which she balanced precariously on the knee-high brick wall. Unfolding a canvas chair, she sat in the shade of the eucalyptus tree as Neville fiddled with the electrical cables, to make sure they were all tightly connected. Jean didn't know anything much about cars herself, apart from how to start one, but had a blind faith in Neville's abilities.

'Take these will you, darling?' He handed her the Registration Certificate together with the Proof of Origin and a Petrol Ration Book belonging to the car's first owner. 'Ah! Here's the original maintenance record. Quite handy.'

'Inside the house?'

'No, we'll keep them all upfront.'

'What are you fitting in there?' Jean leant forward affecting an interest in the enclosed space behind the spare tyre.

'A jack. Extra headlamps. 6V battery. The tyre, obviously. Trickle charger.'

'What's that thing?'

He pulled out a sand coloured car cover. 'Not bad if we had to hide the car for any reason. But I don't think we have the room, unfortunately.'

'I can't see we have the room for anything but ourselves.' The thought of them all packed in like sardines disturbed her somewhat. 'Stewart thinks it's all good fun. He loves squirrelling up in that back compartment.'

'I think we can dump these though.' He handed her out a couple of copies of Volkswagen he'd found. 'The car is featured in the review, so obviously that's why the previous owner kept them. Maybe poke one in the bookshelf for posterity.'

'Darling, do you think perhaps we should get a bigger make?'

Neville Beresford took a long swig of his beer. 'Definitely not. This car is perfect if we have to make a run for it. We need to be inconspicuous. That way no one will take us as wealthy evacuees and try to rob us. Or take me perhaps for a high-profile army officer on the run with the family for example. They're the only ones you see with big flashy cars in the desert.'

'Well, you would know, darling.'

'We will travel light and fast. The only space for cases is where I've removed the passenger seat.'

'You won't get much there.'

'You'll be surprised what I can do.' Neville wiped his hands on an old tea towel.

'I'm sure.'

'And if I give the word "go", we go. OK?'

'Yes, darling.'

'No iffing and butting.'

She sighed deeply. 'Oh, dear.'

'We don't want to end up like Carl, do we?'

Jean took a sip of her gin and tonic. 'The children are on about taking toys.'

'No.'

'I've told them that.'

'The only weight on the car apart from us lot will be spare fuel and water. Everything non-essential has to be stripped out. And those rations.'

'Mary asked me what was in the jerry cans.'

'Tell Mary to keep her cotton-picking fingers off the stuff in the laundry. All is in its rightful place ready to leave. I don't want to be foraging around blind in the night looking for the bloody petrol because she's moved it.'

'You're taking these out, are you?' Jean looked down at the mats. he'd passed out to her.

'For the moment. I have to get to the trunk mat. It just adds to the weight.' He pulled the carpet from the back and added it to the pile of rejects heaped up on their sandy lawn.

'What are these, then?'

'Traction mats. We definitely need them in case we get bogged down in the sand.'

'Gosh. I do think we should stick to the roads.'

'If the unthinkable happens, they'll be full of other refugees and there are the road blocks to think about. We don't want any reason to be stopped. That's when things can turn nasty.'

'Well, I've got my flat shoes,' Jean said, wriggling her right foot.

'You'd better check the children have got good lace-ups.'

'I don't want to leave my lovely rings and bracelets behind, darling.'

He pulled open a leather seat pocket organiser. 'Small jewellery can be tucked in there. I don't know about the bangles. Cans of food take priority.'

Jean climbed into the back seat to try things out.

'I rather like it here, where I can order you around up front,' she said.

Neville gave a smile as he tested the starter motor. The ignition had been intermittent lately and now was the time to fix it.

Jean stretched her right arm out along the top of the back seat. 'I was going to give Gordon and Anita a ring about the dinner party.'

'I'd hold off with that at the moment, darling.'

'Really?'

'And perhaps let's not mention our emergency plans with them anymore, if you don't mind. Nor with Pam for that matter.'

'You think not?'

171

'I most certainly do.'

'Some people are saying that we are jumping the gun.'

'Well let them. We will work things out for ourselves.'

'Well, I agree about Pam. But I don't know it would harm to get Gordon's input on things. I trust him more than a lot of the big talkers here.'

'I don't think we can trust anyone at the moment, darling.'

'Not even Gordon?'

'We don't know what really happened with Ophelia, do we?'

Jean froze for a second. 'You've got a point. I never thought of that.'

'Not saying I have any answers either. Just suggesting it might pay to be cautious.'

'You don't think Gordon had anything to do with her killing herself?'

'I've no idea.'

'It's surely all just talk, isn't it?'

'Gordon is totally infatuated with that woman he's married. That's all.'

'You don't like her at all, do you?'

'She's a Mata Hari type, which I don't go for myself. But some men really do their balls over them. And Ophelia was definitely trying to mess with the relationship.'

'I saw that at the Club. We all did.'

'So best we stay out of it for now.'

Jean quickly absorbed Neville's theory. 'Ooh. I can't imagine Gordon doing something like that.'

'It's possible, you know. Anything is.'

'If it was John I would understand. Much more likely.'

'John's not a bad bloke really.' Neville tucked all the documents into the glove compartment and slammed it shut.

'Well, listen to us, will you?'

A little later Jean raised the subject again, but he had wearied of it. 'People are under great pressure because of the Iraq situation. It's wrong of us to jump to any conclusions, and we don't have to be drawn into a scandal unnecessarily by voicing our opinions in public.'

Jean was more dubious. 'I suppose not.'

'Let's put it this way. Gordon does keep quite a bit to himself when it suits him. For example, he has never explained why he was right next door at Carl's just a few days before he was killed. Which seems odd in the circumstances.'

'Are you sure about that?'

'I'm pretty certain I saw his Saab outside. But when I mentioned it at the dinner party, he changed the subject.'

'I see what you mean.'

Jean gave a deep sigh. It was dreadful when old friends they'd had for years started falling out. Really bad.

Chapter 32

Gordon studied the drawing which Pip Foster had given him highlighting a location in Kuwait City. Somewhere they could meet when required. Code named 'Margaret' it was near the seafront.

Gordon needed answers to several important questions. Firstly, how had he become a suspect in the Carl Sandberg killing? Had Sandberg been a Russian informer when Gordon perhaps inadvisably put him forward as a potential under-cover? If so, Foster should have recognised straightaway the name when Gordon suggested it. Even if he was working for the Soviets, what right did MI6 have to kill him although he could well believe the secret service carried out the odd assassination from time to time.

Gordon's hand trembled with fury. He folded the rough pencil sketch and put it in his pocket. How on earth had he got himself involved in such a grubby mission? The journalist and probable MI6 agent hadn't initiated any contact, even when events spiralled out of control. He was basically unreachable. The phone number of an officer working on the ground floor of the agency building of the British representative was Gordon's sole means of communication.

But on this occasion Gordon had just put the phone down

after leaving another message when the telephone rang.

'You've been trying to get hold of me,' Foster said. 'I assume there's something further to add to the "interview" you gave me on the article.' This was coded language that the call related to Gordon's unwilling involvement in Operation Vantage.

You bastard. You know already why I need to see you, Gordon thought, but said, 'Yes. Something I f-f-forgot to mention which could be interesting.'

'Shall we meet at Margarets? I'm afraid I can't make it until half-past nine this evening.'

As he put down the receiver Gordon could imagine Foster enjoying a whiskey sour on the first floor verandah looking out to sea. Completely unflappable as ever.

So could the British Secret Service have killed Carl Sandberg because he was Agent Alex? But Carl himself had been the one to raise the question about the existence of a Soviet operative active in Kuwait. Had this been some sort of double game designed to put Gordon off the scent?

The drive to Kuwait City took just on an hour. Gordon enjoyed a trip there after sunset. In the day, the experience was different. The desert after dark had a haunting effect on him. Beautiful, mysterious, distinctly feminine.

He drove past the centre where the royal family lived. Kuwait had developed dramatically since he arrived twelve years earlier. The changes had caused conflict and division. The younger generation were drawn to the new exciting experience of alcohol and pop music, while their elders resented the erosion of their proud culture and had not benefitted from the rapid advance of the economy.

Gordon wondered just what would become of the country

in the months to come. Would Iraq invade? And would the Kuwaiti royals hold on to their positions of power? Would they do what they promised their people, to build a fully air-conditioned city? Erect Manhattan style skyscrapers?

He parked the Saab and went straight to the old part, heading for a favourite restaurant unfrequented by the Europeans. Gordon didn't have to order. Farid greeted him and quickly brought the customary hummus and vegetarian falafel, and a dish of majboos diaye chicken with rice.

From nearby minaret towers the passionate call to night prayer began. The lilting chant penetrated the still heavy air, tenacious, unyielding, timeless. The beauty of the sound took Gordon's thoughts and emotions to his estranged wife. His acceptance for what had disappeared so inexplicably between them over the last few days drew a curtain of sadness over him as he idly turned the pages of an Al-Arabi magazine lying on the table. Gordon knew Kuwait had the greatest freedom of expression of all countries in the Arab world. Right then, it felt like a mental prison.

In sombre mood he drove on to the designated meet up, which was a parking lot in front of the beach, eerily lit by two street lamps. At nine twenty, a shape emerged from behind a boarded-up shack. Gordon sat forward to see better and realised it wasn't Foster. He wound down the window and let in salty sea gusts. The half-hour came and went with no sign of the MI6 agent.

Just as he was firing up the ignition, the door rattled open and Pip Foster slid into the seat beside him. 'Sorry about the time, old boy,' he said before rummaging in his pocket for a pack of cigarettes.

Gordon went straight to it. 'Why are Brigadier Mustafa's

people keeping watch on me?'

'Perhaps they are aware we met. You know what Mustafa is like, don't you? Slippery customer. Wears two hats. Runs the police. Also, he's setting up a commando unit ready in case there is an invasion.'

'Was Carl Sandberg's death anything to do with the list of names I gave you?'

He remained silent for a while. 'Who knows?'

'Why would they imagine he was working for the Russians?'

'Someone is, old man. But you were the one who put him forward. Remember?'

Gordon Carlisle couldn't deny that. 'The good news is that I sent the names on to London.' Foster inhaled a lungful of smoke. 'The bad news is that most of them were known agitators.'

'The police had an exact copy of the list he c-c-compiled.'

'Sandberg gave us out-of-date gen. Old information. Which is where the Brigadier's theory of him being a Russian agent comes from. Deliberate obfuscation.'

'So he was murdered but we don't know why or by whom?'

'If you want to know, yes. But if you are suggesting Sandberg was assassinated by those working for MI6, no. You're definitely barking up the wrong tree there. Unless...'

'Unless what?'

'Unless he came up with something else. Only you would know that. Did he?'

'He phoned me to say he had new information.'

'When was that?'

'The night before he was killed.'

'Did anyone overhear that?'

'No. I was at home with my wife at the time.'

'Where did he call you from?'

'The Hubara Club.'

'Not one of the most private of places.' He let the window down allowing the smoke to drift out.

'So he could have been t-t-targeted?'

'I leave for Beirut tomorrow. It's a hotbed of KGB creeps. A haven for spooks from all over for that matter. I'll find out what I can. If a soviet agent has been deliberately silenced, then someone there will know about it. Anyway, if I don't see you beforehand, stay sharp and keep your head down.'

He got out of the car, leaving Gordon to stretch across to rewind his window. But before he could do so, Foster poked his head back in and added, 'Tragic about Ophelia Dickson, wasn't it? Rumour has it she'd been having an inconvenient affair.'

In the darkness, a loaded silence hung in the sea breeze. 'And give my regards to your own, will you?'

A cold fish, thought Gordon, as Foster walked away. He was pleased he'd not given him the satisfaction of knowing Anita had moved out over the Dickson affair.

And he was still pondering the double meaning of Foster's comments about his wife as he lay awake in the bed they once occupied together. The phone rang. It was one thirty in the morning.

Someone had called the Kuwait Fire Department to report an incident out at the Magwa storeroom. There'd been a fire and a fatality. The dead man was Najib, his trusted Palestinian assistant.

Chapter 33

Jean Beresford plonked down into a chair in Pam Quinn's lounge and checked the time on her new automatic Omega. 'I can't stay long because of the children.'

'What is it? Mine has stopped. I'll have to get Matthew to buy me one of those.'

'Neville got tired of having to wind my old manual one. I always forget. So tedious.'

'I like that. No more winding.'

'We've just over an hour before the buses leave school.'

'OK. Plenty.' Pam jumped up from the great round pouffe seat. 'What can I get you, Jean?'

'I'll have tea with the tiniest bit of milk. I'm slimming.'

'Wait there and I'll bring it in,' Pam came back balancing a tray of cups and saucers. 'I suppose you want to hear all about Ophelia, don't you?'

'Not necessarily.'

'I'm not supposed to say anything. It's all very hush-hush.'

'Well, I won't ask then. That's not really why I'm here,' said Jean, suddenly remembering Neville's warning not to discuss the subject and get drawn into gossip.

Pam pulled a long face but her lips silently formed the words. 'She killed herself.'

Jean put a hand to her mouth. 'I had no idea.'

Pam continued, in a hushed voice as she put the tray down. 'Yes, suicide.'

'Where's John?'

'Got the first plane to England. We don't know when he'll be back.'

They sat sipping tea and looking at one another searching for answers.

'I don't know what to make of it all,' Jean said.

'That is all I can give you. So!' Pam shrugged her shoulders in fatalistic fashion 'Poor Ophelia.' She slapped both hands against her thighs. 'More tea?'

'Please. You do realise that, on top of everything we've had the Kuwaiti police all over Carl's house.'

'Yes, because you're right next door to them, aren't you?'

'I think it's made the decision for us. Neville is now seriously talking about me and the children going home to England.'

'It was the weird sweeper who killed Carl, wasn't it?'

'That's the thing Pam. No.'

'Oh.' Her friend looked taken aback.

'They let him go. He was back today, clearing out his room behind the bungalow. That's what's worrying us.'

'What do you mean?'

'Carl left Mia and the kids back in England, didn't he? Maybe he sensed something bad was about to happen.' Jean sipped her tea.

'Didn't you say he'd had trouble with that man? Probably pissed. Got on the drink.'

'Pam. Why would the police release him unless they were convinced he was not involved?'

'Who else would want to kill Carl? It doesn't add up.'

'Oh, I don't know.'

'Maybe you can move bungalows if you are worried. Put in for a relocation. They do come up. Jean.'

'Well, what would we do that for? All that upheaval?'

'I suppose you wouldn't want to leave your garden either, would you?'

'There's Sylvie to consider, too. She's been playing up. You are aware she was there when it happened, aren't you?'

'You did mention it at the pool. Yes.'

'She ran away from the Lloyds' pyjama party that night. It's a precocious American concept. Anyway, she convinced herself she was at our house when it happened. I don't think she was, of course. It could all be in her mind.'

'Well, I've not heard of anyone else leaving Kuwait yet. You're probably overreacting.'

'Perhaps. I don't know though.'

'Better to wait and see what happens next year.'

'But what if war breaks out in the meantime?'

Pam closed her eyes in protest. 'Don't you think that's a bit extreme?'

Pam was doing what Jean's husband advised, but Jean rose to the bait all the same. 'Well, I do. But Neville doesn't.'

'If Neville leaves, he will have to get another job. Plus, he'll lose his pension. How long has he got to go?'

'He won't be forty-five for ages yet.' Jean felt her temperature rise.

'He doesn't act like he's even twenty-five. Stripping that car out. And what's with all this shooting I hear about at your place?'

'How did you hear about that?'

'Stewart told me.' Pam took another sip of tea.

181

'It's just target practice in the back. Neville wants the children to be able to handle a gun. Not that my son needs much encouragement.'

'I don't approve of having firearms about the house. Not when there are kids around. What on earth is he thinking of?'

'You know what men are like.'

'What Neville is like, Jean.'

'He says we women bury our heads in the sand. He might have a point, really.'

'Men and their guns. It's as well there are us women around to stop them all from killing themselves. I don't know how you put up with it. You should stand up to him.'

'Oh I can't. Neville hates women who nag and domineer.'

'I bet he does.'

'Most of the time, I get my way. I just pretend everything's his idea.'

'I know you do. But it's not going to help you if he starts firing guns about the place, is it? So what's the problem with Sylvie? She seemed fine to me.'

'Well, now she hates going to school and yet she's so bright. Thinks she's being watched by some man. I'm worried she could be having a little nervous breakdown.'

'She's too young for that, Jean.'

'Do you think so?'

'Of course she is.'

'I would have too, normally. But you never really know, do you? One thing. All this dreamt-up stuff is beginning to pall, I can tell you.'

'We've been assured they would send in the British army to protect us. I don't understand why Neville gets all these ideas in his head.'

'Neville doesn't want to wait for any army. At the first hint of trouble, we're heading straightaway south.'

'South?'

'He says it's the only way. The airport would be blocked solid.'

'That's just him worrying you, Jean.'

'We'd have to shoot the dog. Load up Mary because we wouldn't leave her behind, poor thing. Neville's done the car very well. Tucked stuff in every nook and cranny.'

'It's no wonder Sylvie keeps breaking down. Neville is frightening her.'

'Oh, I don't think so.'

'Yes, he is. It's his fault. He's scaring her.' Pam did the slapping thing again. 'But you've heard the latest news, have you?'

'What's that?'

'Anita is no longer with Gordon. I said it wouldn't last five minutes.'

'Oh, Pam. Surely not.'

'Well, something must have happened. Apparently,' Pam hesitated and leant forward to increase the drama. 'Anita has moved into Oleander Court. Matthew told me. One of the nursing sisters at Southwell has just gone on leave. She's "watering the plants" for her. Isn't that sweet?'

'I can't believe that, Pam. Poor Gordon. Are you sure?'

'It's what I've heard. What was Anita talking about at the dinner party the other night? Can you remember?'

'I don't Pam. She seemed to be more on edge than usual.'

'Some people worry about entertaining. Not confident enough perhaps. I expect it all got to her.'

'Dearie me. I was going to ask Gordon about where he got

their carpet. He gave me the address of the place, but that was years ago and I've lost it. If I leave, I want to take one back with me for the new house. You can't find out for me, can you?'

'No. You do it yourself.'

'I feel bad now that you've told me about Anita. What if Gordon thinks I'm prying?'

'Don't mention the break up. Or that I told you. Because they could get back together again. When would you be leaving, anyway?'

'Not until January. The children would hate it if we weren't with Daddy at Christmas.'

Chapter 34

Carlisle assumed the incident at the storeroom and secret lab was accidental. But on arriving at Magwa, the emergency crew quickly disabused him of that idea. 'Bomb. Bomb. An explosion caused the fire.'

He was stunned. It was hard to even process let alone accept that Najib Noor, his trusted colleague was a terrorist and saboteur.

Alerted by the Fire Department in the early hours, Gordon and Mansour had been out at the pesticide complex for some time before Brigadier General Mustafa arrived. Although wearing the same serious expression, the Chief of Police was in a more conciliatory mood than when he visited Gordon's house in Main Street.

They stood together, looking over the remains of the burnt-out building.

'Mr Carlisle. Can I ask, when did you arrive here exactly?'

'As soon as I could. The Fire Department rang me at home around 1.30.'

Mansour had identified the body. What was left of it. The blast had blown Najib apart and the resulting inferno rendered his face barely recognisable. A policeman dug into the rubble looking for other human remains.

'You weren't here yesterday?'

'No. The room is kept locked up, anyway.'

'But your worker had a key?'

'Yes.'

'What is this building for, actually?' The Brigadier asked.

'We use it as a storage facility.' It'd been clear to Gordon from the moment he arrived that the devastating fire would have destroyed the anthrax samples. Perhaps that had been the aim.

'For what purpose?'

'Years ago we used this building as a laboratory to research infectious diseases.' Gordon stepped warily around the questions and decided it would be best to be a little economical with the truth. He didn't want to incriminate himself at all costs. If the Kuwaiti authorities weren't already in the know about the lab, it was better not to disclose now how it had housed spores of the biologically produced anthrax.

'And today?'

'Nothing much really apart from filing cabinets and office equipment.'

The Brigadier looked pleased with himself. He'd worked everything out and was proud of it. Pointing at the still smoking ruin he said, 'We now have all the answers. This man was making a bomb. It is reasonable to assume it went off unintentionally. It is most likely he was one of our rebels and this is where he was assembling it.'

'We're lucky. The pesticides in the building next door could have ignited. Then we would have had an environmental emergency on our hands,' said Gordon.

They stood together quietly before the Brigadier interrupted his own reverie to dispute Gordon's assessment. 'As you said, if he'd blown up the insecticide depot, many others could have died.' And followed it up with, 'So why did you give him access to this highly dangerous plant?'

Allowing Najib a key was something Gordon had to ask himself too. While he'd never taken as much to Najib Noor as he had to Mansour, he still liked the man. Had he missed signs that Najib was a security risk? Why hadn't he picked him as anti-colonial earlier?

'I had no idea of his intentions' he said with complete candour, not because Gordon had ever asked Najib about his political views, but because he'd had ample time to observe his behaviour for himself and draw his own conclusion.

'I'm surprised you had no warning before. You didn't mention him when we spoke the other day.'

'There was often fr-fr-friction between himself and some of the other men. Mostly for his pro-Western views. Not the other way around.'

Perhaps it is as well he is dead, Gordon thought. As the Brigadier had pointed out, Najib had access to deadly poisons. Would he have used them on the civilian population? Did he have no off-limits?

'These people can be brilliant at hiding their motives.' Mustafa made a zipping motion across his lips. 'He wasn't even on our radar.'

But Gordon kept to himself the fact that Najib did have access to the anthrax samples.

Uncomfortable under the gaze of the Brigadier's dark brown eyes, Gordon wiped his brow.

Short puffs of wind had little impact on the now insufferable heat. They strolled back towards their respective vehicles anxious to get out of the morning sun.

187

Inwardly, he questioned the facts himself. Why now? Why hadn't Najib destroyed the anthrax samples long ago? When Gordon showed Pip Foster around the facility Najib had turned up too. Perhaps he'd sussed Foster was a British agent. Assumed matters were drawing to a head. If he'd been working undercover for the Iraqi secret service, then he would have acted to destroy the evidence. Cover it by staging the fire.

'Do you think there are any others like Najib still working within the oil company?' Gordon asked.

'Perhaps. But the saboteurs aren't at Ahmadi. The city is where we've found guns and many weapons, explosives. Sometimes in the most unexpected quarter.'

'Najib hired some extra crew the other day because we were short staffed.'

'They could be working for the Iraqis too. It all depends though. Not all Palestinian immigrants are traitors,' said the Brigadier. 'Over the past ten years, many have arrived from the West Bank and Gaza. Teachers. Civil servants. Unskilled labourers. Last year, we had a huge influx of Jordanian Palestinians and they brought relatives and friends into the country. Perhaps he was one of those?'

'He's been with me for seven years.'

Mustafa shrugged, disappointed that it didn't fit with his neat scenario. He scuffed the toe of his shoe in the sand. 'The Palestinians are not Kuwaiti citizens.'

That was the problem, Gordon thought, but said, 'Perhaps they should be. Palestinians make up some of the best qualified surgeons and doctors we have here. They are excellent administrators as well. And they work hard.'

More than any other single expatriate group, the Kuwaiti

Palestinians he'd known had helped shape the country. They occupied an honourable place in local society and felt they belonged.

The Chief of Police disagreed. 'No. Most of them want to return to Palestine eventually. That makes a problem.'

Led by Brigadier General Mustafa, the two decided on a joint course of action. There seemed no mileage to be gained publicising news that a terrorist attack had gone wrong. The community had enough racial tension without adding to it. 'We will keep this to ourselves.'

'Maybe that's for the best.' Gordon agreed but still had to deal with the reality. His faithful worker had been anything but loyal and probably an activist for the Iraqi underground.

'Perhaps Mr Sandberg wasn't killed by the British, after all,' said Mustafa with a glint of menace in his eyes. 'Do you agree we may now have identified the real culprit?'

It was a question that required no direct answer.

As Gordon drove back towards Ahmadi, he shelved any previous thoughts of going to Oleander Court to see Anita and smooth things over. Pip Foster's bitter remarks about her replayed in his mind and Foster's coldness about Carl's death was chilling. Why was he so aggressive? If British agents were indeed capable of murder off book, then Gordon had to be very, very careful. And he didn't want to bring his wife into the mess as well. After all, he still harboured dreams of them getting back together again.

Chapter 35

At around eleven, Gordon arrived back at Main Street, his clothes pungent with the smell of Najib's corpse mixed with the stench of the smouldering fire.

He showered, changed, and sat at the dining room table suddenly aware he hadn't eaten that morning.

Florrie came in from the servants' quarters curious to know why Saab was home and not at work.

'An accident happened at a storeroom, Florrie. A very bad one.'

'Are you hurt, sir?'

'No, not me.'

'That's good, sir.'

She ducked back into the kitchen and whipped up an omelette which she brought back along with a glass of cold water.

'Florrie, any news from Memsahib?'

'No, sir,' she said, pottering around waiting for a specific instruction.

'I'm going into the office after this.'

It was already midmorning and a strong wind now blew in, picking up the sand grains.

'Bad weather, sir,' she said, gazing out the window and

making wide-handed gestures to emphasise her disapproval.

'Yes, I think there's a shamal on its way. You'd better fasten all the windows.'

'I close them. The sand, the sand. It still gets everywhere.'

Florrie was right. Minute particles passed through the smallest cracks. It was as if nothing could be done to keep out a sand storm.

Gordon spread a sheet out over the Grundig radiogram. The sand got into the works and could even destroy the records if they weren't protected in their covers. He fingered through the pile of albums for the Sibelius record, which had done a disappearing trick, before giving up in irritation. It seemed irrelevant now whether or not he return the LP to the Dicksons.

Najib's death, combined with a lack of sleep, dragged Gordon into a depressed state bordering on paranoia. Everything seemed to be closing in around him.

As he joined the local traffic he even imagined he was being followed. But each time he checked over his shoulder or behind in the mirror, there was nothing other than the usual flow of vehicles.

Low on petrol and with a strong chance he would have to make a trip into Kuwait City later Gordon turned off at the first petrol pump.

The already soaring heat and the sand-laden air from the approaching storm added to his irritability. While waiting for the attendant to fill the tank he noticed the Arab driver in the car ahead was wearing the red and white kaffiyeh, a symbol of resistance and solidarity connected with the Palestinian Marxists.

'As-salamu alaykum,' said Gordon warily without the slightest stutter. Peace be upon you.

So they are beginning to show their defiance more openly. A bad sign.

'*Wa alaykumu s-salam.*' And peace be upon you too. The man's voice had the polite phrasing usually adopted in an exchange of formal greeting.

He nodded at the sky before unwinding part of his headdress with a confident motion and brought one end across his face to cover the nose. '*Taqs Sayiy,*' he said referring to the bad weather in prospect, then got back into his old jalopy and drove off.

Gordon waited impatiently as the attendant filled his tank. A gust of wind blew the forecourt dust around in circles. He wished the check scarf was not so political. He'd wear one himself. The headdress was the most comfortable and practical in sand storms.

The sky grew yellow as the sand blotted out the sun. Gordon clambered back into the Saab and continued his journey. He reckoned no sane person would attempt to follow his car in the deteriorating weather.

The death of Najib Noor had progressed to a police paperwork stage, but there were still written reports which Gordon needed to complete. Najib had family to be informed too. While Gordon could fill Najib's position in minutes, the many memories of their time working together would linger on for years.

He kept going over in his mind the earlier conversation with Mustafa who'd half suggested that anti-Colonial pamphlets had whipped up antagonism against the Kuwaiti royals. The photograph made sense now. Gordon's employees often borrowed his car to run errands when the trucks were out.

Had Najib taken the Saab on the pretence of filling it with petrol so he could distribute his leaflets? It was possible.

Najib knew all Gordon's movements by heart. Ever present at meetings, Najib might have overheard his conversations with Sandberg. Perhaps suspected Carl would add his name to the list of potential saboteurs. Dark thoughts played on Gordon's mind. How his most faithful worker had stabbed his friend to death.

By early afternoon, the weather had set in. News reached him that the shamal had already caused the Hubara Club swimming pool filters to clog, and had been closed to the members. Gordon sent Mansour off to inspect the damage to the filtration plant.

'At least you've had a bit of good luck with the Magwa stores,' said Matthew Quinn when they crossed paths in reception.

'You heard about the fire of course?'

'The pesticides didn't ignite. Just as well.' Matthew raised two eyebrows. 'Sad about Najib. He got caught up in it, I hear.'

'He shouldn't have been there at all,' said Gordon, and wondered how much Matthew knew. 'In fact, the Fire Department don't even think it was accidental.'

'Could Najib have been behind Carl's murder as well, do you suppose?'

'They don't have any other suspects at the moment.'

'He'd been with you a long while, hadn't he?'

'It's all hotting up by the look of it. We've been stocking up at home. Reckon if Britain sends in the troops, we'd open up our house to them.'

'That's a good idea.'

'The boys will be in tents. Pretty basic desert digs. Reckon they'd appreciate some air conditioning and a generous supply of alcohol. If it happens. Mind you, if this weather continues we might just need the beer ourselves.' He gave a wry smile.

'It's passing through, I think.'

'How's Anita by the way?' Matthew was being his usual polite self.

Gordon shrugged, not willing to open up.

Matthew downed the rest of his beer in one swallow as he sought to change the subject too. 'Have you seen what Neville has done with his VW?'

'Not yet. I haven't had time with all that's been happening, Matthew.'

'You can check it out tomorrow at the Maynards' cocktail do. He's driving around with all the seats removed, the kids sitting on the car floor sliding all over the place and squealing every time he goes round a corner. If you need to take off into the desert at short notice, it's quite a nifty conversion he's done, I must say.'

Gordon smiled. 'They will look like a bunch of Oakies driving west to California loaded up with everything, dogs, chicken, furniture.'

He returned to the office, parted company with Mansour, found his car and drove back to Main Street. It had been an eventful day. And it wasn't over.

With Foster back in Beirut, Gordon had a lot to do that evening. He wrote a brief report to notify Whitehall that a bomb and fire had destroyed the Magwa facility and killed his worker, Najib, at the same time. He considered it important to keep them informed of the latest developments.

But delivery via the foreign office involved a trip to Kuwait City to get it into the political officer's diplomatic pouch.

Outside the shamal was still sweeping up the surface sand forcing it into rippled waves. But the trip had to be done despite the weather.

The word was already out on Najib. Gordon reckoned it was better for the powers that be to get the news from him directly, rather than indirectly via Foster or even the Kuwaiti authorities. Gordon wondered if he could trust either of them to report the facts.

He ate a quick early supper of salami and canned new potatoes before setting off. The foul weather made him yearn for the spires of Cambridge, a village pub, and a deep green forest. Was he beginning to tire of the desert? And, with the departure of his wife he felt desperately lonely and increasingly isolated.

The Maynards' cocktail party was a further example. He and Anita hadn't received an invitation for drinks. Nor to other functions he'd heard about. A string of people had begun to distance since the episode at the Golf Dance.

The sky looked like a gigantic, dirty blanket looming overhead. Near darkness enveloped Ahmadi. It was if he was being blamed personally for clouds which had recently passed over the normally vibrant expat community.

Chapter 36

Dick White, head of MI6, rocked back and forth in his comfortable black leather chair. He was mid-discussion with his subordinate about the latest rumblings coming out of Kuwait and long experience told him the signs were not good.

The poisoning by organophosphates. Self-inflicted perhaps. But also a method used by Russian operatives to assassinate those who got in their way.

His right-hand man had to be brought up to date quickly. 'They're considered junior-strength nerve agents because they have the same mechanism of action as gases like Sarin.'

'All this is happening against the background of a possible invasion from Iraq. Aided by the Soviets, if the Iraqis cross, they'll want to neutralise the armed forces and kill or capture the Emir of Kuwait. They already have hundreds of agents operating within the Kuwaiti community.'

He picked up the report from twelve months earlier and slid it across the desk. 'Start by reading this.'

INTELLIGENCE REPORT
STATEMENT BY GORDON CARLISLE (KOC ID 155)
PREVENTATIVE HEALTH OFFICER
CASE OFFICER: J.G.C./smj -
REFERENCE: ANTHRAX OUTBREAK/IRAQ BORDER/
FILE: RE2769X

I visit regularly the Bedouin tribes along with one of my technicians, Mansour al-Sook, as an interpreter. These nomadic people are usually suspicious of foreigners, but we have become familiar to them and we respond to their customs. The Bedouin now trust us sufficiently to have us immunise them against some of the many diseases which sweep through the desert regions.

Through these visits we learnt they supplemented their income by weaving carpets which they sell through a trader in Kuwait City. On one occasion, they presented me with a rug which is in my KOC bungalow at 5 Main Street, Ahmadi North. I have owned it for four years.

A friend expressed an interest in the carpet and she asked me where she could buy one for herself. As a courtesy, I visited Kuwait City and identified the shops of two dealers who, amongst others, bought rugs from the same tribe.

The trader told me all their woven carpets had sold, but one buyer had not paid. He'd chased the debt. The man had fallen ill and died, and his widow refused to pay, blaming the dealer. I thought it was trader gossip so I called on the other dealer, who also had sold out of the rugs. He urged me to help him acquire more because they were highly profitable.

We organised a trip into the desert to the Bedouin camp. A surge of polio cases at the time presented us with an ideal opportunity to vaccinate them against the disease which was the main objective. When we located our Bedouin friends, we discovered their chief weaver had died too. Several members of the tribe and some cattle had also succumbed to a mystery illness.

Their symptoms were clinically consistent with those caused by anthrax. The last large epidemic of anthrax in the Middle East occurred in Iran in 1957. We took a piece of weave and ran tests in our laboratory, which confirmed our suspicions. We treated the tribe with antibiotics and can record that those affected made rapid recoveries.

I revisited the carpet dealers in Kuwait City and was able to trace the purchaser of one carpet from the previous batch. When we tested this rug, we found it also contained spores of anthrax, from which I concluded that Bedouin women must have unknowingly sewn them into the carpets. We traced, confiscated and destroyed these along with similar ones likely to be contaminated. I retained a limited set of samples, which are kept in a laboratory at Magwa.

Two weeks later, I went back to visit the tribe who had moved on. When we finally found them, we were able to track out their former movements to discover the original source of the outbreak.

The Bedouin explained how they had arrived earlier

in Kuwait via the northern border with Iraq. Guards at a new Iraqi outpost had intimidated them and forced them to move on.

Other Bedouin I spoke to described the potent smell of chemicals at the same settlement. It is likely they used this facility as part of a Soviet-backed bioweapons programme. However, my assistant has since made a trip back to the location. He reports the building complex is no longer standing.

'Your thoughts?' White pursed his lips and lifted his eyebrows in his usual quizzical way.

'Could be a natural outbreak of anthrax. Or the Iraqis are considering using biological weapons.'

'That was why Carlisle was told to keep it on the QT. Since then, there've been too many unexplained events. I'll list them now.' The boss held up his fingers and started bending them down with his other hand as he counted. 'Carlisle stored samples at a small laboratory, as in the report. We don't know the precise location, as he doesn't say.'

'Fair enough.'

'There's more. The Hubara Club is the major social hub for the Kuwait Oil Company employees. Everyone goes there. An explosive device was discovered close to the pool area. It was not primed. Dismissed as nonthreatening.'

The officer leant forward in his chair. 'Yup. It's getting interesting, sir.'

'Next. We get a list of names of anti-British agitators from a man called Carl Sandberg. He had special access to the oil rigs. Also he gave us a list of those within the Kuwaiti Resistance, committed patriots, and ready to fend off an invasion. Through them Sandberg learnt that the UAR, are building a guerrilla force within Kuwait. This information came via Philip Foster, our man in Beirut.'

The officer raised his own eyebrows. 'And?'

'Someone stabs Sandberg to death on his own verandah. The Kuwait police arrest a sweeper who found the body. An Indian. But he had an alibi, so he's let go.' The MI6 boss bent down another finger. 'Next. Carlisle's lonely little lab goes sky high because a Palestinian working for him was building an explosive device and it went off. The anthrax samples? Gone as well.'

'You think the same Palestinian did the Sandberg killing too?'

'Not necessarily. But we do know this. Last year an Egyptian named Yasser Arafat, an engineer from Cairo, employed in the Ministry of Public Works in Kuwait, set up a group called the Palestinian Liberation Organisation, the PLO. The movement shares the same aims, loosely, as the United Arab Republic. So it's possible the bomber was an undercover agent operating in their interests. And because of Carlisle's work remit, had access to the Hubara Club as well. He could even have planted the first incendiary device.'

'But he's dead now. Is that correct?'

'Yes. However, more concerning is the poisoning of a woman called Ophelia Dickson. The name won't be familiar, but her maiden one was Newton, which certainly will be.'

'The "Newton" who was with us?'

'He's her old man.'

'Right.' The officer's face brightened up as he grasped the connection.

'So, if our theory is correct, there's a Soviet agent operating at the heart of the Anglo-American community. Last place you'd expect which is why it could well be true.'

'Hard to believe they could hide in plain sight, isn't it?'

'There are plenty of British Trotskyites who take the view that we have no right to own the oil anyway. Think it's plunder. Hate the Empire. Probably ex Cambridge or at least one is. Beirut has confirmed all this and the fact that there are communist agents embedded, including one from Ahmadi. Known locally as Agent Alex.'

'So?'

The boss drummed the desk lightly with his fingers. 'We need to know all we can about this Carlisle character. Any ideas?'

'The Kuwait Oil Company asked Ian Fleming to write about the country. Fleming still works for Naval Intelligence freelance as you probably know.'

'Interesting. When's he due to visit?'

'November. The Royal Navy believe they can get useful gen from him in case they are forced to intervene. They would never come to us of course.'

'Never lower themselves. The RN need as much as they can get on Basra because that's where they will land if it is called for. What have we got on Basra?

'Plenty actually.'

'Perhaps we use that to our advantage.' The boss gave a sly smile. 'We'll give Fleming what we've got in return for stuff on Carlisle.'

'Tit for tat.'

'Exactly.'

201

Chapter 37

Slam! Jean watched the two women dart around the tennis court and wondered how they had the energy with temperatures already over 38 degrees.

The ball flew straight and hard from one side of the court to the other. It kept the enviously fit players moving quickly from left to right.

Jean was never good at any sport other than hockey and rounders.

When Pam and her friend Nola left the court, they weren't even puffing.

Nola excused herself because she had to rush off to some other group activity like Whist or Bridge. Jean didn't know which. The only card games she played were Rummy and Snap with the children.

There was a tennis trip on to Beirut, so Nola and Pam intended cancelling next week's Tombola or Housey Housey arrangement, or whatever the game was called.

'You should come along to one of those, Jean. Leave Neville and Matthew in the Blue Bar drinking. Men don't enjoy Tombola as much as the women. It makes for an enjoyable night out.'

'I'm not really a Bingo-type person,' said Jean, crossing her legs. She'd always thought it a bit of a working-class activity, but didn't say so directly because it sounded condescending.

'They do a fish and chip supper with it, too.'

'I spend enough time up here as it is.' Jean said as they settled into the wicker chairs to wait for their children who were finishing their cokes and vanilla ice lollies in the Dolphin cafeteria down in the basement. 'Now even more so. Did you know Mrs Stanley has asked Sylvie to do an act in the Christmas show?'

'You must be proud,' said Pam. 'What is it?'

'She's going to be miming a song. You know Sylvie is very talented at drama apparently.'

'I'd like Helen to do that. How did Sylvie get the part?'

'We're not entirely sure. She won first prize last week for the Twist at the children's dance.'

'I heard about that.'

'Then they approached her yesterday for this little part.'

Pam pulled an impressed face. 'How nice.'

'I think it may help her confidence. Take her mind off all her worries. I've offered to make the costumes myself. So I suppose that also helped her get the part,' Jean added, feigning a little modesty. 'Time to lug out the sewing machine again.'

'I can't sew for toffees,' said Pam. 'I even get the tailor to stitch in laundry labels.' She threw her hair back and laughed loudly.

'You're good at other things though.'

'We'll have to buy tickets early,' said Pam. 'You know how they sell out when the Anglo-American School is involved.'

'What else have you been doing, Pam? We've been a bit on the quiet side ourselves lately.'

'I'm planning to drive to the coast one day next week if you want to come. The Families Beach just near North Pier.'

'No, I won't do that, Pam. It gets so hot down there. I don't mind at the Boat Club. At least you can take refuge in an air-conditioned club house. The children love those awful TV dinners they heat in the oven.'

'The water is so dirty there. From the engines, you know. The diesel spreads everywhere. How do you join that club, anyway? I didn't know you were members.' Pam turned round to face Jean squarely.

'We were thinking about joining and getting some sort of speed boat. But we've shelved that idea for the time being,' Jean confided.

'If Matthew and I joined anywhere, it would be the Cumberland. The yacht club is just near the South Pier. Close by Mina. North of the Shaiba complex.'

'What's that like? I've never been there.'

'Even that smells a bit of sulphur. But not as bad. Matthew doesn't like what he calls stink boats.' Pam laboured the point, blaming the oily sheen left on the surface from the water skiing. She wrinkled up her nose. 'Matthew used to do yachting.'

'They say you're either one or the other, don't they? If you enjoy boating.'

'Oh, I hate the beach too really. You get sand all over the carpets. By the way, did you ever find out from Gordon where you can get one like his, you know, the Bedouin one,' Pam asked.

'No. Neville doesn't want me to bother him at the moment.'

'Is that because of the fire at the KOC storeroom out at Magwa?'

'I hadn't heard of that.'

'There was a funny fire. Just the other day before the big sand storm. Gordon was involved in some way.'

Jean sat forward, excited. 'Oh, really?'

'Out where the hospital used to be. Your children were born at Magwa, weren't they?'

'Both of them.'

'It wasn't the old clinic that was destroyed. But behind it there were some storerooms which Gordon's department managed. Some sort of accident, according to Matthew. But strangely enough no one seems to have heard much more about it.'

'As I said, we've kept away from Gordon for the time being.'

'And you were such close friends too, Jean. Even more than us.'

'You don't want to get tied up with gossip, do you? I've no idea what's going on with them at the moment.'

'Now that Anita's moved out? I saw her driving around in her A30.'

'Did you?'

'Anyway, shall we walk down to meet the girls?' Pam got up. 'They'll be in that place gassing for hours if we don't move them along.'

Jean checked her watch. 'We've got a rehearsal in half an hour in the assembly hall, so that's why we're hanging around.'

'Ah, that's nice. Helen is bound to be jealous of Sylvie being in a show.'

Jean nodded. 'Still, her turn will come.'

They picked up with their two girls in the snack bar, both giggling and flicking straws at one another like five-year-olds.

When the four parted company, Jean took her daughter up to leave her with the show organiser for an hour. As she was leaving the hall and crossing the outdoor complex, she caught sight of Gordon Carlisle, who was checking out the water quality of the swimming pool. It had been closed for a few days to get a thorough clean after the shamal.

'Hello, Jean,' Gordon said when he spotted her. 'How are you? Well, I hope?'

'You'll be popular,' she said, as Gordon got up from his crouched position. 'Opening up the pool again.'

'It'll be usable tomorrow. At least for the end of the summer season.'

'What a terrible storm it was, Gordon.' It was a safe topic for Jean and stayed a comfortable distance from his marriage difficulties. 'I almost got caught in it.'

Gordon towered above her. 'Pretty bad, wasn't it? I had to drive to Kuwait City that day. Almost impossible to see the road.'

'The City?'

'Which reminds me. I promised to do something about the carpet for you, didn't I?'

'There's no rush at the moment.' Jean felt her face grow even redder. 'I feel awful. I have to say thank you for the dinner party that evening.' Jean tossed in a massive fib. 'I've tried to call a few times but not got you or Anita.'

Gordon stammered over his words. 'She's s-s-spending time on her own for a bit.'

'Is that so?' Jean played dumb. But now was forced to ask, 'Anything the matter, Gordon?'

'There's been a lot happening of late. Not all good, as you know. Anita's working on a ph-ph-photographic project.' He stammered on the 'F' sounding syllables for some seconds.

Jean looked away as Gordon struggled with the words.

Perhaps it was time to question her soft spot for him over his stammer. There was probably another side to his character which Anita had discovered.

'Send her our love, won't you?' said Jean, anxious to pull away but equally anxious not to appear rude. So when Gordon called a waiter to offer her a gin and tonic, she made an easy excuse and slipped off.

Chapter 38

Until he ran into Jean Beresford at the club, Gordon had not seen many from his former group of friends for several weeks. People were either too preoccupied with their own private lives to socialise, or still giving him the cold shoulder because his behaviour might have had a bearing on Ophelia Dickson's suicide. One or the other.

Plus, he was separated. Expat Kuwait was a conservative community, at least on the surface. Any whiff of emotional problems or marital instability got talked about. But no one wanted to be involved in any way.

'Well, I'm sure it'll work out,' said Jean Beresford in her kindly manner. 'I suppose it's different when you marry younger, like we did. You're not so set in your ways.'

Gordon had to smile at her unintended lack of diplomacy. He had been a bachelor for longer than most. Instead of getting hitched early twenties, unlike everyone else, he'd played the field. Everyone was used to him being the convenient spare man of Ahmadi society. Several women had asked, 'Haven't you ever been tempted?' as if marriage was an ice-cream sundae to be tasted as soon as possible.

His constant reply had always been, 'No. I don't think I'm

the marrying kind.'

An introvert but someone comfortable in his own skin, what Ahmadi thought about his single status didn't bother him in the slightest. But Gordon didn't care either what it made of his surprise new marriage. But there were certain inferences going around that had indeed caused him concern.

The suggestion he'd been carrying on an affair with John Dickson's wife out of petty spite because his own wife had wandering eyes, did get to him. What was even more disturbing was the rumour that he'd driven Ophelia to suicide. That he tried to divert suspicion by giving a lavish dinner party as if nothing was going on between them.

The Najib affair also hung over him with the insinuation that he'd been sloppy when vetting his staff. It was plain silly to believe that Gordon condoned Najib's behaviour and even sillier to think he sympathised with the man's views.

He knew all the ridiculous things being said. However, he was more worried about matters closer to home.

The words on Ophelia's suicide note kept coming back over and over. Every time they sounded to Gordon as if she'd written to him several times before her death.

Ophelia had loved sending letters in all their various forms to everyone. Scratched-out notes with doodles on the sides, enclosed invitations and little 'thank you' messages with magazine cuttings and tucked-in recipes. Anything to keep a dialogue going. However, he'd not received a thing from her for some time which was not true to her style.

One hot and humid evening, he raised the subject with Florrie. 'You might have to cast your mind back. Do you recall any personal letters arriving for me which I might not have got for some reason?'

The Indian ayah tapped her fingers against her forehead. 'I am thinking, sir.'

Gordon polished his spectacles to give her time.

She walked into the front room. Her flip-flops made the usual flapping noise he was so accustomed to associate with the ayah as she moved around the house.

Florrie stopped at the radiogram. 'I leave all your letters here in the normal place every day.'

Gordon crossed the room and opened a drawer in the dining room cabinet and took out a couple of personal letters, still in their envelopes. One was from his mother and another from his older brother, which reminded Gordon they both still needed replies.

'Do you remember these coming, Florrie?'

She nervously examined both the envelopes.

'Yes. From England.' She gave a small smile.

Sometimes she steamed off the stamps and sent them back to a collector in India.

'Were there any others at all, Florrie?'

'Only some for the Memsahib.'

'But none other than these for me?'

'Maybe others. But not from England.'

'Local letters?'

'Yes.'

Gordon took out a black file which contained two house-hold bills. 'You would have seen these?'

'I don't remember, sir.'

'But they would have been in typed envelopes.'

'I remember now. Yes, sir.'

'Were there others?'

She nodded.

'Hand-written, perhaps?'

'Yes, sir.'

'How many?'

'Two, three.'

'You left them here on the radiogram? As you normally do.'

'Yes, sir.'

Gordon couldn't be sure. Perhaps a letter had come in from Ophelia, which he'd never received let alone had a chance to read. Had Anita got hold of them? Maybe jumped to the wrong conclusion he was still having an affair and destroyed them?

With Anita not talking, he couldn't ask her himself. And Gordon knew it would be wrong to accuse her directly of opening his mail. Let alone binning it. It all seemed to him most unlikely. His wife was more guarded about her independence than possessive of her husband. So much so, sometimes he wondered if she'd ever cared for him at all. Could he have got it all wrong? Not really got her true personality?

He poured himself a drink and slipped a record on the Grundig.

Outside, the wind had picked up, shaking the dry leaves loose and carpeting the front lawn. The sky darkened. Vivid lightning strikes lit up the area followed immediately by bursts of thunder. That means the storm must be very close, Gordon thought as he looked out the window. The skies opened up and great heavy rain drops landed, bouncing off the concrete patio. A fierce cloudburst right overhead..

Living in one of the hottest locations on earth, rain was always a welcome relief. But it led to road closures and flooding. And at that moment, Gordon was drowning in his own thoughts too, engulfed in a depressive wave of sadness.

He missed Anita. Although always a contradiction, still he longed for her to return somehow.

Acting on impulse, he picked up the telephone and called her number. As expected, it went unanswered. But where was she? Kuwait wasn't a country where any woman, particularly a European, should be alone, whatever the circumstances. And it certainly wasn't the sort of night for Anita to be out driving somewhere or other.

He heard the back door close as Florrie went back to her staff room behind the house.

Gordon made a tour of the rooms, checking Florrie had secured all the windows.

The downpour continued unabated for a full thirty minutes. Gordon lit a cheroot and stood watching small craters form in the garden as the rain pounded down on the muddy sand. He recalled how Florrie had told him the Kuwait police had dug up bits of the garden when they'd called round just after Carl Sandberg's murder. What had they been looking for exactly?

But there had been no follow up. Even the investigation into the storeroom fire and Najib's death had gone quiet. Things had returned almost to normal. Mansour now had to cover duties that previously he and Najib shared. Deadlines still had to be met and the stock replenishment from Magwa was on target. Only Gordon's personal life was way off-course.

As an example, there had not been anything back from the report sent through to Whitehall after the storeroom explosion. With Pip Foster back in Beirut, there had been no further talk going around about an Iraqi invasion.

The nearest thing to the world of spies and espionage was

the imminent arrival of the dashing best-selling author Ian Fleming. He had the reputation of being a skilled fixer and a wonderful showman. Everyone in Ahmadi was excited and wanted to meet him. He'd published seven Bond books, and they were fast becoming a global phenomenon. Gordon read every one as soon as it came out.

At least he had that to look forward to and forget for a time all his worries.

Chapter 39

The famous writer, thrust out his hand. 'Gordon Carlisle?'

Gordon wondered why Ian Fleming had singled him out from such a jam-packed reception of local luminaries. But it soon became obvious. Gordon's interest in desert wildlife.

'They promised me you'd help me escape from all this,' said Fleming with deliberate flippancy, glancing around the packed room.

'A real pleasure to meet you. How can I h-h-help?'

Their common interests made for an easy conversation between the two men.

'I'm a terribly keen bird watcher,' said Fleming. 'Of the feathered variety. Few people know I named the delectable Solitaire in Live and Let Die after a rare Jamaican bird. And indeed James Bond was named after an American ornithologist. He's my real type of hero. By the sound of it, yours as well.'

'Perhaps you'd like to see the houbara, one of the native desert birds Kuwait has to offer.' said Gordon.

'Very much so. I get tremendously bored by this sort of thing.'

'That's un-un-understandable.'

'You struggle like I used to when I was young,' said Ian Fleming referring to his own stammer. They struck up an instant rapport, having both been bullied at school because of it. 'I experienced trauma during my time at Durnford as did many others. But I have no great message for humanity. I don't wish to foist my tales of personal terror on others. My books are not too involved or complicated. They are simple adventures for people to read in planes and trains.'

'My favourite is Casino Royale,' said Gordon.

'That was based on my wartime memories in the Naval Intelligence division.'

'C-c-can I ask who gave you my name?'

'Your John Dickson in the KOC Public Relations department mentioned you months back. The deal was I would write a book giving a favourable view of Kuwait. In addition to the fee, he promised to provide me with a few excursions into the desert.'

Gordon nodded, but wondered how much Ian Fleming knew about the reason for Dickson's absence during the visit. 'If you like we could do one tomorrow. I am not tied up at the moment.'

'That sounds just the ticket. An early start, I assume?'

'Yes. Quite early. Say 5.15 while it's still cool?'

'OK. I'm your man. Look forward to it.'

After the function Gordon invited the writer back to Main Street. During the intervening period, Gordon phoned Mansour and got him to organise a hawking expedition for the next morning. Fleming had expressed an interest in seeing Gordon's small zoo of desert creatures and Gordon had, on the way home, driven to his office and picked up a few favourites from his menagerie.

Florrie tutted and shook her head as the glass cages were carried in.

Gordon waved her away. 'Florrie, go and shut yourself up in your room if you are so bothered.'

Fleming arrived by taxi. He strode confidently up the drive and shook Gordon's hand vigorously.

'Why is your ayah staring through the window at us with her face half covered by a shawl?' Ian Fleming asked.

'She's terrified, that's why. Not of you, of course. Come in and see Sally, my lovely scorpion.'

Sally was busy investigating the chair legs, her brown tail raised, ready to strike.

Ian Fleming sipped on the pink gin which a nervous Florrie brought out before rushing back to the kitchen and safety.

'I'm curious to see which one would emerge the winner in a contest between a snake and scorpion.'

'Perhaps we c-c-can organise that some time,' said Gordon, before getting down on his knees to pick up Sally. 'We don't want her going under these slip covers or we could lose her.'

He seized Sally at the tip of the tail just beneath the stinger, gripping her firmly between his index finger and thumb. 'Come and say hello to Daddy,' said Gordon.

'I didn't know you could pick them up like that.'

'It's to stop her whipping her tail prior to injecting venom.' Gordon gently placed the scorpion down on a large glass ashtray for his guest to scrutinise more closely.

'You might want to return her now.' Fleming leant back in his chair eyeing Sally cautiously.

Gordon Carlisle put the scorpion back in her cage.

'Tell me, Ian. Out of curiosity, how do you come up with

ideas for your stories?'

'While my books go wildly beyond the probable, they don't go wildly beyond the possible. My plots are often based on the truth. People say I have a dirty mind.'

'Well, don't we all to a degree? But you have such vivid powers of imagination.'

'We are obviously force-fed adventure stories when we are young. Which is useful. Sometimes the exotic is so terribly dull in real life, isn't it? Like espionage work.'

He gave a questioning look.

Gordon suggested they might have a light supper. 'It seems unkind to get Florrie back in. She's so nervous. Don't you agree? I'll knock something up.'

When Gordon brought in his version of scrambled eggs on toast he found Fleming studying the wedding photos still on show on the sideboard.

'My favourite. Thank you,' said Fleming.

'Anita is away at the moment.' Gordon passed him the salt and pepper.

'You been married long?'

'Barely a year.'

'Marriage can be a miserable existence sometimes,' Fleming observed, as if he understood the situation without going into it further.

They ate in silence, each with their own thoughts.

'I have a favour to ask. I came via Beirut. It's crawling with real British and American spies there. My friend Nicholas Elliott, who I stayed with, is the Station Chief of MI6. He is desperate to get any local intelligence from here. What is going on? As you probably know, the place is a Cold War battleground. Kuwait is currently the number one issue on

217

the map. I promised to take him back a little behind the scene information and a box of local truffles as payment for my stay in Beirut. Can you help me on where to find them? Living here you must know what's what.'

'The rain has brought out a particularly good crop this year.'

'By the way, is there any truth in the rumour that someone working for you murdered a British engineer?'

'It's a possibility,' said Gordon. He realised their friendly meeting hadn't been entirely without other motives.

'Why do you say that?'

'Because we can't be sure. Najib Noor had been with the company for eleven years. And in a department I run for seven of them.'

'But his name was on a list of suspected pro-Iraqi Palestinians.'

'No, I don't believe it was.'

'It wasn't? Are you sure?'

'Absolutely. Unless it's another list I don't know about.'

'This was information given to MI6 in Whitehall via Pip Foster.' It was obvious Ian Fleming had been fully briefed.

'He wasn't on the list that came from my contact Carl Sandberg.'

'Are you sure about that?'

'Obviously, if I'd seen his name I would have put the police on to him straightaway. Long before he blew himself up out at the storeroom at Magwa.'

Fleming took out another cigarette and fitted it into the holder. 'Obviously you would have, yes.' He looked at Gordon, assessing his integrity, wanting to believe him. 'Perhaps they got their wires crossed.'

'Brigadier Mustafa confirmed he wasn't a person of interest

to them. Otherwise, they would have been watching him. And not me.'

Fleming raised his eyebrows 'Where do you fit into the equation exactly?'

Gordon recounted fully his meeting with Pip Foster. How he'd introduced Sandberg into the mix, and bore guilt for the connection between himself and the man accused of Carl's murder.

'Are you sure you didn't see his name on the list?'

'Yes, absolutely. I wrote out a copy before I passed it on.'

'Sounds like it's up to me to check on the facts again. I must get back to the Guest House. I hear we have an early start in the morning. In the meantime, I'll have another of those excellent pink gins.'

Chapter 40

Gordon Carlisle was a trifle apprehensive when he got up at four thirty the next morning. Perhaps it was natural. He was about to drive miles into the desert and would be hosting a world-famous VIP. If anything went wrong he knew they wouldn't be able to get help out there easily.

It'd been Ian Fleming's idea. He was keen to see the real Kuwait. The romantic origins of the country and people excited him far more than the civilised, pious image he was expected to project in his work. That had been the briefing right from the start.

For security reasons the hunting trip had been arranged in secret by Mansour. Fleming didn't want the news to get out as he knew others would want to come and didn't want to cause offence to them unnecessarily. There was little time to organise things. Just the bare essentials could be taken. Included in last-minute preparations were hip flasks of coffee, dough to be made into chapati, bars of chocolate, basic medical supplies and last but not least plenty of alcohol.

Gordon set out at five to pick up Ian Fleming, who was ready and waiting outside the Guest House, nattily dressed in an appropriate hunting jacket and trousers. The first light of dawn appeared as they drove away together in the Saab heading for the pre-arranged rendezvous, where the real desert began. Mansour sat waiting in his vehicle loaded up with the camping equipment.

For the next leg of the journey, they'd go with the hawkers. Fleming wanted to savour the complete experience at first-hand.

Gordon parked his car alongside the Arab falconer's vehicles, an ancient land rover and a seven-ton truck loaded with more camping equipment. After the customary greetings Ian and Gordon climbed into the back seat of the land rover, while the falconer took up the one alongside the driver. The falcon, hooded with a leather cap, perched quietly on the Arab's gloved wrist, obedient but nervous, moving from one claw to another when the vehicle hit the odd rough patch.

Gordon's pulse raced a tad faster than usual. With the sun just up every bush cast a long blue eerie shadow as the small convoy of truck and jeeps made its way northwest. As the sun climbed higher the desert lost its strong shadow line marking out the undulating sand hills and took on harsher tones of gypsum white and olive-grey broken only by the tough Arfa bushes.

'Can we stop here for a bit?' Ian Fleming asked the driver as they reached a well ringed with palm trees. He took out his camera and photographed the oasis and its desert Arabs filling camel skins with water as their own driver topped up his radiator.

'Perhaps we should keep moving,' Gordon said, aware of the passing time and also of a growing unease in the distant reaches of his mind. Something seemed wrong, though he couldn't put a finger on exactly what.

He started at the faint sound of gunfire away in the distance but concluded it had come from a gang out hunting wild dogs. This was a common practice in order to keep down the incidence of rabies endemic amongst the greyhound-type salukis and other feral breeds.

The convoy moved on and continued deeper into the trackless desert, driving straight over the clumps of bushes blocking their way from time to time.

After two uncomfortable hours, the driver pulled up and announced they were there. 'Houbara place,' he announced.

'Shall we?' said Ian Fleming, anxious to get out from the sticky back seat as soon as possible.

Gordon had been on many trips and was always fascinated by the life and death battle between hawk and houbara. But he had never felt an excitement tempered by such unease and couldn't understand why.

The hawker produced a piece of string from his pocket, lifted the hawk's wings and tied together the three outer primary feathers on each wing.

Clambering up onto the back of the open truck, he un-hooded the hawk and raised it high up on his right hand. The hawk pivoted his head around and surveyed the country with his huge black eyes.

'If the houbara sense danger, they lie flat and are almost completely invisible,' Gordon whispered to Fleming, well aware the slightest sound could scare the birds.

'Whoa-hoa. Whoa-hoa.' The hawker's weird long-drawn-out call, intended to entice the houbaras to respond and cock their heads up, floated out across the landscape.

Everywhere stayed silent, waiting. Gordon still couldn't identify the tingly feeling in his body.

'Whoa-hoa. Whoa-hoa.' The bird handler's call rang out again in the motionless morning air followed by a humourless staccato 'Ha-ha-ha-a-ha'.

The hawk spread its wings wide and flew off over the hamdh bushes. High in the air Gordon and Ian could see the hawk as it swooped down on its prey. The hawker rushed towards the target, gown flapping high behind him.

'We follow now,' said Gordon as they joined the sprint forward.

At the scene of the kill, the triumphant hawk had already torn fresh scarlet meat from the houbara's small breast. The hawker pulled the hawk away and rehooded it quickly. The driver of their truck drew his knife and in a practised ritual cut the bird's throat.

With the first kill behind them, Gordon's trepidation eased a bit.

'We will stop here for a while,' he said to Mansour who passed the order on to the hunting team.

Mansour set out the picnic lunch for the hungry party. They ate heartily, washing it down with bitter coffee boiled up on the open camp fire.

'We will head back shortly,' Gordon said to Ian Fleming. 'But the chief hawker just said to me he'd like to give his bird another couple of runs. Is that OK with you, or do you need to get back early?' Gordon asked.

Fleming was well up for the extended hunting experience. After lunch, they drove further on and again released the bird. This time, it flew much further. This forced the party to jump into their vehicles and tear off in hot pursuit. Turning and twisting at high speed, they narrowly avoided rolling over. Gordon was relieved when they finally caught up with the hawk which had already devoured its catch, and sat perched proudly on its victim surrounded by a carpet of the houbara's white feathers.

Gordon jumped back as, with a great swishing sound, four houbara rose from right alongside the wheels of their jeep.

Focussing on the chase he had failed to notice in the distance the raggedly dressed gang on the search for feral dogs. They stood staring at the hawking team. Mansour leapt to his feet and rushed to the truck to get a rifle. The gang stood silently watching it all before remounting their jeep and speeding off in a cloud of grey sand.

'Were they about to cause trouble, do you think?' asked Ian Fleming.

'It certainly looked that way,' Gordon replied.

They'd had a close shave. But had they wanted to kill Ian Fleming? Or were they targeting Gordon? Was he next on the list to be assassinated?

Chapter 41

Gordon and Ian had little to say to one another and sat in silence for the same rough ride back from the desert. Instead they emptied the hip flasks and each thought over the day's events.

After dropping the author at the Guest House Gordon went to Ahmadi police station and alerted them about the armed gang they had seen while out hunting.

Apart from that, the expedition had been a success. It was obvious Ian Fleming had enjoyed it immensely. The trip was a welcome distraction, but perhaps not suitable material for inclusion in his work on Kuwait.

The typescript needed not just oil company approval but a nod from the Kuwaiti Government. The possibility that they might have been mugged was neither here nor there. Someone in the government would edit that out anyway. There was no point in Fleming writing it up.

In the evening, tired, but relieved about the overall outcome, Gordon drove slowly back to Main Street. By the time he got in, he felt nauseous and his vision had been affected by heat stroke.

He plonked down heavily and enjoyed the peace and quiet of the house. Gordon's head still throbbed from the whisky as well, but he needed to think clearly. Something Fleming had said earlier nagged away at him and he tried to recapture the essence before it faded away.

Shuffling in through the kitchen, Florrie interrupted the process. She stood beaming from ear to ear.

Anita had dropped in during the day.

'She waited for you, Sahib,' Florrie said, proud to be the bearer of good tidings.

'I went on a trip, Florrie.'

'So sad you were not here, sir. Maybe she wants to talk.'

'That's very sweet of you, Florrie.' The ayah was excited at the prospect of a reconciliation.

Gordon would have been elated normally, but this evening was different. Only half listening, he focused on why he still felt so uneasy.

He'd latched onto something vital and was afraid of losing it. So he asked Florrie to prepare him some supper hoping that way to get Florrie out and back into the kitchen and give time to concentrate in peace.

He paced the room while Florrie tinkered around in the kitchen, muttering cheerfully to herself as she prepared his supper.

Throughout the solitary meal, he ran through everything. On what he'd been told by British Intelligence. They knew all about Najib. Fleming had not followed up with Beirut on the Sandberg spy list because of the early morning timing of their trip. Gordon checked his transcribed hand-written copy of Carl's original but found no mention of Najib Noor or anyone else working within his department.

And he went back over the conversation he'd had with Ian Fleming the previous day at Main Street, trying to remember the exact words. What was the sequence again?

Pip Foster had passed on to MI6 that Najib Noor was a listed Iraqi agent. Gordon had not been in touch with Foster since the fire, though. He'd been unable to contact him, so how could Foster have learnt about Najib? He wasn't on Carl's first list. Could Foster have added the name himself? And if so, why? Had it been perhaps a spy's intuition, a guess without real evidence? Had he simply nailed Najib as a traitor? If so, why hadn't Foster tipped off Gordon himself about it?

Florrie came out and cleared the table.

'Sir is very tired,' she said sympathetically.

Gordon rose and stumbled forward to the front room. Fatigue made any deep concentration difficult.

'You go to bed, Florrie. I'll be OK.'

He heard her finish up and the back door close as she headed to her sleeping quarters. Gordon lit a cheroot, and found he was able to concentrate properly again.

Pip Foster had let Gordon know that he was a British agent. That had been confirmed by Ian Fleming, who knew the Beirut Chief of MI6 well enough to have stayed as his home guest en route to Kuwait. Foster spied for the British. But were any spies to be believed or trusted?

He trusted Foster, but should he have done so? He'd introduced Carl Sandberg to him. Sandberg had told Gordon about a Russian informer working undercover within the local community.

Gordon inhaled and held the smoke in his lungs before exhaling slowly. It helped him resolve a complex puzzle as he savoured the sweet taste of the expensive tobacco. Foster's apparent indifference to the murder of Carl Sandberg came back to him. The reaction didn't make sense.

Perhaps Pip Foster wasn't who he said he was at all. Could he have been passing on duff gen to the British Government all along? Was that possible?

Did that mean Pip Foster was a double agent? Perhaps even Agent Alex himself? And could Carl Sandberg have got on to it and paid the price with his life?

Gordon dropped off, but woke twenty minutes later with the cheroot still alight, and grasped between his fingers.

Exhausted, he climbed into bed but couldn't sleep. The memory of when he and Najib had worked together setting up the new office came into Gordon's mind, how they'd shuffled round the cabinets and desks together. Gordon sat bolt upright. Why hadn't he thought of it before?

In the darkened room, one thought moved to the next. On the night of Carl Sandberg's murder, Najib had worked late helping Gordon. Mansour, who would normally be there too, was away doing a slaughterhouse inspection in South Ahmadi. Mansour had the truck they shared, so Najib went home on the bus. This meant Najib couldn't have killed Carl.

So an innocent man was being blamed for the murder? As his boss, Gordon owed it to Najib to find out who. And what if it hadn't been Najib making the bomb at all? Perhaps he'd interrupted someone else who was in the middle of it? Did that mean that person had killed Najib and then covered by setting fire to the lab?

It was now clear. There were traitors at work within the system. Gordon realised he must be on his guard or he would be drawn in further himself and not necessarily with a good ending for him.

With his mind in a turmoil, another thought occurred. If he was correct about a dubious British agent passing on false gen, who would believe him anyway. Gordon Carlisle, a minor Kuwait Oil Company employee.

Despite reasonable efforts to avoid it, Gordon had still somehow allowed himself to be sucked into the murky world of espionage. And despite best intentions had become a major player. The last thing he needed.

Once again he went over the sequence of events which had brought him into contact with Pip Foster in the first place. John Dickson had called Gordon to introduce the journalist. He'd said at the time Foster had specifically wanted to meet Gordon. But who'd given John Gordon's name in the first place?

With Ophelia out of the picture and Dickson now back in the UK taking care of his personal matters, speaking to the head of PR was not an option.

Gordon realised he had to find out much more about the journalist. Where could he go to do so? Who else had Foster interviewed for his article? Had Gordon been the only one? He doubted it.

If Gordon could get hold of a copy of the published piece on Ahmadi, he'd be able to contact the other interviewees. That would help and confirm or deny his theory.

Chapter 42

Security tightened up around Ian Fleming after the hunting trip. It could easily have become a diplomatic disaster. Gordon got a rap over the knuckles from Head Office. What had he been thinking taking such risks? If they had been attacked or even robbed it would have made world news, and the Kuwaitis blamed for their lack of protection for a global personality and former British intelligence officer. Any contact between them was to be avoided in the future. The writer had a job to complete and must be allowed to get on with it without further distraction.

As far as the Kuwait police were concerned, the incident was a non-event. Arab bandits had always roamed the desert outside of the law. Thugs had struck on unsuspecting adventurers, after money and watches. No doubt they'd round them up sooner or later and deal out Arab justice.

Gordon felt exonerated when he learnt later that Ian Fleming described the experience as one of his most enjoyable in recent years.

Some weeks had passed since Anita moved out of the KOC bungalow, but Florrie told him she'd dropped by just the day before. It was a hopeful sign. He still harboured dreams of Anita regaining her senses as he saw it, but they needed to talk in person. There were questions that needed answers like what had happened to the missing letters Ophelia sent. And really important questions about her loyalty and whether they had a future together anyway. All that couldn't be resolved in a simple phone call.

Anita had not given Gordon her flat number within the Oleander Court complex, but he drove there all the same. Perhaps he might run into her by chance or see her car parked nearby. However there was no sign of either Anita or the car.

He went to the local shops on the off-chance she might be there. If not, at least he could pick up a copy of the Daily Telegraph with the article Pip Foster had written. He didn't know what the schedule was or whether the newspaper had already published it. But there were no copies available anyway.

Discouraged, he dropped into the Hubara Club. Often, the receptionist would cut out a relevant story on Ahmadi and post it on the society board for members to read. Killing two birds with one stone was an appealing thought. Check the board for the latest and check the club for Anita. The pool was closed. However the members still crowded the terrace and lounge, gossiping, drinking but there was no sign of Anita.

Rather than go back home in a depressed state Gordon decided to drive into the city. It was the weekend and he had nothing else to do. Florrie was on high alert at home anyway, ready to pass on to Anita the message that he wanted very much to see her.

He hated Kuwait City during the day when the sharp sun emphasised the heavy concrete constructions of modernity. The capital was masculine in every form. Street vendors, men draped in white robes, taxi drivers, builders banging away and the endless blast of car horns gave a sense of tension. Gordon always enjoyed a visit to the souk, a relic from the comfortable past. The familiar cries, the wonderful smells of saffron and cinnamon hanging in the air from the maze of stalls lifted Gordon's morale and gave him a warm and pleasant feeling of hope. Perhaps things would work out in the end.

He wove through the kiosks offering olives and goat cheese, fruit, berries, and apples and felt at peace. There was also an outside chance he wouldn't be dining alone. So he loaded up with humous, chapati and tahini to brighten up the evening meal.

Gordon decided to drop in on the carpet stall he frequented. He'd promised to do so for Jean Beresford more than once. This was a good opportunity. But when he reached the shop he saw it had changed. The new proprietor now traded in Arab tea pots, desert scarves, key rings and other souvenirs. Not a rug in sight.

'I'm looking for the shop which used to be here.' The young boy serving couldn't understand Gordon's accented arabic.

At a corner stall nearby an older man hunched over his radio, muttering under his breath. But he was willing to engage. The previous owner had died suddenly, he told Gordon.

'What happened to the rugs he was selling?'

His button eyes flickered, wary and distrusting.

'Lorry came. Gone away. I know nothing.'

The old man turned away. He didn't want to talk about the shop anymore. Then the penny dropped and Gordon saw things in a different light. Following the storeroom fire and with the vendor shutting up shop, all links to the anthrax trail had been severed. Perhaps it was just as well.

When he got back to Main Street, Florrie was busy poking a wire into the sole plate of the iron trying to unclog the steam slots.

'I'm not understanding why this happens, sir. I clean it all the time.'

'It's just a buildup of starch,' Gordon explained, grabbing a beer from the fridge. 'A drop or two of Memsahib's nail varnish remover will clean that off in seconds. Wait until the iron cools though.'

Florrie gave one of her familiar tuts of annoyance. 'I need to do your shirts, sir.'

'Has Memsahib been in touch today at all?' he asked hopefully.

'No, sir. Someone called and left her something.' She gave up on the ironing and disappeared, returning with a large brown envelope. As she handed it over, Gordon noticed her worried expression. As if she sensed that she was being pulled into more complicated troubles over the mail and other things she didn't understand and couldn't control.

'Did he leave a name?'

'Yes, sir. Mr Evans.'

'A first name?'

She couldn't remember. 'Would Sahib like anything to eat?'

'I'll make myself some humous, Florrie. Leave the shirts until tomorrow. I'll have a go at the iron later.'

Gordon studied the sealed envelope. Who on earth was Mr Evans? He thumbed through the directory until he found several entries with the surname Evans. But he could hardly phone around.

The room darkened as the sun set with the speed typical

233

at equatorial latitudes. Gordon crossed to the radiogram and sorted through the LPs. At least with Anita not around Gordon was at liberty to play his favourite music. But he still couldn't find the Sibelius record Ophelia had lent him. And it irked.

He called out to Florrie. 'Have you moved any of the records? There's one missing.'

'It must be there, sir.'

Florrie came into the room, lifted her sari and knelt down on the carpet. She diligently turned over each individual record cover, looking long and hard at the pictures on the front.

'Leave them, Florrie. You won't know which one I'm after.'

He reassured her she wasn't to blame. Then dismissed her on the pretence he was tired. Gordon didn't want her to see him going through them himself. And also so she wouldn't see him check Anita's mail again to find out where it had been posted. He felt angry at the way his wife had reduced him to such petty behaviour.

On a jealous impulse Gordon steamed open the envelope. Inside he found a set of blown up colour photographs of the Shuwaikh Port and a brief note.

'Dear Anita, I developed these pictures by accident when I found a roll of film on the floor. You might as well have them. Give me a ring some time. Tony.7438.'

He ground his teeth against one another, annoyed to have let himself down. As he reglued the envelope Gordon realised how paranoid he had become. Imagining infidelities or worse; conspiracies which might not exist.

Anita had been out in the open about Tony Evans all along, and it was Gordon who'd forgotten his name. She'd used dedicated facilities and processing hangers for her photography ever since arriving in Ahmadi. The letter was over a straightforward matter and the tone friendly, but not intimate. It certainly didn't mean they were sleeping together.

But their own relationship needed urgent attention without a doubt. Gordon decided he would confront her in person. If she was having an affair, he'd have to accept it as a fact.

The following day, he called in at Oleander Court, tracked down the manager of the complex, and asked him outright if she had seen Anita Carlisle.

'Nope. No longer here.'

'She's l-l-left?'

'We live in a Muslim country. These flats are for single women only. We have a rule no men are allowed to visit or stay overnight. I asked her to leave because of it.'

Gordon now had confirmation of his worst fears.

Chapter 43

First thing the following morning, Gordon decided to put his marriage problems on the back burner for the time being. He didn't have any answers. Was he just hanging on to hope instead of facing realities on it all?

What more could he do? After all he'd tried everything. Catered for her every whim. Cleared out all his bachelor junk. Even suggested she restyle the whole house if she wanted to. Out had gone his collection of Arab artefacts with their curving lines and interwoven vines and leaves; in their place had come the monochromes and matching linen. As Gordon buttoned up his shirt ready for work, his eyes caught sight of the Arab rug in the bedroom. The one which Anita hated and declared so vulgar, but the one which Jean Beresford so admired. With the carpet vendor in the souk out of the picture he had an idea.

There was the unresolved question of why Carl Sandberg passed on a list of names with Najib's significantly missing. Gordon reasoned that he might clear that if he got access to Carl's bungalow. Living next door, the Beresfords kept a key. If he could go through Carl's belongings there was a chance he might learn more about his contacts.

Gordon looked up the Beresford's number in the Ahmadi

phone book and dialled it.

Jean answered straightaway but sounded awkward. 'I didn't recognise your voice at first.'

'I thought I'd drop by and see you both after work.'

'I will have to check with Neville first, Gordon.'

'Of course. But I've got a gift for you, Jean. I've been meaning to drop it off.'

Reluctantly Jean agreed. Gordon knew she would not want to be seen as rude and ungrateful.

As Gordon collected his thoughts he addressed the question of what excuse he would use to get into the Beresford house and while he was thinking this through, Florrie burst in and began on her household duties. The distraction drove him to escape into the bedroom.

Down on all fours, he began to roll up the heavy carpet. He was focussed on keeping the edges straight, but his eye still caught something else, which looked like a piece of folded paper trapped at the rear of Anita's vanity unit.

Somehow it had survived all Florrie's sweeping and vacuuming. He finished rolling up the rug and went back to get out the envelope. Gordon rocked the vanity forward and the smallish pink envelope dropped down on to the tiled floor. Although addressed to him, it'd been opened, and the contents removed.

Gordon's hand shook slightly. Had it contained the missing note? The postmark torn in the opening process was illegible, but the handwriting was unmistakably Ophelia's. He recognised the large, flowery, feminine letters at once.

Gordon slipped the envelope in his pocket, heaved the roll of carpet on to his shoulder and staggered out to the car. He packed it in ready to deliver after work.

Watering the garden with the hose, Florrie turned in his direction and tutted with disapproval as Gordon loaded the carpet.

Taking the envelope out of his pocket, he walked over and showed it to the ayah.

'I found this behind the dressing table in the bedroom.' She studied it and continued with the watering.

'Is this the letter we spoke about?'

'Probably, yes sir.' She looked down at the wet grass.

Gordon felt a sudden tightness in the chest. This was confirmation of what he had done his best to ignore. That Anita had opened any letters from Ophelia Dickson and then destroyed them. Under the circumstances, it seemed chilling. It meant she'd spun the reason she'd walked out on him a hundred and eighty degrees. He'd never picked her as the jealous type but obviously he had been wrong.

That day at the office, Gordon reflected on the unpleasant possibility Anita had lied about not being in touch with the Dicksons. He wondered what it meant for both of them. Was the relationship reparable and could Gordon ever put the duplicity behind him? Start again?

Both the Dicksons had always been a bit of an enigma in themselves. On first impressions, Ophelia was the classic Ahmadi wife, somewhat superficial. But she kept concealed the other sides of her personality.

They went back a long way. Gordon had met both the Dicksons when they first arrived in Kuwait with their two toddlers. Straight away, the three of them had hit it off. Enormous fun, the Dicksons gave great parties and were ever at the top of the social ladder, invited to everything.

Only after both their children were shipped off to English

boarding schools did Ophelia begin to hit the bottle. She always struck Gordon as someone who hadn't quite reached her intellectual potential. She'd worked at Bletchley Park as a decoder for one of Turing's deciphering units. Ophelia once told Gordon that her father had served in the Foreign Office in some capacity. No great detail was ever given.

Where were the contents of the envelope? What was so important in the note that had caused Anita to leave him so abruptly?

He tried to catch up on projects which now pressed in on him. But instead wasted time chatting to Mansour about the hunting trip with Ian Fleming. His assistant had organised it so well. Other than the threat posed by the Arab gang it had all worked out beautifully.

Gordon could depend on him when needed, knowing he could master administrative tasks with confidence. After Najib's death, Mansour had had to take on far more. He was a solid worker and full of surprises.

'When I get the photographs from the trip developed, I'll give you copies,' said Gordon.

Mansour had been a fan of James Bond all along and excited about the visit of the author. His rapid action in diving for a rifle when the gang approached had not gone unnoticed. 'You moved pretty fast. It could have ended up rather badly.'

Despite the agreement Gordon had made with the company about secrecy over the hawking expedition, Matthew Quinn had heard all about it. He stopped Gordon when they passed one another in the hospital corridor.

'Ian Fleming has been telling everyone about your little safari. A bit of a spirited affair, I gather.'

'Well, it was unique. If he had a yen to see the adventurous

239

side of Kuwait, he got a full measure of it.'

'People complain that he's not been turning up at the arranged events. He is always around at your place, apparently.'

'Only on a few occasions really.'

'Interesting. Well, must be off.' At that the former close friend rushed off down the corridor. 'Things to do. People to see.'

It was obvious to Gordon that he was still persona non grata. Nothing much had changed in recent weeks. Those who once sought his company now distanced themselves. What were people saying about him behind his back?

Chapter 44

Jean Beresford was delighted with the red and brown patterned carpet.

'Are you sure we can't give you more for it?'

They'd just agreed on a very modest price for what Jean knew was a highly valuable item. Gordon had initially refused to take a thing but reluctantly agreed to accept a token payment.

'I will be able to r-r-replace it. The Mutafiqs migrate southwards from Iraq every year. They'll be back again soon enough.'

'You got it from the tribe themselves, didn't you?' Excited, her eyes lit up at the romance of it all.

'I used to drive out there to talk them into getting vaccinated.'

'Did you get any pictures?' Jean's son Stewart lay stretched out on the new rug.

'Well, I did, actually.'

'Cor.'

Gordon dug out a photo of the Bedouin women beside their broad black tent weaving a new roof from sheep's wool. 'They sew these six strips together to form one large panel. As you c-c-can see from the next picture, they're very proud of their repairs because they have to withstand the harshest of weather.'

'I'd like to live in a tent.'

'No, you wouldn't,' said his mother. 'Hard to imagine it is that windy out there.'

'It certainly is. They renew the centre sections as that's the area which takes the most battering.'

'Do you go out there much, Mr Carlisle?' asked Stewart.

'Not very often. What do you think they enjoy the most when I go?'

Stewart looked vacant. Gordon passed over a photo of himself in which he stood cradling armfuls of chocolate bars. 'Of course that is only in winter when it is freezing out there.' Next to him stood a striking man, tall, with gaunt, proud features and a wiry black beard.

'Can I see too?' Sylvie asked.

'That is your carpet spread out on the sand.' Beside it were other similarly colourful rugs, all in the traditional tribal designs. 'They tend to weave them in summer so they can peg their work out when there isn't a chance of rain ruining it.'

'Not that we get much of that,' Jean said.

'Surprisingly enough, there's been more than usual this year.' This jolted Gordon's memory. He had forgotten Ian Fleming had asked if he could get some truffles to take back to Beirut.

'The shop you thought we could buy a carpet ourselves closed down, you say? Why do you think that was?'

'He could just have gone out of business. The anthrax scare put people off trading.'

The rug, they agreed, would go nicely with the Moroccan leather pouffe and footstool Jean had picked up on a recent trip to the village of Fahaheel.

On the sideboard sat the de rigueur gleaming Arab coffee pot. 'They're a bugger to polish,' said Jean. 'But when I saw the shine on Ophelia's, I had to up my game.'

There was an awkward silence on the mention of the name.

'How is the house in England coming along?' asked Gordon, anxious to change the subject

'Well, they've laid the foundations, but not much else. If I go ahead to England without Neville, I'll be able to visit. English builders seem to take forever, don't they?'

'So you're definitely leaving, are you Jean?'

'Yes. I think it would have been on the cards anyway. It'll mean staying with Neville's parents for a bit. I doubt our house will be ready for months yet.'

Neville Beresford strode into the room, wiping his hands on a towel. 'I hate working on the car. Grubby business. Here's a beer. It's very kind of you, Gordon. You didn't have to, you know. We have paid you, haven't we?'

'He won't take the right money for it. I've tried.'

'Not at all. To be honest, Anita n-n-never took to it too much.'

'I don't know why. I think the colours are wonderful.' Jean gave him a look. 'You promised you could get another one for yourselves.'

'Easily. Unlike us, the Bedouin are at liberty to cross the border wherever they like without any paperwork. Well, between Kuwait and Iraq and Saudi Arabia, that is.'

'We've got the children on their own passports now.' At this, their excitable son rushed into his bedroom and returned with a BOAC junior jet club book and badge.

'He's very proud of that.'

'Can I show you my lizard?' Stewart asked.

'You have one?'

Jean raised her eyes. 'I let it go, Stewart.'

'Oh. Not again,' he whinged.

'Why not run along and play in your room, children? We adults want to talk.'

After they'd scurried out, Gordon turned the conversation to where he wanted it to go.

'You don't have a spare key to get in next door, do you? I was hoping to look through for something of mine I lent him before they stripped Carl's place.'

'As a matter of fact, I do, Gordon,' said Jean. 'Neville and I used it to let the house packers in. They've crated up everything. The old company furniture was left. The rest is to be shipped back.'

'Oh, so that's taken care of, is it?'

There wasn't any excuse to enter the place.

Gordon thanked them both for their hospitality and got up to leave.

'If Anita changes her mind about the carpet, please feel free to take it back any time. And you should both come over for dinner with us one night next week.'

'Absolutely,' agreed Neville, and tried to sound as though he meant it.

Gordon suggested Jean might like to bring Stewart to visit his office at the hospital to see his collection of desert animals.

'Don't encourage him, please. He brings in all manner of things as it is. He'd dig up half the garden if you told him he'd find a lizard.'

'One small thing, Jean. Do you recognise this handwriting?' He took the pink envelope out of his pocket. 'Is that Ophelia's?'

'Just one moment. I'll check.' Jean picked up a pile of old invitations and flicked through them. 'It's Ophelia's. For sure. I thought it was. I just had to make double certain. Why do you ask?'

'There were photos inside taken of us all at a party,' he lied. 'I wanted to make sure they hadn't come from someone I hadn't thanked.'

'Talking of photographs. Some good ones of you and Anita at the golf do. They've put them up in the reception cabinet. You probably won't have seen them. They only went up this afternoon. A bit late, don't you think? After all this time?'

Gordon drove straight over to the Hubara Club. An extensive set of pictures from the formal event sat pinned in rows on the green felt backing. A couple of other people scoured the board looking for ones they were in.

'There you are in that one,' said a woman, pointing to the photograph of Gordon alone, posing in a wicker chair and staring straight into camera. There was no sign of Anita. Maybe Jean had got the wrong end of the stick.

But just as he was about to give up, he caught sight of the one Jean had been referring to. Anita was snuggled up next to Pip Foster, whispering something in his ear. His heart missed a beat. Anita's expression said everything about the relationship.

Chapter 45

Gordon returned home from the Beresfords to find Anita sitting quietly in the lounge. She wore a tight, compressed expression, wary of his reaction at her unexpected reappearance.

There was no sign of Florrie. Out in the kitchen, she moved around as quiet as a mouse.

'Welcome home,' Gordon said. 'Nice of you to drop in.'

'You sound angry.'

'Hurt, more like.' That was honest.

Anita studied her fingernails. 'I'll go if you wish.'

'You must know I don't want that.'

He placed his keys in their normal place.

'The carpet's gone from the bedroom.'

'I-I-I assumed you wouldn't mind. The Beresfords have got it.'

'I thought it was something special to you.'

'I can get another if I need to.'

'How was the hunting trip?'

The hem of her dress rode up several inches as she crossed her legs.

'You heard about that?'

'From Florrie.' In the distance they heard the kitchen door

open and close as the ayah retreated further to hide away out of trouble in her quarters.

'Of course. You came around that day, I heard. We weren't back until quite late.'

'Oh yes. And with that great author of yours?'

'Did she tell you that too?'

'No. I worked out he would be here. Why else would you organise a hunting trip with so little notice?'

'Did you pick up what happened to us?'

'No. Do tell.'

'We ran up against one of the feral gangs out there.'

He expected some response, but Anita sat unmoved.

'Really?'

'We call them desert pirates.'

He sat back, undecided whether this was the right time to ask her why she had tampered with his mail.

'Are you sure it's OK for me to be back here?'

'Of course.'

'At least say it as if you mean it.' Her eyes filled with tears of self-sympathy.

Gordon swallowed hard. There was no good time, so it just came out. 'Why did you open letters addressed to me?'

It was obvious the accusation came as a complete shock. Anita frowned and shook her head in bewilderment. 'I don't know what you mean.'

Gordon took the envelope from his pocket. 'I found this behind your dressing table.'

She plucked at the slip cover and leant forward to see. 'What is it?'

'You know what it is.' Gordon strode across and waved the envelope in her face.

247

'I've never seen it before I don't think.'

'You're lying,' he said. 'It's in Ophelia's handwriting.'

'Oh. Then perhaps.'

He stared at her for a moment. 'So?'

'The invitation? They sent one months back.'

'I c-c-can't recall.'

'Don't you remember they had a party and we couldn't go?'

Gordon had forgotten all that. Anita's triumphant expression said more than words. She was about to win the day.

He took back the envelope and stared at it again.

'But it's addressed just to me?'

'She never wanted to accept you were no longer a bachelor. You said so yourself.'

He was struck dumb, embarrassed and lost for words.

'Did she ever ring here for me?'

'You know she did.'

They heard the back door open, and Florrie glided into the room.

'Your supper is ready, Sahib and Memsahib.'

Florrie had laid out plates of whole fried sole along with a large bowl of basmati rice on the dining room table.

Gordon waited for the ayah to retire before again trying to clear the air.

'Where were you on the afternoon Ophelia died?'

'I was here preparing for the dinner party. You know that.'

'But that morning, you said you would check to see if they were coming.' Gordon fastidiously prised loose the fine fish bones and deposited them on the side of the plate.

'Yes, you asked me to do that.'

'Did you go over there that day, Anita?'

'I said I'd phone them.'

In frustration, Gordon drummed his fingers on the table. 'Did you go over there? Did you have a row with her?'

Anita put down her silver ware. 'You're scaring me now, Gordon. If anyone was likely to cause a scene, it was you. Perhaps you were still seeing her behind my back?'

They heard the back door open again. Both fell silent as Florrie came in to see if they needed anything.

'Thank you, Florrie. But perhaps you can leave us now.'

'Yes, sir,' said the ayah, only too happy to escape any involvement.

Anita jumped up to take over and threw down her napkin on the table. 'Why are you attacking me? You're the one creeping around all the time. What were you doing at Oleander Court for example? Don't you realise that was the reason they asked me to leave?'

She had a point there, Gordon acknowledged. He'd made several trips over to the complex. He gave a deep sigh.

'Were you checking up on me at Oleander Court?'

Gordon wasn't ready to admit it.

'Why are you so concerned about this, anyway?'

'I suppose I feel guilt over Ophelia's death in some way.'

'If anyone should feel guilty, it's me. After all, I'm the one who married you and cut short anything you might have had going between you.'

Anita cleared away the condiments as Gordon sat staring down at the empty place mat deep in thought. She pushed her chair back under the table. 'I had no idea you were such a Lothario when I met you.'

He gave a shrug as he recapped in his mind all her responses.

'I'll get you a drink. I think we both need one.' The mood between them had calmed somewhat and Gordon was anxious to keep it that way.

'I'm thinking of going back home myself,' she said quietly as they sat in the lounge together.

'I don't want you to leave me.'

'But perhaps it's for the best.'

'That's up to you.' He sipped a neat whisky and swirled the ice around in his glass.

'I think it's more up to you than me.'

'And there's really nobody else?' He looked her straight in the face.

'You swing from one side to the other,' she said in a coyish way. 'First, you accuse me of plotting against your ex-lovers. Now of having an affair.'

'I know I've been like that lately.' He sought a measure of common ground.

'While we're at it, something came for you the other day.' Gordon took out the Manilla envelope from the sideboard drawer.

Anita tugged open the sticky seal and peered inside for a brief moment. Her face paled.

'What is it?' he asked, pretending he didn't already know.

'Just some photography. Tony Evans sent it over.'

'Anything interesting?'

'Not really.' She downed the remnants of her gin. 'Are you going to grill me all night? Or mix another drink and then take me to bed?'

His wife handed Gordon the empty glass and left the room with the envelope. Gordon wondered how she'd managed to avoid answering any of his questions in a straightforward way. Was she being devious or was it all just part of the mystery that is woman?

Chapter 46

The following couple of days were rather surreal. For once, Anita seemed keener than Gordon to patch up their relationship. As if she sensed he wasn't as starry-eyed over her as he'd once been.

They slept together again and often. The natural scent of her skin smelt as good as when they first made love. He was as intoxicated as ever by the sound of her voice, the charisma of her personality. He wondered how it had come about that he was now living with an almost new version of the same woman. And he was happy, but at the same time wary.

There was no more talk of her leaving Kuwait. The new Anita excised the old one in a rather schizophrenic way. And paradoxically, the new Anita did everything to get life back to how it'd once been.

She played his favourite music in the lounge. Piled up his books neatly. No longer mocked him when he crawled right underneath the radiogram, seeking perfect reception from the BBC World Service.

Gordon didn't question on how the change in attitude had come about, nor try to get clarification on where she'd been during the Oleander Court phase. Not that he had been convinced by the earlier explanation she had given. What they had rediscovered in their relationship was too exhilarating to risk. Once again Gordon looked forward during every hour at work, for the time when he could drive home to the bungalow and his wife. Florrie bustled around the place wearing a happy expression on her usually bland face.

On Wednesday afternoon Gordon arrived back from work to find Anita trying on clothes she'd previously kept hidden away.

'We've been asked across the road for drinks later.'

He got the impression she'd engineered it, just to spread the word of their reconciliation. They'd not spoken to the Goodwins for some weeks and Gordon looked forward to seeing them again.

'I've got a shampoo and set at the club later,' she announced. 'You can drive me if you aren't too busy.'

He was elated to see Anita adopting the role of a classic wife. It hadn't been a part of their married lives up until then. 'I'll drop you and pick you up.'

'Haven't you got books to take back to the library? It's just next door.'

Later that day, she emerged from the land of the towering hairdryers with a very tall bouffant. Starchy and formal.

'What do you think, Gordon?'

'It's different, but I like it.' In two hours the free spirit he married had morphed into a local version of Brigitte Bardot.

Since their reconciliation Gordon had been careful to keep clear of any contentious topics of conversation such as politics. But as they were dressing for the party, Anita raised one herself.

'What do you think will happen here? Do you expect the United Kingdom to send in the army?' She got the words out as she applied a generous layer of mascara.

'Probably.'

'The days of Britain defending a colony are gone, surely,' she said, now applying pink lipstick and then rolling her lips against one another to even it out.

The evening went off without a hitch. Anita fitted in with ease. It was like she had never disappeared from their lives for those intervening weeks.

The following day she spent in the kitchen. The pressure cooker whistling away was a sound Gordon hadn't heard since her abrupt departure.

'What's cooking that smells so delicious, darling?'

'Christmas pudding.'

'That's over a month away.' Gordon half smiled, somewhat bemused.

'You make them six weeks ahead. Didn't you know that? It allows the flavours to intensify. You get that black colour.'

Anita's transformation all seemed too good to be true. 'Are you going to make the cake as well eventually?'

'Of course,' she said. 'You see, I want to be the perfect wife for you.'

'I always knew you would be. That's why I married you.' He couldn't stop the small, happy thrill coursing through every fibre. By conforming as she had it went beyond anything he had ever hoped and promised a predictable, stable future for them as a couple.

'What do you normally do here at Christmas? Should I ask?'

'There seemed no point before you. This year is different. We'll cut down a branch of a tamarisk tree, decorate how you want, with lights, tinsel.'

'Do we have any?'

The need for decorations required an impromptu visit to Fahaheel. The weather had drawn in and there was a distinct edge to the November air. Anita took her camera along. They bought everything in sight. Silver baubles, strings of tinsel and streamers. On the way home they stopped and Anita took pictures of a herd of donkeys grazing by the roadside. The early idea of Anita putting her collection into book form cropped up again.

'It's a shame you didn't discuss that with Pip Foster when he was out here. He may well have had some contacts for you.'

'Yes, that would've been a good idea,' she said, avoiding all eye contact.

It was the perfect opportunity for Gordon to mention the photographs taken at the dance. 'There's a picture of you two together at the Hubara Club. Have you seen it?'

'No,' she said and changed the subject.

That evening he suggested dinner there, so she could see it for herself. He was in the bathroom fiddling with an awkward cufflink when she walked in and wrapped her arms around his waist. Gordon hardened as Anita pressed her body against him. Her fragrance and touch was filled with the promise it held for later, when they could be together naked in bed, free of all constraints.

'I-I-I'd like you to meet Ian Fleming before he leaves, if it can be arranged.'

'Why do you want me to?'

'He's charming. And witty.'

'And inventive.'

'He's certainly imaginative.'

'Like your so-called attack in the desert?'

'I can assure you it happened.' He stroked the arms, still

clasped around his waist.

'You've given him the perfect idea for his next book around that.'

'Which is?' he asked, genuinely intrigued.

'Soviet-backed Iraqis want to liquidate James Bond while he's on a visit to Kuwait to send a message to the imperialist British to get out of the wealth producing colony.'

He blinked at her in the mirror, taken aback. 'What was that?'

'It's a great storyline, don't you think? You boys with your guns and fantasies.'

'Now you're mocking us.' Gordon turned round, disappointed at the shift in tone.

'Gordon, you know how I feel about sexist authors.'

'He writes for entertainment. And he's very good at it.'

'So you think sex with Vesper Lynd in Casino Royale is all the spicier, because it has the "tang of rape"? That makes for good entertainment, does it in your opinion?'

'You have read some of his books then?'

'One or two.'

'Now it's all coming out.'

'Only as a feminist study. Who but a chauvinist calls a woman Pussy Galore?'

'It's original.'

'He writes a load of rubbish.'

'His books are very popular. You can't deny that.'

Gordon changed the subject and they spent the evening in light banter on neutral topics. And when he got the opportunity to see Ian Fleming one more time before his departure, Gordon made sure it would be done without Anita in tow.

Chapter 47

Jean Beresford called Pam anxious to get something off her chest.

'I think I've made a bit of a faux pas,' she said.

'Oh, Jean. What have you done this time?'

'I've just been with Gordon Carlisle and I think I said the wrong thing.'

'I do that sort of thing all the time.'

Jean took a drag on her cigarette. That was a relief in itself.

'Where did you see him?'

'I took the children to get their vaccinations at the hospital.'

'We've got ours to do.'

'Gordon invited them to see his new office, so we went on there afterwards.'

Aware this might be a longish call, Pam asked her to hold on until she'd lit a cigarette herself.

'Stewart wanted to see those awful snakes and things Gordon keeps,' said Jean.

'He likes creepy crawlies and beetles, doesn't he? I don't know where he gets that from. Just being a boy I suppose.'

'Definitely not from me,' said Jean, between puffs. 'Anyway, it was while we were in there I happened to mention about Anita being on that tennis trip to Beirut.'

'What tennis trip are you going on about?'

'The one you went on.'

'I didn't go. It was Nola who went. Not me.'

'I thought you said you saw Anita Carlisle there with the tennis team.'

'No, Jean. I said Nola saw her there. But not with the tennis team.'

Jean's heart rate crept up a beat. She wished she'd not rung now. 'Oh. I misunderstood you.'

'You can't just get on the team, Jean. You have to be selected.'

'Oh, I see.'

'And I wasn't picked. Not this time.'

'I thought you were one of the best.'

'Only when I double with Nola. She played county league when she was younger. That's the only time I win, Jean. I'm not nearly as good as her.'

'I don't play myself, so I don't know the difference.' Jean flicked off the grey ash and took another drag.

'The tennis team is very competitive. I wasn't lucky enough to get in on this one.' Pam took a breath. 'Exactly what did you say to him, that was so wrong anyway?'

'That you saw Anita there.' Jean inhaled another lungful rather nervously.

'Why did you do that? I didn't mean for you to pass that on to him.'

Jean's heart hit over 100 beats per minute. 'So was Anita there or not?'

'Well, she was. But she isn't with the team yet. Not even on the waiting list. And I think I'd object if she was selected over me,' said Pam. 'And I wasn't selected!' she repeated in a shrill voice.

'Well, it probably won't matter, anyway. You know. That I mentioned it to Gordon.'

'Nola went so she could spend time with "you-know-who". Loverboy. She saw Anita at the bar canoodling with someone apparently.'

'Oh, I don't know about you two,' said Jean, who wanted to be off the phone now.

'Well, it's not me, is it? It's Nola who's up to things.'

'The thought of all that messing around doesn't make sense. If Neville did anything like that… I don't want to think about it.'

'You don't have to.'

'No. We're still as silly with each other as when we first met. Anyway, I'd better go.'

'So what did you tell Gordon then?' Now Pam wouldn't let it drop.

'Obviously the wrong thing. I didn't mean to. It just slipped out. He did look a bit taken aback, I must say.'

'You do get things twisted at times, don't you, Jean?'

'I wish I hadn't opened my mouth.'

'From what I've heard, they're back together again.'

'Yes, he said something about that afterwards.'

'Oh well. Ho-hum. It's too late now.'

'I thought I'd let you know in case Gordon brings it up with Matthew. Perhaps you could say I got my wires crossed.'

'I don't know who Anita was with. Nola said she'd seen him somewhere before, but couldn't remember where. She didn't think he was with KOC.'

Jean heaved a loud sigh. 'Well, I don't know what to do now.'

'Best to do nothing. He'll probably forget all about it.'

'Do you think so?'

Jean rang off and went back to her sewing machine and Sylvie's Christmas show outfit.

There was a sluggish whirring sound as she pressed down on the foot pedal and tried to take her mind off the awkward phone call, but was too het up and cross with herself. Instead she fed length upon length of material in too quickly. Twice it snarled up.

'Damn,' she said to herself. *Concentrate. Concentrate.* But her thoughts still lingered on the conversation she'd had with Pam.

She finished stitching the last few inches, lifted the presser foot from the green satin, and snipped off the loose threads.

At twenty to four, the children came off the bus to find their mother in one of her bad moods. They saw the look on her face, knew what it meant and scarpered off into their rooms.

There was a loud din coming from the back of the bungalow. Jean got up and stormed into Stewart's bedroom, and found he had spread out scores of toy soldiers across the width of the carpet.

'What are you two doing?' Jean shouted at her children. They deserved a yelling because they were fighting again. It gave the perfect outlet for her own frustration at herself.

'He hit me in my sore arm.' Sylvie held it up in evidence.

'Well, she won't play soldiers with me,' said Stewart. 'She promised she would.'

'Don't hit your sister.' Amber, the dog, started whining and barking, uncertain as to which side of the argument she should back. 'Or I'll tell your father. Then there'll be no more target practice. Do you hear me?' The quarrel reached a crescendo and then died away.

259

'Ha ha,' said Sylvie, pulling a face at her brother.

'And clear up the mess this minute. Don't leave it for Mary to do each time. I've told you about that before.'

Under his breath Stewart hissed at his sister. 'Well, if I can't do shooting, you can't either.'

'I don't want to fire stupid guns.'

'Why not?'

'Because.'

'Because you're no good, that's why.'

'I don't want to be good, though, do I, dummy?'

Stewart began collecting up the toys.

'Well, if you were better at it, you could shoot him. Kill him.'

'Shoot him and kill who?' Jean shouted, feeling her anger rise again. 'Who are you talking about?'

'Him. The man,' said Stewart, removing a matchstick from the barrel of a miniature cannon.

'I don't want to hear that type of talk,' said Jean. 'Do you understand me?'

'What's going on?' Neville had arrived back from the office only to walk into a full blown domestic.

'They're fighting again,' Jean was annoyed with herself for not having been able to control the children. 'Who are you talking about shooting, Stewart?'

'I'm not talking about shooting anyone. She is.'

'Who is?'

'Sylvie.'

'No, I'm not.'

'Yes, you are. You're always going on about him. And yet it's me who gets the blame.'

'Who, Sylvie?'

Her daughter's face puckered up. 'No one.'

'OK. That's it.' Jean yelled and pointed her finger at both of her children in turn. 'I don't want to hear any more talk about guns from either of you.'

'The man who killed Uncle Carl!' screamed Stewart. He threw the cannon into the corner of the box and turned on his sister. 'You're the one who started it. And now you've gone and got me into trouble. I hate you.'

'I hate you too.'

Jean looked over at Neville. 'Which man, Sylvie?'

'It doesn't matter.'

'She says she saw him at the hospital yesterday.'

'Will you shut up?' Sylvie screamed at her brother and burst into tears.

Jean slammed the door and turned on her husband. 'Look what you've done with all this target shooting. I told you it wasn't right for them. This is not what I want for our children, Neville. It has to stop.'

Chapter 48

Gordon Carlisle sat at his desk and opened the Telegraph Jean had left for him. It was thoughtful of her to drop the newspaper in on her visit to his office; as typical of her as it was to blurt out local gossip without thinking. Which is why her passing statement about Anita being in Beirut had floored him.

The dates made sense. A trip to the Lebanon would account for some of the time his wife had been absent from Oleander Court. But not all. Had she decided on a whim to fly to Beirut on a sightseeing jaunt? Perhaps. It really was none of his business since they had been separated by that stage. But it was puzzling to say the least. Jean had passed on what she'd heard third hand. The protectorate was rife with rubbish rumours and it all could have been just another one.

Gordon dismissed the matter and turned to the newspaper. As he smoothed out the pages he caught sight of Pip Foster's feature in the middle section, illustrated by a few photos. There was a short paragraph on the Ahmadi public health facility and a mention of Gordon by name. Otherwise the article was devoted to an economic overview of the growth of the country and its development leading up to independence.

There was not a word on Carl Sandberg nor of the political

situation simmering away just beneath the surface.

As he refolded the sheets neatly he noticed one photograph which looked familiar. He couldn't be sure, but the image of a woman completely draped in black, against a modern backdrop, looked like one of Anita's best photos.

He tucked the newspaper under his arm when he left work that day. Anita was in slacks and a jumper watering the garden when he walked up the patio path.

'Hello, darling. I've got something to show you when you come in from that.'

He spread the paper out over the dining room table, with the photograph in full view.

'Is this one of yours? It certainly looks like it.'

'Oh, it was used, then?'

'How did Pip got hold of it?'

After a brief pause she said, 'I gave it to him.'

He left her reading through the piece, her cheeks still flushed from the gardening.

'Can I fix you a drink?'

'That would be nice,' she said, taking in the article.

Gordon made as if he had to get a fresh tonic from the crate outside the back door, but went to their bedroom instead. He searched guiltily through her bag and found the passport. Gordon flipped through it, stopping at a page with Lebanese entry and departure stamps.

His heart pounded, and he felt a surge of jealousy so intense he wanted to smash his fist against the wall. So that was what she'd been up to. *In Beirut with that bastard Foster.*

Gordon marched back to the lounge and found Anita sitting calmly, both legs crossed.

'When were you going to tell me?' He held out the open

passport in front of her.

'That I went to Beirut?'

'Yes.'

'I had to deliver the negative for the photo. Or Pip wouldn't have used it.'

'Are you having an affair with him?'

She didn't answer for a while, but he no longer needed one. She gazed at the fireplace for a few seconds.

'Not anymore.' She turned, her face pale and fearful.

'So you had one?'

'We were involved. Yes.' She looked away.

'How involved?'

'We were married.'

Gordon felt as if the ground would open and swallow him up.

'You were married to Foster?' At the shock his brain went into overdrive. The photo at the Club with the two of them looking like an item now made sense.

'It was a long time ago.' She turned slowly towards him.

'Wh-wh-when were you going to tell me?' He slammed the passport down on the table.

'Well, I'm telling you now.' Anita ran her fingers through her blonde hair and gave a sigh. 'I never expected him to come here to Kuwait.'

'Did you know he was a British agent?'

She allowed their eyes to connect for a few seconds. 'Of course. I knew he had a position with MI6.'

He shook his head part believing, part disbelieving. 'So why didn't you say?'

'Because I wanted to stay married to you. I didn't think you would understand. And obviously you don't.'

Suddenly, it was clear. All the friction between them. Why the relationship had soured since Foster's arrival. Her absence the afternoon he'd returned home after he'd first met Pip. Then again, her blank looks and lack of preparedness on the afternoon of the dinner party. Had she been to meet him?

'Yes.' She closed her eyes. 'I told you I'd been married before. When he learnt I was out here, he got in touch. He was determined to learn more about you.'

'So that was the note. "My Darling". It was for him?'

'You weren't supposed to see that. I couldn't say what I wanted in a letter.'

'There was a call here. A silent one. Was that him too?'

'Probably. Wondering where I was.'

'You went to see him instead.'

'I didn't want him destroying our lives together. He is a very jealous man too. I thought it needed a delicate touch.'

'So that was why he said "Send my regards to your wife". I never told you that.'

'He said it in a bad way. I'm sure of that.'

'But you still went after him?'

'I travelled to Beirut to tell him to leave us alone.'

'Am I supposed to believe that?'

'I love you. It's that simple. You accused me of jealousy the other day. How could I be jealous if I didn't have feelings for you?'

'Was Foster the one who visited you at Oleander Court?'

'Yes. He hasn't given up on me.'

Gordon stood silent, processing it all.

'Do you want me to leave you?' she said plaintively.

'No.'

'Are you sure?'

'Yes, but I need some time to absorb all this. It's a lot to take in to say the least.'

The Desert Motoring Club was where Gordon went for male company. He didn't blame Anita for what he'd learnt, but rather himself. Swept up by her allure, he'd shut out all the details of her past life. Ophelia Dickson had nailed it. Before he proposed to Anita, what had he known about her? Next to nothing. He wanted to believe she loved him but doubts remained.

All this brought back their chance meeting at the Sibelius concert and how she'd bewitched him from the start with what seemed to be a shared passion. Her glamour and sophistication had overwhelmed him. It was almost as if someone had schooled her for the part in his life.

Had someone set her up to meet him 'by accident'? What if she also worked for MI6?

The transition of Kuwait into an independent free state closely bonded to the British Foreign Office in London was of paramount importance. Sandberg had suggested the British were even prepared to colonise the country just to save the oil for the UK.

Gordon had to face the possibility that he'd been well and truly duped. But why would MI6 have targeted him other than that he was single and so able to marry and embed one of their agents in Ahmadi? Unless British Intelligence believed for some reason he was Agent Alex. Which meant that his life could be at risk from none other than his own wife, Anita.

Unable to go back and face her across the dining table he sat in the deserted bar and got stinking drunk.

Chapter 49

Little Sylvie Beresford thought she was going to die. She knew she was locked inside the back of a covered truck, but that was all she knew. Where had they taken her and how far away from home? What was the time now? The truck had parked there for what seemed like forever. But how long had it really been? One hour? Two hours?

In the distance, Sylvie could hear a dog barking. It was different from the yelps Amber made when she got excited. She could just hear Arab voices too, not far away.

Think clearly, she told herself, trying to recall everything that had happened. She knew someone had drugged her because she remembered the awful stinky cloth the man held against her nose and mouth. And later, when she woke up, how he spoke good English when he asked her her name.

Was he a good person or a really bad one? She didn't know. Only that she was terrified of him with his weird shaped hand with only three fingers.

She wanted to cry, but knew it wouldn't help. What was the point? Nobody would come.

Sylvie willed herself to go over again what had happened. She forced herself to count back the hours to when she was at school to help work it out.

They'd taken a spelling test, and she'd scored ten out of ten. She remembered that and how they'd marked their own work from the board. Then the bell rang for end of school. How everyone rushed out of the class like crazy. They wanted to be first to get to the buses lined up ready at the front of the school. They all piled on together. Stewart and Peter Goodwin were ahead, not that they would sit with her anyway. They never did that. Stewart was always at the back with his goofy friends.

But when they got to their bus stop, Peter was off first. Stewart had charged up from behind to keep up with his idol. He had pushed her aside.

'Get out of the way, stupid,' Stewart said and did what annoying younger brothers do all over the world, elbowed her back and pushed past.

As if that wasn't enough, he'd blocked the aisle by grasping the upright seat backs either side with his outstretched hands and kicked behind him. Kick, kick, kick.

'Stop it,' she'd said. 'You are such a jerk.' The bus driver, both hands still holding the steering wheel, looked around, his face part swaddled in a check head cloth, and urged them to clear off.

Stewart tumbled out down the metal steps, making the usual unnecessary clattering noise. He always did the same thing every single ride on the bus. Swung sideways on the bar at the bottom before jumping down into the sand. Then rushed off.

'Wait for me,' she'd called. But of course he didn't.

The stop was only a short distance from their house. Even so, they were supposed to walk together back home.

'I'm going to play with Peter,' he shouted, then ran flat out after the boy whose parents allowed BB guns, banned in the Beresford household.

'Wait!'

That's when it happened. As the North bus drove off, an Arab man had stepped out from a clump of thick tamarisk bushes and dragged her back in there. It'd all been so quick. He held the wet horrible rag over her face. She remembered that clearly and that was the last thing.

How long ago was that, though? Ten minutes, or ten hours?

Sylvie held her breath trying to understand the scuffling noises coming from outside the truck.

She heard the noise as the driver slammed the door closed and the sound as the engine started. The old truck rattled, groaned, and shuddered forward, bouncing down the road.

Terrified, Sylvie tried to scream, but nothing came out. Thrown about she tried to hold on to the side panels but her arm ached too much from when he'd held her so roughly.

Where was Stewart? Why hadn't he seen her being taken away? Or had he run straight ahead and not looked back? Whatever, she knew her parents would be furious.

'You're supposed to come home from school together,' her mother said when Stewart had rushed off ahead and left her behind the week before.

'Why? She's older than me.' Stewart's cockiness both amused and at the same time made his mother a little proud that her son had such self-confidence.

'Just so I know where you are.'

'It's only a few houses,' her brother had said.

'You'll do as I say.' Sylvie's mother wagged an imperious finger at him.

But Stewart was like so many boys. He didn't always obey his parents no matter what the consequences.

Sylvie propped herself up. Where was the truck heading now? Perhaps the man was driving her home. She closed her eyes and willed him to do so with all her might, listening to every move of the vehicle. It came to a brief stop. She heard clearly the sound of the indicators clacking away and then the engine revving up as they drove off again. Somehow Sylvie identified the swishing sound of a fast-moving car going in the opposite direction and then it was back to the regular beat of the truck engine.

After what seemed like an age, but really wasn't, they ground to a stop. Sylvie counted up to ten in her head. The man opened the cover and sunlight flooded in.

'Come, we change cars.'

Sylvie recognised him immediately as the same one she'd seen next door when Mr Sandburg was killed.

'Please, can I go home? Please.'

'Yes. But not now. Later.'

Her heart leapt at the sound of the "yes". She would be back home again soon. He'd just said so.

'Where am I?'

'It doesn't matter where you are.'

Sylvie started to cry. More than anything, she wanted her parents, to see and to be held by them again.

A dusty black car sat parked next to the truck. The man in the driver's seat wore traditional headdress too. Sylvie's abductor opened the back door and pushed her in.

The new driver started up and drove off for a short distance into a local settlement. Sylvie felt she was close to her home somehow. The houses were similar to hers but smaller and built more closely together. The driver pulled in next to an untidy looking bungalow. He got out and jerked his thumb in the direction of the side entrance door.

Sylvie nervously obeyed the sign and entered into the kitchen, where a large Arab woman was waiting. She looked Sylvie up and down with a sympathetic expression, took her by the hand and led her into a sparsely furnished room. The woman pointed to a rolled- out mattress indicating that this was where Sylvie should sit.

Chattering in Arabic, she opened a side door and pointed at a hole in the floor which smelt very bad and served as the toilet.

Timidly, Sylvie went and sat down silent and obedient on the mattress. She'd do as she was told. The Arab woman ushered in a small child. The toddler installed herself on the seat of a small plastic car and manoeuvred around with her tiny feet. Then she got off and squatted on the floor opposite Sylvie staring at her with her dark brown eyes.

The woman went out and came back bearing a broad brass tray with a plate of chewy bread and two mugs filled with water.

Somehow Sylvie felt she would be safe after all. Perhaps she'd not be killed if she was nice and behaved properly. She smiled at the woman, who smiled back.

When would her own mother come looking for her and how would she find the place anyway? What would her parents be doing right now? The thought of home was too much and she couldn't stop it. Tears ran down her cheeks.

The small child disappeared, but returned holding a battered doll. She held it out to Sylvie to make her feel better.

But it didn't help. Sylvie cried so hard that her new friend took fright. She ran over and buried her face in the woman's voluminous black skirt.

Chapter 50

Brigadier General Mustafa al-Ramiz al-Sabah stroked his chin considering the next step. He'd been tracking Carlisle's movements for weeks. Not in person, but by delegating the task to half a dozen members of his intelligence unit. But today was different.

'For now we wait here,' Mustafa said to his driver. The surveillance had paid off. They were now close to nailing the suspect for a range of crimes. 'Don't get any closer.'

One wrong move could end in disaster and result in the needless death of an innocent child.

At long last forensics had identified the substance dug up in Carlisle's garden. It was the same pesticide used to poison the wife of oil company executive John Dickson.

'How does he think he'll get away with it, driver? Stupid.'

Mustafa made a mental note to bring Matthew Quinn up to date. After all, he'd collaborated with the Kuwait police laboratory in the analysis work on the poison. What a fantastic result.

All the evidence was conclusive. The unit had sighted Carlisle mailing off letters at the post office, all of which had been intercepted, opened and scanned for content. They'd identified the Saab as one used in the drop of anti-colonial pamphlets behind a garage in East Ahmadi. Carlisle had also been present when the fake incendiary device was found at the Hubara Club, obviously intended as a warning that attacks on the British were to follow. Who'd planted it? Probably Carlisle himself.

Then there was the fire at the old Magwa hospital, his store room destroyed and one of his accomplices killed while manufacturing an incendiary device.

And it all added up, the strange behaviour of the man himself, in taking Ian Fleming, the iconic author, out on a hunting trip knowing there were feral gangs operating in the area. If the writer had been killed it would have been a great embarrassment to the royal family and the state.

The Brigadier General smiled to himself. How satisfying. His theory had now been confirmed by hard evidence. Carlisle was acting as a Soviet agent, controlling and inciting pro-Iraqi protesters to violence. It was likely he was also responsible for the duplicitous death of his long-term friend, Carl Sandberg, which he had blamed on his subordinate.

'This man is a calculating criminal and a danger to our state, Abdul.'

Despite himself Mustafa was rather impressed. Who would have suspected the tall, urbane Englishman of being a traitor to his own country? The English had a history of double agents and traitors, however. Carlisle was not unique. And he was equally willing to sell out the Kuwait royal family by siding with the militant Iraqis, all to help Soviet interests. Probably for cash as well.

Brigadier Mustafa was certain an inspection of the Carlisle home at 5 Main Street would turn up further evidence of his guilt. Perhaps photographs of strategic engineering works, for example, or drawings of the port and information on other potential targets to strengthen the Iraqi invasion plans.

Brigadier General Mustafa hadn't believed it initially. But now he was doubly sure Gordon Carlisle was the nebulous Agent Alex, the one who had caused significant damage to property and thus undermined the country's stability.

How easily the Russian informer had infiltrated the Anglo-American community. From within his trusted position, he could send information about potential oil and gas targets to the Soviets in Beirut without being suspected.

And now an innocent child had been abducted. The Kuwait police received a phone call from what must have been Carlisle's Arabic-speaking accomplice. He'd offered the girl in exchange for the release of ten saboteurs who faced execution for their role in recent terrorist attacks in Kuwait City.

The mother had been inconsolable. She'd rung the police, and they went straight over, sirens and blue lights flashing. The young victim hadn't come home from school, though her brother was certain she did get off the bus.

It was dark by the time they interviewed the Beresford parents. A difficult time of day to start a search.

Apparently the girl had told her mother that she thought she had been followed. And also claimed to have witnessed the neighbour's killing, but no one believed her at the time. Thought she was a story teller.

Now, from whichever angle they looked, Carlisle's name was attached in some way. 'It is quiet on the road this morning, Abdul.'

'Yes, sir. Very quiet.'

Mustafa watched idly as the cars passed by. Company employees driving to their offices, delivery vans and maintenance men going about their daily chores and open-backed trucks filled with labourers off to carry out repairs to the tarmac roads. A normal morning.

Mustafa shifted forward in his seat. A school bus pulled out, blocking his view of the beige coloured Saab for a time, the very bus Sylvie Beresford would have been on normally. As the bus drove off, the brigadier had Gordon Carlisle's car back in sight just as the Saab took off.

'Let's go, Abdul.'

The police knew every minute detail of Carlisle's routine. So, at the end of Main Street the brigadier expected him to turn left towards his office. But today he did a right and followed the road before pulling into a garage.

'Now we will learn everything.'

Mustafa ordered his driver to pull off to the roadside. 'We can see from here what he's doing.'

They watched as Carlisle disappeared inside and then returned with a garage worker who pushed a car jack ahead of him. The mechanic popped the hub cap off, jacked up the car and spun loose the bolts with his wrench and set about changing a tyre. In ten minutes flat, the mechanic had tightened up the wheel nuts. He went round examining the remaining tyres, pushing on them with his feet.

There followed a brief discussion between the two men as they stood by the Saab. Mustafa couldn't hear a word but imagined he could. It was crystal clear to the Chief of Police Carlisle was preparing the car for a long journey deep into the desert, perhaps to where the child was held.

'Abdul, we must bide our time. The terrorists would have kidnapped her after she stepped off the bus.'

'I'm sure you're right, sir,' agreed the driver, never one to question his master's conclusions.

'What is taking so long?' Mustafa felt his face twitch with anger and impatience. They had to move fast before any harm befell Sylvie.

Kidnapping of a child under eighteen carried the death sentence in Kuwait, so it was obvious those concerned would try anything to achieve their objectives. The saboteurs were about to be sentenced. If the Kuwait police could locate the Beresford child quickly, then the plan to get to them freed on an exchange would come to nothing.

With all the tyres checked out, Carlisle got back into his Saab and drove off.

Brigadier Mustafa 's driver immediately followed on at a safe distance. Once again, the car did not take the route expected out towards the desert. Instead, it did a one eighty and turned up in the direction of Southwell Hospital.

'He's headed for his office.' Perhaps another ruse, thought Mustafa. Pretending as if nothing has changed.

Mustafa had worked on several abductions over the years, but never on a case involving a European ten-year-old child. His previous experience covered the trafficking of victims on to Saudi Arabia. But even that was rare.

However, this was no ordinary kidnapping, but a high-profile political exercise.

'Put your foot down. Hurry up, man.'

When Carlisle pulled up outside his office, the police vehicle ran up right alongside. The brigadier jumped out, hand ready on his 38 revolver.

Brigadier Mustafa watched Carlisle as the man wound down his car window, his face set in an angry frown.

Mustafa leant into the car. 'Mr Carlisle. We need to talk.'

Chapter 51

Gordon had read the classic work by Kafka twice. Now it was as if he was the main character in *The Trial.*

The novel told the story of a bank clerk arrested and prosecuted by a remote, inaccessible authority, the nature of his crime revealed neither to himself nor the reader.

But Gordon never expected the nightmarish situation to happen to him. When he wound down his window that crisp morning, it was playing out for real. Brigadier General Mustafa was the master inquisitor. There'd already been several interviews previously, none of them pleasant and all vague and undefined. But this time the charismatic Chief of Police openly accused Gordon of Soviet espionage, kidnapping a child and two murders. And then, thrown in for good measure, the insinuation that he was guilty of urban terrorism, all of which carried a capital sentence.

They sat opposite one another in Gordon's office, and for one silly moment he wondered whether he'd be better off making a run for the border. He knew that the Kuwaiti detention centres were places you didn't always come back from. Gordon blinked nervously astounded by the number and seriousness of the accusations.

'These are very serious allegations you are making, Brigadier.'

'We have been watching you for some time, Mr Carlisle.'

'What you're suggesting is ridiculous. Preposterous, in fact.'

'Which part is so unacceptable to you may I ask?'

'Well, take Mrs Dickson for example? Why would I want to poison my friend's wife?'

'Unlike our culture, yours doesn't allow you to have more than one wife.'

'That's ins-s-sane.'

'Perhaps she was causing you problems with your current situation. So you decided to get rid of her.'

'I have no current situation. Nor any interest in Soviet politics. Nor in planting incendiary devices. Nor, for that matter, distributing anti-colonial leaflets.' He glared defiantly at Mustafa .

'But you're a committed commie, are you not?'

'Of c-c-course not.'

'You don't look like one I must admit. But then the communist individual is no longer a "type" exemplified by a coarse revolutionary with a time bomb ticking away in his briefcase. Instead, they are skilled at working underground for the purposes of embedding themselves in the social fabric. Is that not yourself?'

'It couldn't be further from the truth.'

'You described your society as materialistic, did you not? And the Kuwaitis as having a ruling class.'

He opened the file which he had set out on Gordon's own desk. The Brigadier held up an airletter which Gordon had written to his brother in England, which clearly had been intercepted.

279

'You have had my letter for a while, obviously.'

'I'm afraid you will have to write to him again.' Mustafa tapped the letter. 'You speak of a "witch-hunt", of "reactionary forces" in Kuwait. Do you not?'

'Common expressions from the broad English language, as you would appreciate, having spent time at Sandhurst, Brigadier.'

'You talked about the exploitation of certain Palestinian workers when we spoke the other week.'

'We were having a general conversation.'

'You can't deny you have strange interests? Even your friends we have interviewed suggest you are an unusual man.'

At last it dawned. The recent distancing by his usual social group was a direct result of the police investigations into his background.

'Your worker Mansour Sood is an active member of the pro-Palestinian movement.'

'Mansour?'

'You pretend you did not know that?'

Gordon eyes widened. 'Indeed I did not. No idea.'

'And that he was an undercover agent for the Iraqi Secret Service?'

Mansour was the traitor and not Najib. How could Gordon have missed it?

'Who also murdered Mr Sandberg on your orders?'

'That is absolutely not true.'

'Where was Mansour on the evening your friend was killed?'

'He was out working on a spraying operation at the time.'

'You said that Najib was here with you.'

'Yes. He was.'

'Which gave you the alibi you needed. You sent Mansour to kill Mr Sandberg because he was about to betray you.'

Gordon shook his head. The shock of it all had sent a trail of perspiration running down his forehead. Inside the office the humidity wasn't made less bearable by the smell coming from the animal cages.

Of course it had been Mansour. Who else knew his every move, had access to his car and even, on occasions his own house? Not for one moment had Gordon suspected him of disloyalty let alone that he was behind the killing of Carl.

'Well, you must have evidence if you are accusing Mansour of that.'

'Where is he now?' The Brigadier fixed Gordon with a cold stare.

'You mean you don't have him?'

'No. And now a child is missing.'

'This is the first I've heard of it. When was this?'

'You know when. Yesterday evening.'

No wonder I hadn't heard sitting there at the Desert Motoring Club on my own getting plastered.

'You kidnapped the Beresford child.'

'What, not Sylvie surely?'

'It was easy for you to do because her parents are your friends. She knew you and therefore trusted you when you picked her up in your car yesterday.'

The news was staggering and stunning all at once. 'Sylvie Beresford is the one missing?'

'Of course. You intend to trade her off to release the saboteurs we hold in Central Prison.'

Gordon thumped the desk angrily. 'You are wasting time here with me if Sylvie Beresford has been kidnapped or worse?

If Mansour has her, then we have to find him now. Jean must be beside herself.'

For the first time Brigadier Mustafa had a moment of self doubt.

'So where would you suggest we begin?'

Gordon dug into a drawer. 'I have his home address here.'

'And so do we. We've already been there. We turned up at his house, but there was no trace of the child. The neighbours said they saw a car with a white girl inside. So it's possible he took her to his own place first.'

'He's not acting on my orders. Believe me.'

'Do you have an idea where they could be?'

'I don't know. Could be anywhere. No. Wait a minute.' Gordon had a momentary flash of inspiration. 'I have just had an idea.'

Within minutes, a posse of police cars roared into the desert. They raced across hard sand and towards the former Iraqi outpost Mansour and Gordon had 'discovered' together on the trip over six months ago.

As he sat in the back of the police vehicle barking frantic directions Gordon went back to the time when they first came across the Soviet structure.

Mansour insisted on going with Gordon when he had the hunch about it. They'd been out together trying to locate the wandering Arab tribe who told them how to get there. Gordon remembered Mansour's reluctance to follow the Bedouin's specific directions and his pretence he'd never seen the complex before when they did find it.

It'd been Mansour who went out again alone to see the complex and when he returned told Gordon the building had been destroyed, with just foundations remaining. If the place was still there, it'd prove Mansour a liar. Also probably a spy, a killer and now child abductor. Also a pro-Palestinian activist who'd pulled the wool over Gordon's eyes from the start.

What was just as concerning was that the police had discovered pesticide identical to the one used in Ophelia Dickson's poisoning. Mansour would not have had access to nor a motive for killing Ophelia. That must mean it was a personal affair unrelated to Arab politics.

To Gordon, by eliminating Mansour Sood as a suspect left just one person who'd have a reason to bury the pesticide in the front garden. Perhaps for the same reason she'd hidden the letter. Gordon's own wife. Had Anita poisoned Ophelia? It seemed impossible to accept.

Before he could even begin to grasp the horrors that would open up, they had to find the ten-year-old child.

Chapter 52

Above all, Sylvie wanted to live and somehow go back to the life she knew. All the things she loved so much. The swimming pool, fun games, and above all her family.

How she wished she'd never fought with Meg and the others at the sleepover. They hadn't said anything that bad. She should have just played along and ignored the teasing. Not run away like she did. Put up with that idiotic Meg laughing at her. Then she would never have had the terrifying experience of walking alone through the black night. Or seeing the fight on the verandah. And she wouldn't have laid eyes on the man who killed Mr Sandberg. Now it was too late to turn back the clock.

She wanted to see her mother and fathers' faces again so much it hurt. Where were they right now? Why hadn't her parents come to find her when she needed them to so much? They'd talked about leaving, hadn't they? Escaping from Kuwait and the troubles. If only that had happened before. They'd have gone all together in the car across the desert to safety.

But then they'd have had to shoot Amber. Sylvie didn't want to think about her darling dog being shot.

At long last, Sylvie realised she really did have friends. They were silly sometimes. But perhaps she'd been unfair on them too. What she'd give now to go on the swings at the school field, or play hide and seek even at Meg's house.

Then there was the show. Would she be back in time for the Hubara Club Christmas show? She was miming the song, for goodness' sake. She'd got her first big chance, just her alone on the stage. She'd been the one picked out to perform Connie Francis over all the others. Glasses or no glasses, she was the best at pretending to sing and never missed a funny movement.

They'd all been so jealous of her getting the song. 'Stupid Cupid.' What would happen now? Would Mrs Stanley give the part to someone like Meg? Even though daft Meg was a terrible copy-cat, she still couldn't do any of the fun actions correctly. When Sylvie wagged her hips, everyone smiled. She would never get the chance to do mime again ever, a dream gone and she'd always wanted to star on stage so much. To make-believe she was a real singer.

Memories from her last birthday flooded in. What fun it'd been. Her mother had spread out the tablecloth with the chicken and toys pattern and covered it with plates of iced buns and chocolate fingers. Then she'd brought in the cake made in the shape of a house surrounded by the pink candles. Sylvie blew them all out in one go. There'd been tons of presents to open. Everyone said Sylvie always had the best parties of them all.

She longed for a coke with a straw how they served it at the club. Imagined sipping it ice cold, the fresh taste. Remembered how it arrived served on a round silver tray with the straws bouncing up and down in the bottles and how

Stewart had thought it a bright idea to suck his coke up and blow it out through the straw to see how far he could reach. Disgusting.

She'd screamed at him when the sticky drink drenched her swimming costume. But she wouldn't shout at him anymore. Never, ever again. More than anything, she missed her annoying brother. Where was he now? What if they hadn't fought that day over playing soldiers? Or if she'd allowed common sense Stewart to tell Mummy and Daddy about the man with the weird hand sooner?

The memory still gave her the creeps. What sort of man only had three fingers on his hand? His name was Mansour, he told her. He worked for Mr Carlisle, didn't he? That's why she'd seen him at the pool that afternoon, testing the water for the chlorine. But why did Mr Carlisle hate her so much that he asked his man to grab her and keep her away from the family like this? Wasn't he a friend of theirs? Didn't mummy and daddy go to his flash dinner parties all the time and sit at the same table at the club? And hadn't Mr Carlisle given mummy his super carpet as a present? She'd been so thrilled and happy to get it.

Mr Carlisle even gave Sylvie and Stewart Christmas presents. And when he got married, his wife had taken Sylvie's photograph on a launch trip just as they were leaving the smelly old jetty. Sylvie might never pose for a picture again in her entire life. Or see her cosy bedroom full of all her things.

Mansour told Sylvie she would never manage to escape, because they were so far into the desert now that the police wouldn't find them and because they were in a secret place. A hundred thousand miles away, it sounded like. When the government released certain prisoners, Sylvie could go home. Otherwise she'd stay there until they did.

Sylvie knew Mansour was telling the truth because they'd travelled such a long distance getting there after leaving the house. Rolling over the sand dunes, driving deeper and deeper into the empty desert. She'd never been so far away from her parents in her whole life.

At one point they passed an Arab camp. The women all wore long black robes and there were dozens of them. They terrified Sylvie because you couldn't see their faces, only deep-set eyes peering out from the hooded garments.

Mansour had told her about his mission. How he didn't plan to hurt her because he had a lovely little daughter of his own. Sylvie guessed that was the toddler with the doll she had seen when they first stopped. If Sylvie was patient and good she would be able to go home again when the time was right.

Sylvie felt Mansour cared about her a little and if she was quiet and did everything she was told, she might live after all. He even taught her some Arabic words and made shadow puppets with his funny hand, which he said was a birth defect, whatever that was.

The house was small, every spare corner filled with leaflets and various boxes of equipment. She'd been with him all night now. One long, long, night.

Early in the morning Mansour told Sylvie he had to drive to Ahmadi for business and leave her on her own. He'd return with food and maybe some games or a book to keep her amused. She mustn't open the door to anyone under any circumstances. She agreed to everything because she wanted the whole thing done and finished. If not he might kill her like he'd done her Uncle Carl next door. She so wanted to get back home and play ball with Amber again.

Three slow hours passed. The room darkened suddenly. Sylvie jumped back, terrified at the sight of the black-clad figure peering in the one window to the room. She realised at once that it was one of the desert women. What did they call them? Bedar, bedwin or something? The woman began knocking on the window. Knock, knock, knock.

And now she could hear the sound of women's voices too. Other Arab women now pressed up against the window trying to look in.

They were so, so scary. Sylvie shrank back against the wall.

Now someone was pounding on the door with something extra heavy, like trying to break it down. The spooky women must be going to take her even further away. Like Mansour said, she mustn't open the door, or she'd end up in some faraway land and never see her parents and brother ever again.

Sylvie crawled across the room until she reached a tiny cupboard standing in the corner of the room. She tugged hard at the handle and crept in pulling the door closed behind her. Deadly quiet, but shaking in fear, she closed her eyes and prayed for the fear to go away.

Something heavy smashed away at the door and Sylvie heard a splintering sound as the hinges gave way.

Then she heard a man call out in english and it sounded just like Mr Carlisle's voice.

'Sylvie. Sylvie. Are you in there?'

Chapter 53

During the drive back from the desert, Sylvie Beresford sat in silence. Gordon wondered whether it was because she was traumatised or just shy. He in fact knew little about the workings of children. But it was odd nevertheless. The little girl sat huddled up.

She didn't even seem happy to have been freed, her eyes full of fear as she stared out the window.

'Where are we going now, please?' The convoy of police cars failed to reassure or convince her she was really on the way home.

Although Sylvie appeared confused and very afraid, nevertheless she remained the polite child Gordon had always known.

'Are you okay, Sylvie?'

'Yes, thank you, Mr Carlisle.'

'We're going to get you back to your mummy very soon.'

'Thank you very much.'

But a storm of anger still raged inside Gordon. How could he have been accused of kidnapping an old friend's child? She'd been at his house many times when she was younger. They were that close. It seemed inconceivable that he was a suspect.

Jean Beresford was waiting anxiously outside on the verandah when the police cars drew up outside her bungalow.

Nearly hysterical with worry, her face bleached of all colour,
she clasped and unclasped her hands.

Poor Jean, Gordon thought. This last twenty-four hours
must have been hell.

'Mummy,' Sylvie cried and the girl tumbled out of the back
seat and ran into her mother's arms.

Mary, standing back at a respectful distance, stood wiping
her eyes on the hem of her sari. Stewart watched wide-eyed
from the corner of the garden where he'd been kicking a ball
about, highly impressed by the arrival of so many police cars
in their normally quiet street.

'Where's Neville, Jean?'

'He's out looking for her.'

Gordon turned to the police and shot a quick question in
Arabic to the inspector who promptly despatched a car to
search for Neville and give the good news that his daughter
was safe.

'That's quite understandable. He must be beside himself.'

'My baby,' Jean cried, holding Sylvie close to her bosom and
not letting her go for an instant. She started to cry.

'This was not my doing, Jean. I can assure you.'

Jean wiped her eyes and nodded. Gordon then realised he
too was crying. The sight of reuniting his friend with their
daughter was just as heart-breaking in its own way.

'I didn't know where she was,' Jean wailed. 'All alone and
frightened.'

'Would you like me to wait until Neville comes back, or
would you rather I left now?' Gordon understood that he was
still under suspicion to an extent.

'I don't know what to do,' Jean replied, still overcome by it all.

'Mummy. Can I have a coke?' asked the little girl, wiping her glasses, which had steamed up from the tears.

'I'll get it,' Stewart yelled. 'Can I have one too, Mummy?'

Gordon looked up as he heard the chugging beat of a VW engine down the street as Neville Beresford drove up, with the Kuwaiti police car in close formation.

Neville leapt out of the VW Beetle and gave Gordon a look filled with a mixture of suspicion and loathing.

'Darling,' shouted his wife. 'She's home. And she's fine. It wasn't Gordon. He had nothing to do with it.'

Neville took in the news straightaway.

'My worker Mansour abducted her. I am so sorry.'

Neville turned to see Sylvie's smiling face and gave the deep sigh of an exhausted but relieved parent.

'Thanks for bringing her home, Gordon. I assume it was you who found her. Where was she?'

'In a remote desert property Mansour knew about and had access to.'

'Do you want to come in?' Neville asked.

He's always civil, Gordon thought.

'No, I'd better be heading off. I have to go to the police station to make another statement. At least there's an arrest warrant out for him now.'

'Good. Oh, I suppose you know John Dickson's back?'

'Really?'

'He's been involved in some way. Perhaps you'd better give him a ring when you get home.'

'Will do.'

But before any phone call, Gordon knew he had to raise

with his wife the question of the hidden pesticides the police found in their garden. When he got in, Anita was in the bedroom and packing a suitcase.

'You're back, I see,' she said, in an attempt to cover the embarrassment at being caught out once again.

'Where are you going now? It looks like you're off without even bothering to say goodbye again.'

'I was going to talk to you. I think you know what about?'

'Not entirely, no,' he said honestly. The matter could have been connected with her infidelity, the pesticide, or a thousand other things. Barely controlling his temper at her selfish behaviour, he asked, 'Did you know Sylvie Beresford had been abducted?'

Anita's face paled, and acquired a neutral, spaced-out expression. 'Yes. Jean rang here looking for you earlier.'

'We've found her. And she's back home with them now.'

'Who's we?' she asked, abandoning her packing for the moment.

'I went with the police. But Mansour took her. All this time, he's been a pro-Iraqi activist. He killed Carl. Sylvie saw him there when it happened. And he was present when the Beresford children came to my office two days ago. She recognised him straightaway by his deformed hand. But obviously Jean told you that.'

She stared at Gordon hard and long.

'Did he molest her?'

'I don't think so. His motives were purely political. Release of the saboteurs they're holding in the prison in Kuwait City in exchange for Sylvie.'

'Where did you find her?'

'Mansour ran his operation from an outpost up near the

Iraqi border which was used to harbour chemical weapons for the Iraqis when they attacked.'

'Well, that's amazing. Can I get you something to eat, Gordon?'

He didn't answer and searched her face, looking for any sign of guilt or involvement.

'Please stop staring at me like that.'

The jangling of the telephone broke the conversation. 'I'll get it,' he said and left her to her packing.

'Gordon? It's John Dickson.'

'Neville s-s-said you'd returned.'

'I think we should meet. Rather urgently.'

'Of course,' Gordon agreed.

'Is Anita there?'

'Yes.'

'I need you both to pop over for a bit. Do you reckon you could do that? I'll explain when you get here.'

As he replaced the phone. Anita came out of the kitchen. 'Who was it?'

'John Dickson. He wants us to drop by. No doubt it'll be over this whole Beresford affair.'

'You go, Gordon. I'm not feeling too well.'

'I told him we'd both be there,' he said firmly. 'I think we should. The least we can do. To pay our respects.'

'Perhaps make it a short visit,' she said.

Her eyes darted around the room, looking for personal effects she'd overlooked.

'Of course.'

'I'll just do my hair.'

Twenty minutes later, Gordon led Anita out of the front door of 5 Main Street, wondering when would be a good time

293

to raise the subject of the insecticide found in the garden.

He opened the passenger door to let her into the car. She sat and swung her legs around as he closed it with a bang. Whatever transpired in the future, he knew that their fairy tale love affair was over. If Anita wanted to leave Kuwait Airport on the next Air India Super Constellation, that was fine by him.

Chapter 54

Mansour Sood drove the work truck back into Ahmadi. He was seething. Angry enough to kill. His plan had worked so well up until that point. He was certain the Kuwaiti authorities were about to release the prisoners. But having returned to the desert hideout and found the girl gone, he quickly realised what must have happened.

Someone had betrayed him. Given his identity as Source 687 away to the police.

His wife confirmed the worst. Law enforcement had turned up at their home to arrest him. They'd taken away the leaflets directing the faithful on how to help the cause of Arab unification.

Doubtless the police would use the pamphlets as evidence against him. Proof of his involvement with the underground movement which supported the Iraqi aims. Mansour knew he had to work fast. He told his wife he would return shortly to collect her and his daughter. They'd make their escape over the border.

Had he secured the prisoner swap, he would have been feted as a hero in Iraq. Perhaps some producer would make a film about how he had saved the brave comrades. The movie would've been Mansour's big break into fame and he'd make history. He had been prepared to martyr himself just to make that happen.

Now he would have to flee without anything to show. It was a bitter pill to swallow to end in that way. Overwhelmed by intense feelings of humiliation, he vowed revenge on the informer who'd betrayed him. The one who'd given him away to save their own skin. Mansour cursed under his breath. Agent Alex would meet the same fate as the other traitors. Die like Sandberg and Najib.

Early evening Mansour reached Main Street and parked up on the vacant lot next to the Carlisle bungalow. He could see their Saab standing on the drive, unguarded. Holding the magnetic bomb with its mercury tilt switch activator in his right hand Mansour crept forward using what cover there was from the suburban shrubbery.

But a rush of evening traffic interrupted the plan. One, two, three cars streamed past. It was too dangerous to clamp on the device then. He went back to his truck and waited.

The road went quiet again and Mansour made a further attempt, but this time noise coming from the garden of Carlisle's property forced him to pull back again.

Mansour could almost make out the english words. It sounded as if the couple were about to leave the house and go off somewhere together. His ears pricked up at the crunch of footsteps as they walked down the path and the murmuring sounds of a vague agreement between them.

Mansour retreated into the truck, placed the explosive device on the passenger seat, and waited. Where were they off to? He wound down the window and heard the Saab's engine start.

Time was running out. He must put his escape plan into operation soon before the police closed in. On impulse Mansour decided to follow.

He opened the glove box and took out his Smith and Wesson 38. When he got close enough he would shoot the traitor Agent Alex in the temple.

The Saab drove off along Main Street, then turned right. They must be going to the Hubara Club, Mansour reasoned and kept a good distance so he wouldn't be noticed.

He thought back over other opportunities missed. Like the plan to ambush the hunting trip and kill the author Ian Fleming as well. Alex would have got the credit if that had worked. But the men he hired were unprofessional, spineless and useless. They took the dinars and hadn't followed through.

Carlisle's Saab came to an abrupt halt after it turned off 6th Avenue and into the driveway of a well-kept bungalow. Mansour pulled to the side and waited.

It was a beautiful evening. The large red disc of the setting sun sent long streaks of pink and purple across the Kuwait sky. In the distance, Mansour could hear the call to prayer from the nearby minaret. He alighted from his truck, sank on his knees, and prayed to Allah.

When was the time to strike? With the 38 in hand he crept through the gate and concealed himself in the thick foliage at the lower edge of the garden. Inside, the property lights blazed brightly. The couple had disappeared into the house. Mansour wondered how long he'd have to wait for the right moment.

A long slow twenty minutes passed and Mansour began to despair. What was keeping them? Time was critical.

He returned to the truck. Replacing the firearm in the glove compartment, he took the explosive device and made his way back up the drive.

He must work quickly. Perhaps there was going to be a party inside. If so, other guests would soon arrive and he didn't want to be caught in the act.

Using his elbows, he scrambled underneath the Saab, and attached the explosive to the chassis of the vehicle. The magnets would hold the bomb in position.

Satisfied the device was secure, he activated the tilt switch and ran back to the truck. Mansour knew the level switch would close as the car bounced over speed humps on the road as it headed back to Main Street.

Now all he had to do was leave the country as soon as possible. His job was as complete as he could manage within the short time frame available.

Mansour reversed up and drove back home. On the way through to South Ahmadi, he stopped off at his old office intent on setting loose his boss's favourite most venomous animals. People would be scared to death of them. Mansour smiled at the thought.

Unlocking the office door, he switched on the light. Eaten up with hatred, he set about trashing the office. He yanked open the filing cabinets and tossed the papers all over the floor. Did the same to the drawers and their contents.

Then he turned the scorpion container upside down and watched with interest as the creature scurried away.

Still consumed by anger he picked up one of the large glass containers and hurled it against the wall where it smashed into a myriad of pieces.

The remaining creatures wriggled free as Mansour overturned their glass pens, alert and on guard at the unusual activity. The viper swayed its broad head from side to side ready to strike.

Mansour took the snake's cage down and sat it on what remained of his boss's desk. He opened the top and plunging his hand down, pinned the snake's head against the bottom of the enclosure, then lifted and placed the writhing animal on the floor.

Then with the lights still ablaze he fled, leaving the office door wide open.

Forty minutes later he arrived back at his modest home in the southern suburbs of Ahmadi. He'd instructed his wife to pack and be ready to leave immediately on his return.

No sooner had he stepped inside and saw her huddled in the corner than he realised she wasn't alone. The next thing he heard was the unmistakable sound of a gun cocking right behind his ear. Mansour Sood begged for his wife and daughter to be spared as he was dragged away in handcuffs by the police.

Chapter 55

John Dickson opened the door wide to the Carlisles and glanced from Gordon to Anita, then back again to Gordon.

'Hello there. Come on in.' He stepped back and waved them into the lounge.

Gordon recognised straightaway the record playing in the background as the Sibelius *Finlandia* which he'd been looking for high and low. How had it got back there without him knowing about it?

'You recognise that of course?'

Gordon nodded and the sudden chill as they stepped into the cold room made him shiver involuntarily. The air conditioning was full on, unnecessarily so for the time of year and he was just in shirtsleeves.

'I'll go and switch that off, shall I? Make yourselves comfortable. I'll get you a drink. Beer, Gordon? Anita?'

Gordon looked over to Anita and caught the barely contained fear in her face.

'Gin and tonic, please. '

'Take a seat. Make yourself at home,' John said, before disappearing in the direction of the kitchen. They both could hear him talking in hushed tones as he organised the drinks.

John reappeared smiling happily. 'Great you found Sylvie, wasn't it?'

They waited while John settled into one of the leather club chairs that flanked the couch.

'I have some big news for you about Pip Foster. Our journalist come MI6 man has just defected to Moscow from Beirut. He was a double agent. All made a bit of a buzz in London I can tell you.'

Gordon felt as if someone had stepped on his grave. He turned to his wife to gauge her reaction. Anita's face had paled to stone, but her eyes displayed a polite interest.

For a moment the room fell quiet but the silence was broken by the cracking sound of an ice tray out in the kitchen.

'Are you sure, John?'

'Does that surprise you so much, Gordon? After all, you were the one who raised the alarm about him in the first place. By the way, Fleming sends his regards.' John looked steadily at Gordon with his clear blue eyes.

Gordon's mind was going a million miles an hour, trying to digest the news, plus rationalise why John was in such an ebullient mood.

Gordon thought he saw Anita's lip tremble for a moment.

'First I've heard of it too,' she said.

'He skipped a dinner party in Beirut a couple of nights ago and boarded a Lebanese freighter bound for the good old Soviet Union.'

'Staggering,' Gordon said. His suspicions had proven correct. But it was still a great shock.

'Didn't even wait for you, Anita. Such a shame.' John's eyes rested on Anita's pale face.

Her hand shook as she reached into her clutch bag and

301

pulled out a handkerchief, something to fiddle with.

'I don't know what you mean,' she mumbled in an almost inaudible voice.

'Well, that was the master plan, wasn't it? To fly to Beirut to join Foster?'

'Is that true, Anita? Speak up for God's sake.' Gordon didn't need an answer. It was all in her face. 'Who did you get all this from?' he asked.

'Ophelia. That's who.' John called out over his shoulder and shouted, 'Come in my darling.'

The apparition from the past, the woman everyone had taken for dead, glided into the room bearing a full tray of drinks. She banged the heavy load down on the side table, before smoothing down the sides of her bright pink dress.

'You look like you've just seen a ghost, darling,' she said with a quick smile and handed Gordon a glass of super cold beer with a nice frothy head. 'How have you been?'

'W-w-wonderful to see you're recovered so well, Ophelia.'

'Before you ask, we've been back for over a week. People always ask that, don't they? When did you get back? As if it matters.'

Ophelia handed a gin and tonic to Anita and said with a vindictive smile, 'Did she tell you, Gordon? She returned my record finally. I'd been asking for it for ages. Very kind of you, dear.'

Having passed out the drinks, she slid into a chair and held up her glass, 'Cheers everyone.'

Anita's eyes were full of fear and a bead of sweat had broken out on her forehead. She shifted in her seat, her hand shaking as she raised her glass.

'She brought it back with the letter I'd written you. I doubt you ever got to read it though, did you?' Ophelia lit up a cigarette from a fresh pack of Peter Stuyvesant.

John interrupted. 'I showed it to him, the letter.'

'Instead, she used it to make out I'd killed myself. It was you who slipped poison in my drink when you were over that time.'

Anita's face crumpled and flushed pink.

'It's time to put the cards on the table,' John said, lifting aside a golf magazine, which covered a 38 revolver.

'How could you not know who she was, Gordon?' Ophelia closed her eyes, put her head back, and shook it from side to side.

'Some hard decisions need to be made now,' John said, taking hold of the weapon and placing it on the coffee table in front of him. He looked long and hard from Gordon to Anita.

Gordon had a surge of pity as he saw the fear in Anita's eyes.

'What are you going to do with me?' she whispered.

Gordon struggled to get the words out. 'D-D-Did you poison Ophelia's drink?'

Anita didn't reply. Her lips compressed into a tight line.

'But why?' Gordon stared at his wife. 'You knew there was nothing between us.'

'Oh, darling. It wasn't over you. Don't flatter yourself,' 'I should be so lucky. It was on Moscow's orders. That's why.'

John took a sip of whiskey. 'Well, on Foster's orders to be precise.'

'I do believe Gordon still does not get it.' Ophelia spoke as if he wasn't even there. 'Really! How can you be so dense?' She leapt to her feet and downed the rest of her gin in one go.

'Your sweet wife is Agent Alex. She works for Moscow Centre.'

Gordon felt as if his life had become suspended in time.

Ophelia crossed the room and poured herself another drink. 'Of course, Whitehall is delighted,' she announced from the cocktail cabinet. 'Nailing you Anita. Makes up for the enormous embarrassment over Pip Foster's betrayal and defection.'

'Let's th-th-think this through, shall we?'

'There's still one possible way out of this for you, Anita,' John said, swinging his foot up and down in an attempt to relieve the stress.

'There's not really. ' Anita sobbed and tears flowed down her cheeks.

'Let's get something down on record.' John picked up the revolver and crossed over to where he'd set up a tape recorder. 'Before Ophelia gets too pie-eyed.'

Ophelia swirled her drink. 'Let's not go down that route, shall we, darling? I'm not the snake in the grass here, am I?'

'Does this mean that our marriage was always just a sham?' Gordon felt a mounting anger as all the pieces fell into place.

'You might as well tell us,' said Ophelia. 'Or I'll press charges for attempted murder on top of everything else. Kuwaiti prisons are not the most hospitable places, Anita. Or should we call you Alexandra?'

Ophelia flicked off ash in the general direction of the ashtray. 'Your age was what got me. Passing yourself off as a thirty-two-year-old. Wish I could do it. Knock three years off and get away with it.'

'Darling, bitterness does not become you,' said John.

'I think Ophelia has every right to be bitter,' said Gordon.

'Thank you, Gordon.' Ophelia's eyes also welled up.

Anita clasped her hands together. 'I'm sorry for what I did to you, Ophelia. Really.'

'Took me fucking weeks to get over it you know. Sick as a dog I was.'

'You have to open up. Explain everything, Anita.' Gordon couldn't bring himself to use his wife's real name.

'When Ophelia wrote the letters to you, I knew she'd found out about me.'

'My father was with MI5. I never told you, Gordon. That's why we were hosting that weasel Pip Foster at the dance,' Ophelia explained.

'Anita. Speak to us,' Gordon growled. 'You came here the afternoon of the dinner party. Right?'

Anita remained silent.

'Yes, she came and brought the record back,' said Ophelia, stepping in for her. 'You played the jealous wife rather well, I thought. Leave my husband alone. He means the world to me. Come to dinner by all means, but don't try any tricks. Blah, blah, blah. So let's be friends. Here. Drink this!' Ophelia let out a short laugh. 'Fortunately, I didn't down the damn lot.'

'OK.' John interrupted. 'I've got this machine working now. A bit of quiet so we can get what Anita says down on tape. Gordon. To put you fully in the picture, as you quite clearly are not, we flew back to England. Ophelia went into the London Clinic. Recovered, obviously. We all decided to keep her safely out of the way for a bit. Until we could be sure Alexandra was the Soviet mole. And not you.'

'Me?'

Chapter 56

The first part of the deal struck between the Dicksons and the Carlisles was for Gordon's wife to confess all she knew about the Soviet ring operating in Kuwait. This would be relayed back to London. If she didn't comply, she would be handed over to Brigadier General Mustafa with all that implied for her future.

John Dickson switched on the tape and started by asking Anita to state her full name.

'Which one?' she challenged.

'All of them.'

It was pitch black outside by now so Ophelia stood up and crossed to the bay window to close the curtains. 'Is that your car out there? If so, you've still got your side lights on.'

Gordon excused himself and went out to switch them off. He was grateful to escape the surreal proceedings for a time. When he returned, Anita sat smoking a cigarette and in full swing. Idly, in an almost detached way, Gordon wondered whether she was disappointed that Foster had left her behind when he crossed over to the USSR. But he no longer cared. Anita's complex personality and double existence had not been a figment of his imagination, after all.

But how could he have been so blind, keep burying his suspicions time and again? It could only be down to unquestioning love.

Gordon stared at the woman he had married as she coldly recorded the events and details of their life together. She still held a fascination for him, but for different reasons. Ever an enigma. Who was she really?

Having completely recovered her composure, Anita made the statement with little emotion or concern about the effect it might have on him.

'Coming here was an assignment I was given. Moscow Centre arranged for me to meet Gordon. They wanted someone on the inside of the Anglo-American society here for Operation Palm Tree. He was single and ideal for purpose.'

'So the marriage was for political reasons?'

Gordon sensed John half enjoyed deballing him in revenge for having slept with his wife.

'Yes.'

'Only that?' asked John.

'Not entirely.' She turned to Gordon with a light smile. 'I've grown fond of him.'

'He is your husband after all.'

'Not because of that. Marriage is a capitalist concept. It's not really necessary.'

'But you were also married to Pip Foster once, weren't you?'

'For a while. He ended it. Not me.'

'You were fond of him, too?' John took a handful of peanuts and shovelled them into his mouth.

'Yes, but I didn't want him in Kuwait. I think he came to check up on what I was doing. And what Gordon was doing too, for that matter.'

'Foster knew you were spying for the Soviet Union too?'

'Of course.'

'And you knew that he was a double agent?'

'Pip had been passing British secrets to the Soviets since before I was born. He can be quite frightening. I wanted him to leave us alone. In return, I promised to send through photographs of the oil plants they wanted.'

'Did he kill Carl Sandberg?'

'It was Pip who organised it, but Mansour Sood carried it out. He's been a deep cover Iraqi agent for years.'

'Did you know Foster planned to defect?'

Anita hesitated. 'We spoke about it in Beirut. We were supposed to go to Moscow together.'

The sound of a moth fluttering at the window disturbed the silence.

'So, like I said, basically he dumped you.' John downed a triumphant slug of whiskey.

'Yes.'

'You can tell us what you know. Starting with, why were you sent here?'

'To connect with the sources already established. And make new ones, particularly those with oil field connections.'

'Are you the only KGB agent who's penetrated British intelligence in Kuwait?'

'There are Arabs working in the city. I don't know who they are.'

'And in Ahmadi?'

'No one else I know of. I'm the only one. Gordon is not involved in any way. It was all about undermining the colonials and to help with the planned invasion by Iraq.'

'How will the operatives be used exactly?'

'Blow the oil fields. A heavy smoke screen from the burning

oil will make it harder for strikes from the British once the Iraqis invade. Also protect Iraq's military movements from attack by the RAF if they come into it. Our people are passionate about the cause. Considering Kuwait's wells are sharp drilled to drain the oil from neighbouring countries, they believe they're morally on the right side of things.'

'When is all this to be carried out?'

'Once the invasion begins.'

'Which is planned for when exactly?'

'That I don't know. If I did, I would tell you.'

'How many fields are targeted?'

'A few to begin with. There are hundreds of them, as you know. The smoke and debris collectively would hamper any defence by the Kuwaitis and British. Or the Americans if they get involved.' She paused. 'Also, as I understand it there is a plan to dig fire trenches near the oil fields. Three metres wide and deep and roughly a kilometre long. All to frustrate the advance of coalition ground forces.'

'What else has been planned?'

'A deliberate oil spill from some of the fields. To hinder a landing by sea of the British Royal Navy.'

Anita continued on for a full half an hour detailing the objectives.

'What happens to me now I've told you all this? With Pip having left Beirut, I thought of returning to England but I suppose that's impossible now.'

John Dickson turned off the tape recorder with a clunk, signalling the end of the interview.

'If you go back there, you'd be arrested. Imprisoned, possibly for a long time.'

She grew flustered and upset. 'You said there was a way out.

309

I can't stay here now.'

'You were on your way to Moscow anyway, Anita,' said Gordon. 'Why not go there?'

John picked up on it. 'We can arrange that. On one condition. You agree to work there for us, for MI6.'

Anita couldn't hide her relief as she visualised an eventual reunion with Foster. 'You'd let me do that?'

John leant forward, rubbing his hands together. 'Follow Pip. Tell him the net was closing in on you. But you keep in touch with us. If not, there will be consequences.'

Her face clouded over. 'If Moscow Centre think I've been turned, they'll kill me.'

Gordon took off his glasses and wiped away the sweaty steam which had formed. 'From what I see, it's your only option, Anita. Do what you have to do.'

'I'm sorry, Gordon.'

'There's a plane leaving for Beirut in the morning,' said John. 'We will be in touch with MI6 tonight and make sure they get you on from there to Moscow. The line will be that with the publicity around Foster's defection, you were now exposed. You had to escape before MI6 closed in.'

Gordon fished out his car keys. 'You go back in the car and finish packing. I'll stay and sort things here with John and Ophelia. Get a taxi back later.'

Anita stood up on shaky legs. 'You're a good man, Gordon. Thank you.'

After she'd gone, the three of them sat in silence, exhausted by the tumultuous outcome.

They heard the Saab engine start up and the car reverse slowly down the drive. The headlights flashed a farewell through the window in a brief full beam.

'Have we done the right thing letting her go?' said Ophelia. 'I suppose she can't do any more harm, can she?'

'I don't think so. Not now.'

'Might get you to put something on this tape too, Gordon,' said John. 'It'll help to clear your name.'

All of a sudden the windows shook, followed instantly by the sound of a huge explosion.

'My God. What on earth was that?' Ophelia jumped up.

John Dickson made for the door but Gordon beat him to it and was out the front in seconds. 'Something's gone up,' he shouted.

He dashed across the garden and out into the street. Just past the first speed bumps, he could see the Saab. But smoke and flames had engulfed the car.

Throwing himself at the driver's door, he struggled to open it. A second explosion threw him back into the sand at the edge of the road. The flames flared even higher and within seconds there was nothing he could do.

Chapter 57

Three days before Christmas, everyone was out getting in last-minute food supplies before the holiday shut down. The supermarket parking lot was full but eventually Jean found a space for her little Morris Minor car near the front. She'd had to do two laps to find it.

The December morning was fresh and pleasant and the air filled with the buzz which always happened during the festive season. It didn't matter that there was no snow on the ground. Christmas was still Christmas in Kuwait. Jean had been playing nothing but "Here Comes Santa Claus" and other Bing Crosby records for weeks in the build up.

When Jean got to the entrance, she saw the Quinns leaving the check out. They saw her and waved, so she went over to say hello. Matthew manoeuvred the trolley, which was full to overflowing out of the checkout line.

'He's giving me a hand for once,' Pam said. 'I can't lift this load on my own. You're a true gentleman, aren't you, dear?'

'I try to be.' Matthew gave a good-natured scoff.

'Are you all prepared?' Jean asked.

'I think so. Food nearly done.'

'It doesn't matter how early you start, you're always rushing at the end. I've still got a list as long as your arm of stuff to buy Stewart and Sylvie. Haven't you?'

'No. I'm finished now,' said Pam. 'All stopped. Everything wrapped. I think children today are too spoilt as it is. They get far too many things.' She gave a disapproving glance in Matthew's direction.

He smiled guiltily. 'They're only young once though, aren't they Jean?'

'He just gives the kids stuff to get them off to their rooms and give us some peace. Don't you, dear?'

Matthew continued to grin in an amiable fashion. Jean had always seen him as a very easy-going husband who Pam nagged far too much.

'There was something I wanted to ask you about Boxing Day, Pam.'

'We're seeing you then, aren't we?' Pam peered into a plastic bag. 'Don't expect anything great. It'll just be cold turkey.'

'Nothing but that for the whole week, I think,' said Matthew, looking down at the enormous frozen carcass which hogged up most of the trolley space.

'Neville and I were going to invite Gordon over on Christmas Day so he wouldn't be alone. That's why. If we can get him to come. After what happened to Anita.'

'A terrible thing her killed like that,' said Pam. 'Who would've thought it?'

Jean shook her head. 'They'd just made up between them, too. He's heartbroken. Hard to entice him out. Did she die outright, do you think?'

Matthew nodded and looked down gravely. 'At least it would have been pretty quick.'

'No one seems to know exactly what happened. Gordon won't talk about it. Have you heard anything, Matthew?'

'Not really. Something wrong with the car, they say. Engine exploded apparently.'

'I don't like driving at night,' said Jean. 'I think it's fine if you do a lot of it. If you're out of practice, you can get dazzled with all the headlights. You certainly can't see those awful speed bumps, can you? I don't know why they don't remove them. I would.'

'Poor Gordon,' said Pam with a deep sigh. 'It must be hard on him.'

'Which is why I was wondering if I should mention your little shindig on Boxing Day. Your get-together. Or should I not? I didn't know whether you had invited him already?'

'I hadn't Jean, because I wasn't too sure who else was coming.'

'Just an idea,' said Jean.

'Of course,' said Matthew. 'Great idea.'

Pam raised a finger. 'But the Dicksons will be there. She rang to confirm yesterday. I don't know if that makes a difference. But it'll probably be all right.'

'Ophelia looks very well, doesn't she?' said Jean. 'I bumped into her at the Club the other afternoon. That was a surprise to me.' Jean was dying to learn exactly what happened to her.

'Yes. I told her we were all rather surprised when she disappeared without a trace.' Pam frowned. 'Which is true.'

Matthew looked to the floor and the hint of an awkward smile appeared.

'Obviously I got it wrong about the you-know-what, though.' Pam looked over at Jean.

'Me too, Pam. I don't know how that happened.'

'She went back to England. Something to do with her father being ill. Well, we can ask her ourselves when we see her, can't we?' Pam closed her eyes to add a little emphasis.

'Her son having problems at school, was what I heard,' added Jean with a questioning look. 'The children are both out now. Apparently, John and Ophelia were at the airport when the plane landed and someone saw them. It was two hours late. So the parents all cheered when it finally touched down. The flights are never on time, though.'

'No, Jean.' Pam shook her head. 'They cheered because Kuwait National Airways Company were thinking of suspending their flights and they wouldn't be able to get their children out if that had that happened. In case of the invasion.'

'Oh, that was the reason, was it?'

'The invasion talk seems to have stopped. We go on waiting, waiting, waiting.'

'Well, we're still umming and ahing ourselves. To up and leave is a big decision. I've packed up a few cartons for Kuehne and Nagel shippers though, as a precaution. Things seem to have settled down a bit, according to Gordon.'

'As if he would know,' said Pam, always ready to slight him.

'He's had quite a bit to do with the British authorities recently over his member of staff, he told me,' said Jean, squaring it up. 'All about the Arab who took Sylvie. I don't know exactly what, though.'

Matthew put his bit in. 'It'd be all over Mansour. He was with the guerrilla movement. I knew the chap well myself. We all did. He's worked for the company for many years. In and out of the offices. '

'Thank God Gordon had an idea of where to find her.' Jean stroked the nape of her neck. 'I nearly went out of my mind with worry.'

'You must have done.' Pam wrinkled up her nose. 'The

315

creep should be strung up. That's what I say. No mercy.'

'I don't know what's going to happen to him now.' Jean shivered at the thought of Mansour's body dangling at the end of a rope. 'I can't go back over it. Neville was driving all over Ahmadi like a lunatic, looking for her.'

'Anyway, we'd better get on before this big bird decides to defrost.'

'I must do the same.' Jean edged in the direction of the entrance. 'And we've got the Christmas Show later. That's been wonderful for Sylvie. Taken her mind off things. They think she's very good in it.'

'I'm sure she is,' said Pam. 'We've bought our tickets. So we might see you there.'

'I'll say goodbye for now, then.'

'And don't forget to ask Gordon if he wants to come over on Boxing Day,' said Pam over her shoulder.

'Yes.' Matthew tugged at his ear. 'It'd be good to have Gordon along for a few beers.'

'When I next talk to him, I'll do that.' Jean said brightly.

'Please,' said Pam. 'But tell him to leave his snakes and things where they belong. I don't want those ghastly creepy crawlies in my house.'

Matthew laughed outright. 'At least he caught them before they bit anyone. Only Gordon could do that. They think Mansour let them out when he smashed up the office. Right through the hospital, they were. I took a picture of Gordon holding up the viper. They've used it in *The Kuwaiti* this week.' He chuckled.

'Ooh. I'll take a look. He's a bit of a hero, really, isn't he, our Gordon?'

Chapter 58

Gordon studied The Times Middle Eastern Coverage. The headline read 'Russian Spies Betray Britain'.

An inquiry reveals that a former correspondent for The Times and The Telegraph and also MI6 agent has defected from Beirut to the Soviet Union after being outed by an unidentified civilian in Kuwait. Philip Foster, 52, has been named as part of a communist spy ring operating in the Middle East tasked with passing on classified information to the KGB. The Soviets are known to support anti-imperialist forces throughout the Third World.

Foster's treacherous duplicity has almost certainly led to the loss of several British agents over recent years along with the passing on to the USSR details of important defence strategies in place. See what happened in Kuwait on the following page...

... Continued from front

This is a picture of the "master spy" taken at a dinner dance at the Hubara Club in Ahmadi in July 1960. He is seated next to another member of the Anglo-American community.

The photograph was taken during his recent visit to the State of Kuwait. No doubt the lady he is pictured talking to was unaware that her urbane dance partner was actively involved in the mission to "drive the British out of Kuwait."

According to sources, plots included recruitment of pro-communist agents to carry out sabotage and executions, a chemical weapons attack on the expat community and the possible assassination of Ian Fleming.

In his colourful life Foster has been married three times. Firstly to an English woman who worked in a shoe shop in Chichester, then to a Soviet photographer employed by TASS and lastly to a lecturer at the London School of Economics.

Events surrounding Foster's time in the oil-rich State resulted in the hanging of a Palestinian terrorist in front of the Interior Ministry in Kuwait City for the murder of a British oil worker, and the abduction of a ten-year-old child. It is thought the Palestinian was in close collaboration with the defected agent.

The hunt for other Soviet agents operating in the Middle East has been stepped up ahead of the independence of Kuwait next year.

Gordon Carlisle put down the newspaper and took another look at the bugging equipment he found in their bungalow. Amidst Anita's personal possessions there were a range of tiny electronic devices, some the size of sugar cubes. He reckoned they might be useful to him if he took up the offer to work for MI6 in the future.

In his mind he went back to when he first met Anita at the concert in London. Everything had gone right until the day Foster had arrived in Kuwait. From then on, everything changed. But had Foster not turned up when he did, Gordon would never have discovered his wife's hidden side. He shuddered at the thought of living a life based on half-truths.

Idly Gordon wondered which category Anita fell under. The cross examination and breakdown at the Dicksons had been all too brief and he'd never had the opportunity to learn everything about her. Was she an ideological spy? The type who believed Soviet ideology was nobler and of a higher moral level than the uncontrolled freedoms embraced by the Western world? Or had she just been compromised by her two-year relationship with Foster?

But there was something about a double agent which aroused dramatically opposite emotions. A distaste for the absence of any moral compass in the individual and at the same time a sneaking admiration for the glamour and excitement such a life must entail.

Foster's deception went back years. Wherever Foster was now, Gordon knew that he had played a major role in it all, the potentially unmasking of Foster. Gordon didn't expect the press to reveal that Anita's real name was Alexandra Yuri, her original maiden surname. He took a good swig of Smirnoff and lit up a cheroot.

Florrie came through the door to ask if he wanted something to eat. Gordon looked at his watch. 6 pm. Yes. It was time for salami and gherkins.

THE END

Contemporary History of Kuwait and Iraq

In 1958, Abdul Karim Qasim seized power in Iraq, the Hashemite monarchy established by King Faisal I in 1921 under the auspices of the British. King Faisal II, Prince Abd al-Ilah, and Prime Minister Nuri al-Said as well as many other members of the Iraqi royal family were murdered by the military. Baghdad Radio announced that the Army had liberated the Iraqi people from domination by a corrupt group put in power by "imperialism".

The Hashemite regime had been a reliable ally of the West as it tried to hold back the Soviets. The change of power produced a volatile situation. Uncontrollable mobs took to the streets of Baghdad. Several foreign nationals staying at the Baghdad Hotel were killed in the chaos that followed. The British Embassy was ransacked and a member of staff killed in the process. Iraq became a republic.

Cross currents of communism, Arab and Iraqi nationalism, anti-Westernism and the 'positive neutrality' of President Gamal Abdel Nasser of the United Arab Republic played out their effects in the region.

This raised fears of a domino effect and that the pro-Western oil regime of Kuwait would fall to united Arab nationalism.

By March 1959 Iraq withdrew from the Baghdad Pact, a military alliance between Iran, Iraq, Pakistan, Turkey and the United Kingdom. In its place it created new alliances with left-leaning countries, including the Soviet Union. Because of their agreement with the USSR, Qasim's government allowed the formation of an Iraqi Communist Party.

In 1960, an Arab League declaration repositioned the Iraq-Kuwait border two miles north of the southernmost tip of Iraq's Rumaila oil field. This led to an ongoing dispute made worse when Iraq alleged that Kuwait-based drilling was tapping into their oil fields.

On 25 June 1961, after Britain handed over authority to Kuwait, Qasim announced that Kuwait would be incorporated into Iraq. As well as massive oil reserves, the State of Kuwait had broad access to the Persian Gulf. The military threat resulted in a call by Sheikh Abdullah III Al-Salim Al-Sabah for British protection. Operation Vantage was launched on 30 June 1961. Air, sea and land forces were in place within days.

The Kuwaiti combat contingents were led by Brigadier General al-Jaber al-Sabah and Colonel Saleh Mohammad Al-Sabah. They commanded the Kuwait 25th Commando Brigade and the Kuwait 6th Mechanised Brigade.

Iraq did not attack and British forces were replaced by those of the Arab League. The UK had withdrawn completely by 19 October 1961.

Qasim was killed in a coup in 1963 and Iraq recognised Kuwaiti independence. The military threat receded but Britain kept forces in abeyance until 1971.

Despite the unstable history between Kuwait and the leadership of Iraq, the Kuwaiti military acted in alliance with the Iraqi military during the Six-Day War between Israel and Arab States, primarily Jordan, Syria and Egypt. It also participated with a token force during the Arab-Israeli conflict in October 1973.

On 2nd August 1990, under the leadership of Saddam Hussein, Iraq invaded Kuwait. The Emir of Kuwait, Jaber Al-Ahmad Al-Jaber Al-Sabah escaped to Saudi Arabia. Iraqi troops attacked his coastal residence of Dasman Palace, killing the Emir's younger half-brother, Sheikh Fahad Al-Ahmed Al-Jaber Al-Sabah. After several hours of heavy fighting, the Palace fell after a landing by Iraqi marines. Republican Guard tanks rolled into Kuwait City. By 3 August, Iraqi forces occupied the country and declared it to be the nineteenth province of Iraq. Kuwaiti civilians were ordered to replace their car licence plates with Iraqi ones.

Kuwaitis founded a formidable underground resistance movement made up of military personnel, police, and ordinary civilians. During the seven-month occupation the resistance worked to undermine the Iraqi regime. They established a clandestine satellite telephone service which was used to send out written reports, maps, photographs and even directed coalition air strikes.

This led to the First Gulf War on 16 January 1991, and ended with an Iraqi defeat and retreat from Kuwait on 28 February 1991. As a parting gesture the Iraqi troops set fire to 600 Kuwaiti oil wells.

Author's Note

This book is a work of fiction but inspired by real events. I was born and brought up in Kuwait and I vividly recall the period and what it was like living under the threat of invasion by Iraq in 1960 and 1961. My father, Ian Byres was the Preventative Health Officer for the Kuwait Oil Company based in Ahmadi.

At the end of 1960 Ian Fleming came to Kuwait to write a book about the oil industry which was commissioned by KOC. Due to objections by the Kuwaiti Government it was never published.

During the stay he got to know my father very well and spent many days at our bungalow at 5 Main Street. They had much in common. Both had the same Christian names, were of Scottish extraction and shared a great interest in exotic creatures which sometimes broke loose from my father's personal zoo. I recall one contest between a viper and scorpion on our green carpet when Ian Fleming was there. He went out with my father on one of his hawking expeditions into the desert which he later described as one of the highlights of his time in Kuwait.

During that period the great charmer Kim Philby, based in Beirut, made a tour of the Gulf States including Kuwait and he modelled for the character of Pip Foster in *Our Man In Kuwait*.

Philby himself eventually defected to the Soviet Union

in 1963 when doubts about his loyalty were about to be confirmed by US and British secret services. His defection shocked the tight expat community of Ahmadi at the time who felt it reflected on their own integrity.

Acknowledgements

This book owes much to the generosity and support of many. Appreciation to John Levins who wrote *Days of Fear* from whom I learnt much about what did happen when Iraq eventually invaded Kuwait. To Colonel Hamish de Bretton-Gordon OBE who was there during the Gulf War. Former commanding officer of UK's Joint Chemical, Biological, Radiological and Nuclear Regiment and NATO's Rapid Reaction CBRN Battalion, his fascinating book *Chemical Warrior* is a must read. Also the Kuwait Oil Company and many of the 'Kuwait Kids' such as Cynthia and Nicholas Bagge who grew up alongside me and helped recall detail.

Thank you to my editor Victor Johns for his painstaking work. Dr Ivor Burfitt deserves a shout as my medical advisor. As do everyone at New Century who helped get *Our Man In Kuwait* on the reading and promotional circuit as well as W4 Films, Simon McQuiggan at Muse and Fahar Faizaan for his enthusiasm to get this story made into a movie.

My appreciation also to the book bloggers, reviewers and colleagues on Twitter and Facebook, not forgetting Anne Cater for her publicity service. Also the very talented photographer Alastair Hilton for my author pics.

A special thanks to friends like Katherine Scholfield who described the excruciating pain when she was stung by a scorpion a little smaller than 'Sally'. With love to my family, in particularly Arabella, Brooke, Rhys and Dempsie Lee Williams. Also my long-suffering husband Donald Burfitt-Dons who encouraged me for so long to put the story to paper. My beloved mother Olive Byres, and brother Laurence Byres, though long deceased, were daily in my memory as I relived the years in Kuwait. And last but not least my father Ian Byres who, to me will always be the one and only James Bond of the Desert.

Louise Burfitt-Dons is an author and a screenwriter of TV movies shown on networks worldwide. She was born in Kuwait. Married to Donald for forty years, Louise has two daughters and a granddaughter. Home is now Chiswick, London.

🌐 https://www.louiseburfittdons.com
🐦 https://twitter.com/louiseburfdons
📘 https://en-gb.facebook.com/louiseburfittdons

✉ https://louiseburfittdons.com/readersclub

Also by Louise Burfitt-Dons

The Karen Andersen Thriller Series

The Missing Activist

He's disappeared. So why's no one looking?

Vivid, clever, utterly compelling, THE MISSING ACTIVIST is the story of an outsider's attempt to uncover a deadly conspiracy at the heart of a Westminster political party.

In this **HOUSE OF CARDS** style grassroots thriller, an off-the-wall Private Investigator battles the lofty establishment.

The Killing of the Cherrywood MP

Taut, hardboiled, detailed and funny, **THE KILLING OF THE CHERRYWOOD MP** covers the search for a neo-Fascist extremist with a vendetta against former ISIS brides.

In this **political** thriller, and continuing on from **The Missing Activist**, our off-the-wall Private Investigator goes rogue to save her own skin and foils another deadly terrorist plot.

The Secret War

'With chilling premises and twists and turns at every page, **The Secret War** is definitely the perfect read for lovers of Dan Brown and Blake Crouch thrillers.' *BooksTechnica*

Private Investigator Karen Andersen probes deep links between the Chinese Communist Party and a British university in order to thwart a deadly plot.